SENIOR MOMENTS
ARE MURDER

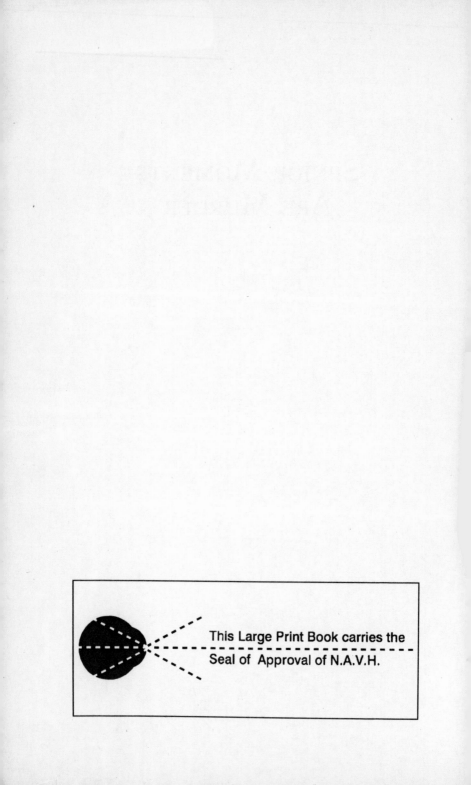

This Large Print Book carries the
Seal of Approval of N.A.V.H.

A PAUL JACOBSON GEEZER-LIT
MYSTERY

Senior Moments Are Murder

Mike Befeler

WHEELER PUBLISHING
A part of Gale, Cengage Learning

GALE
CENGAGE Learning™

Detroit • New York • San Francisco • New Haven, Conn • Waterville, Maine • London

GALE
CENGAGE Learning

LIBRARY OF CONGRESS CATALOGING-IN-PUBLICATION DATA

Befeler, Mike.
    Senior moments are murder : a Paul Jacobson Geezer-lit mystery / by Mike Befeler.
        p. cm. — (Wheeler Publishing large print cozy mystery)
    ISBN-13: 978-1-4104-4116-4 (softcover)
    ISBN-10: 1-4104-4116-4 (softcover)
    1. Retirees—Fiction. 2. Murder—Investigation—Fiction. 3. Memory disorders in old age—Fiction. 4. Venice (Los Angeles, Calif.)—Fiction. 5. Large type books. I. Title.
    PS3602.E37S46 2011b
    813'.6—dc22   2011031402

Published in 2011 by arrangement with Tekno Books and Ed Gorman.

To Kaden and Adam

ACKNOWLEDGMENTS

Many thanks for the assistance from Wendy and Laura Befeler and Virginia Brost and editorial support from Deb Brod, Tracey Matthews, and Roz Greenberg.

CHAPTER 1

I awoke with a start. The head of a woman I didn't recognize rested on the pillow next to me.

Who was she, and why was she here? For that matter, why was I here, wherever here was?

Shafts of light filtered through the opening between two matching curtain halves, white cloth decorated with light-pink flowers and turquoise leaves. These curtains and the room didn't look the least bit familiar to me. And I'd never been one to have flowered decorations.

I pinched my cheek. Yes, I definitely was awake, but I was in a strange bed.

I had no clue how I had ended up in this bedroom.

As I turned over, the woman continued to breathe in a gentle rhythm.

I stared at her, trying to figure out what was going on. Silver hair cascaded over the pillow. An attractive dame.

Pressing my palms against my temples to try to squeeze out some memory had no effect.

Think.

I took a deep breath to calm my rapid heartbeat. It wasn't good for geezers like me to get overanxious.

Reviewing what I remembered, my life had been ordinary, just a regular guy growing up in San Mateo, attending UCLA, enlisting in the Navy during World War II, running an auto parts supply store in Los Angeles and living with a wife and one kid, Denny. I regarded the female head next to me. This wasn't my wife Rhonda.

Then it came back to me. Rhonda had died of cancer after we retired to Hawaii. She was buried in the Nu'uanu Cemetery on Oahu.

But after that — one big blank.

So where was I, and who was this young chick, probably in her late seventies, next to me in bed?

I'd never been one to sleep around. One wife was all I could handle.

I regarded her again. She was attractive with her small nose, high cheekbones, silver hair halfway down her forehead, and blanket tucked under her chin. What did the rest of her look like?

I could peek, but didn't know if that was kosher in this situation.

Damn. What had I got myself into?

I continued to listen to her soft breathing. Her lips moved like she was mouthing words in a dream. But she didn't snore. Nothing worse than to be stuck with someone who snores. One time in the Navy I had a bunk mate above me who snored. That was hell.

I still had no clue who she was or where I was.

I thought of shaking my companion awake, but she looked too peaceful lying there. I turned back the blanket on my side of the bed, swung my legs into space and plopped down onto a hardwood floor. I wriggled my toes. Didn't seem at all cold.

Time to reconnoiter.

I found a pair of brown Bermuda shorts and slipped them on. At least they fit me. Then I discovered a T-shirt with a picture of an orange hibiscus on the front. Had I become an octogenarian flower child?

Maybe aliens had abducted me, and I was in one of those Twilight Zone zoos. Or maybe I was right here, wherever the hell here was.

I parted the curtains to spy a small yard

and the back of a white two-story house. Two green trees guarded a garden of red, orange and white blossoms. At least this place wasn't Alaska in winter.

Exploring my domain, I found a living room with matching green-flower-patterned couch and easy chair, a bathroom and a kitchen with the basic appliances. I knew what to do with the bathroom, anyway.

After that, with a sense of relief, I investigated further and found two beat-up black suitcases, resting against the wall in the bedroom. I inspected the name tags. Sure enough they had my name, Paul Jacobson, with an address in Kaneohe, Hawaii. Additional detective work uncovered an airline itinerary with the remains of a boarding pass for Paul Jacobson on a flight from Denver to Los Angeles.

So my recent travels must have taken me from Hawaii to Denver to Los Angeles. Why would I have been in Denver? Well, my son Denny, his wife Allison and my granddaughter Jennifer lived in Boulder, Colorado. Maybe I had been visiting them. The last I recollected, Jennifer was about six years old. A little spitfire.

But why did I end up here? I could remember squat about any of it. So here I was, in some little flat I didn't recognize. I peeked out the curtains again at the nice sunny morning. Looking to the side, I could see into the neighbor's yard. Everything green as could be. I must be somewhere around LA, but I couldn't tell for sure.

My lady companion continued to silently saw z's. I thought again of waking her up, but who was I to disturb her? I watched the gentle rise and fall of the blanket as she breathed. We must know each other if we'd spent the night together. I pushed the palms of my hands against my forehead.

Think.

How did I get here? What was going on?

I admired her face again. I felt a sensation in my chest. Was that lust? Anticipation? Indigestion?

What the hell? I decided to take a little stroll. Finding tennis shoes and white socks, I completed my walking attire. Outside, I descended a freshly painted set of green wooden stairs to the ground floor. Below where I had been sleeping, I found a two-car garage. Inside, a white Toyota Camry and a blue Subaru nestled side-by-side. Both had California plates. I wondered if either was unlocked and, if so, maybe I could find some identification. I tested the door handle of the Camry. Locked. Then the Subaru. Success. It opened.

I rummaged through the glove compartment, discarding an air pressure gauge, two pencils and an open pack of breath mints, and found a registration slip. Had the name of George Kanter. No idea who he was. Address in Venice, California. So, unless the car had been stolen, my old body had ended up in Venice.

For all the years I had lived in the Los Angeles area as an adult, I hadn't spent any time in Venice. Never had the inclination or need to go there. I'd covered both sides of Venice, traveling to Santa Monica and Redondo Beach, but had missed Venice. Particularly after the war, it had a bad reputation and was said to be run-down.

I surveyed the inside of the garage. Cans of paint lined a shelf, a power lawn mower rested near the front wall, and tools hung neatly on a pegboard along one side. Well-maintained place, just like I always kept my garage when I had one.

I heard a scraping noise behind me and spun around, my heart suddenly pounding harder than was safe for an old fart. A gray tabby cat jumped from a shelf down to the concrete floor of the garage and sauntered over to rub against my leg.

"You gave me quite a fright," I said, reaching over to give her a scritch under the chin.

A tag dangled there from a blue collar. I squinted in the dim light and made out the identification "Cleo" with the additional names of George and Andrea Kanter and an address in Venice Beach, California. Damn. There was that name Kanter again. Was I being held hostage by a Mafiosa family named Kanter or something?

"How did you get in here?" I asked Cleo as I scratched her behind an ear.

She turned her head to the side in appreciation, and emitted a gentle humming purr that I could also feel as a vibration from her throat. Then I noticed a cat door at the bottom of the people door.

"So this is your place to come when you're outside and you need to hide." I petted her and she arched her back. "That's what we all can use — a safe haven. I wonder why I'm here."

Cleo had no good answers for me, so I exited the garage with her following me.

I looked over a three-foot-high hedge into the next yard to see a freshly cut lawn and bright flower garden. This neighborhood looked like a quaint residential area. Small houses, well kept up.

I opened a white wooden gate which led into an alley as Cleo scurried out with me. I picked a direction and meandered down the alley, admiring the rows of covered garbage cans that stood sentinel beside each backyard gate. Cleo tagged along for half a block then got spooked and dashed back to the safety of her yard.

I ambled onward until the alley intersected a larger street. I turned around to lock into my defective brain the path I'd followed.

I used to have a superb memory, but now I couldn't even remember where I was. Being old was the pits. But I could picture the room where I had woken up perfectly. And the attractive woman who had been in bed with me. My heart jumped. At some level she was very important to me. Was it love? What a strange sensation. Some connection there, but I couldn't put the pieces together.

Being careful to pay attention to my route, I turned a corner and, lo and behold, I spotted a canal. Damnation. Venice really did have canals.

The morning sun shone on a white bridge up ahead, spanning the waterway. I heard the chirping of birds and smelled the aroma of lilacs drifting in the gentle breeze from one of the yards near the canal. Across the waterway stood an eclectic collection of houses. One old wooden house was brightly painted in pastel colors and balloons hung from a tree, probably from a celebration the

16

day before. Next to it stood a modern, off-white two-story with a metal railing surrounding a deck on the second level. A neatly trimmed hedge bordered both sides of the canal and across from me floated a small wooden dock with a white rowboat and red kayak moored.

It felt good to be alive. At my age waking up was a victory in its own right. I stretched my arms. Life was good. I just didn't know what the hell I was doing here.

A seagull swooped by, its wings collapsing as it splashed-landed in the canal. No other animals of the human variety were out enjoying the beautiful day. I leaned over to look more carefully at the canal. The seagull floated with folded wings as concentric rings expanded across the water from the force of its landing. Then I leaned farther over the hedge and looked straight down. From under the water a vacant face stared up at me.

CHAPTER 2

My heart raced and my mouth went dry. I had to brace myself to keep from falling into the canal and landing on the body in the water. I caught my breath and looked more carefully. It was a man, probably in his forties, in a blue sports shirt, long pants and shoes. Ripples from the seagull gently washed across his face.

I spun around, scanning in all directions for anyone else in the vicinity. Then up the pathway, I spotted a man who had just entered the walkway with a dog on a leash beside him.

"Hey, there." I waved to him. "Do you have a cell phone?"

He raised his head. "Yes, I do."

"I hate to bother your morning stroll, but could you call nine-one-one? There's a body in the canal."

The man, who had approached to within twenty feet of where I stood, visibly paled.

He stumbled, caught himself, then yanked his dog and approached me. He extracted a little gadget from his pocket, punched some buttons and handed it to me. "Here. You talk to them."

"How does this contraption work?" I asked.

"Just hold it to your ear and talk."

My fingers shook as I pushed it against the side of my face. I gave my name and explained that I'd seen a body in the canal.

The dispatcher asked me where I was.

"Hell, I don't know."

I handed the phone back to my companion. "Where are we?"

He grabbed the cell phone and in a high, shrill voice identified himself and our location. He agreed to stay on the line until someone arrived.

I regarded him more carefully. He wore running shorts, tennis shoes, a T-shirt that read "Los Angeles Marathon." He had short curly brown hair and stood my height, approaching six feet tall. Probably in his fifties. His dog, a black cocker spaniel with white trim, waited patiently while all this was going on.

"You from around here?" he asked.

"I'm not sure. I woke up in an apartment over a garage a few blocks away but I don't know what I'm doing here."

He looked at me askance, obviously wanting to ask more questions, but just then both of our heads turned at the sound of a siren. A white van with a red light flashing from the roof pulled to a stop and parked on a bridge at one end of the canal. In a few moments two men with a stretcher raced down the path toward us.

When they reached us, I said, "You can slow down. He's dead."

I pointed to the body. One of the men climbed over the hedge, dropped down, and splashed into the water which was approximately three feet deep.

He lifted the body up, and his companion reached over to help drag it up to the sidewalk.

I watched, seeing no visible sign of cause of death. One of the paramedics placed a blanket from the stretcher over the body and reached for a cell phone.

By this time a small crowd of early-morning types had gathered — several coffee-cup-toting neighbors and another dog walker. They all seemed to know each other and began yakking up a storm, undeterred by a dead body.

Then another man strode along the path toward us. He wasn't your casual early-morning stroller, as he wore a dark suit and solid blue tie. Definitely seemed out of place in this setting. He stood all of five-foot six, a skinny squirt probably in his forties with dark hair, a thick mustache that matched dense eyebrows, and rimless eyeglasses. His brown, forceful eyes scanned our little conclave.

"I'm Detective Quintana," he announced. "A call to nine-one-one was placed from a cell phone belonging to Richard Nelson. Is Mr. Nelson here?"

My dog-walking buddy waved his hand and stepped forward.

Quintana and Nelson spoke in undertones for a few moments, and then Nelson pointed toward me.

I smiled and waved back.

Quintana's mustache twitched. He reached up and tweaked it as he gave me a piercing stare.

Moments later he marched over to me and stood with his nose inches from my chin. "You placed the call on Mr. Nelson's phone. May I please see some identification?"

I reached for my back pocket. Bullpucky. "I guess I don't have my wallet with me, but my name is Paul Jacobson."

Quintana tapped his right foot. "Mr. Nelson said you acted evasive when he asked why you were here."

"That's because I woke up nearby not knowing how I got here."

He eyed my eclectic outfit. "Are you living on the streets?"

I laughed. "Hardly. I just can't remember anything from yesterday."

"A little too much wine?"

"Nope. I hardly touch the stuff. My memory isn't too hot, though."

"Can you remember what happened earlier, Mr. Jacobson?"

"Yes. That's all very clear in my mind."

"Then please recount your activities this morning."

I summarized waking up, taking a stroll, seeing the canal, finding a body and flagging down Nelson.

"Pretty good memory regarding today's events," Quintana said.

"I used to have a photographic memory." I tapped my temple. "In fact I could recite our conversation so far word for word. But before this morning the last thing I recall is living in Hawaii, then there's a big void. Apparently, I came here by way of Denver."

"How do you know that?"

"I found an airline ticket folder with my name on it in the place I woke up."

"You wait right here, Mr. Jacobson. We

need to talk some more, but I need to speak to the other people who have gathered."

He proceeded to work the crowd, writing notes on a pad.

I looked upward. Bright blue sky, not a cloud anywhere. Too bad such a nice day had to be spoiled with a floater.

Another man arrived, snapped on latex gloves and began poking at the body. It gave me the same queasy feeling as when a proctologist prepared to give me an examination. Next appeared a woman with a camera to shoot pictures of the dead man and the canal. I couldn't imagine a job doing that — having to snap photos of all the suspicious deaths that must take place in the Los Angeles area.

Finally Quintana returned to me. "Now, Mr. Jacobson, please take me to the place where you woke up."

"I'll be happy to give you a guided tour of the two streets I know in this strange city."

He gave me a dismissive wave of the hand, so I turned and retraced my morning route. I bestowed on myself a mental pat on the back for paying close attention earlier.

Quintana trailed closely on my heels. When we arrived at the apartment above the garage, I pointed. "Up there."

"Let's go take a look," Quintana said.

"Um . . . there may be a woman sleeping in the bedroom."

"Your wife?"

I scratched my head. "I don't know who she is."

Quintana squinted at me. "We'll go up the stairs, and you can check first."

He followed me up the wooden steps.

I knocked on the door and then entered.

A woman in a robe emerged from the bedroom. "Paul, there you are. When I woke up you were gone. I was worried about you."

"I hate to ask this, but who are you?"

She laughed. "You obviously didn't read the note on the bed stand."

"No, and we have a visitor. Detective Quintana is outside and needs to check on what I'm doing here. Maybe you can enlighten both of us."

She stared at me, then pursed her lips and shook her head. "Are you getting in trouble with the law again?"

"Again? All I know is I found a dead body in a canal on a walk this morning, and now Detective Quintana is questioning me."

She put her hand to her mouth. "That's terrible. Do you know who it was?"

"No. But I don't know who you are, either."

A smile returned to her face. "Well, invite

the detective in, and I'll help clear up things."

I opened the door to a scowling Detective Quintana, whose mustache twitched as I ushered him inside.

"I'd introduce you, but I don't know who you are," I said to the woman, noting she was an attractive old broad.

She reached out her hand. "Hello, Detective. I'm Marion Aumiller. Paul's fiancée."

"Fiancée?" I said with a gasp.

"That's right, Paul. You and I have a marriage ceremony scheduled this afternoon."

I plopped down on the couch. This was too much for my addled brain.

"Let me give both of you a brief summary," Marion said. "First of all, Paul suffers from short-term memory loss. He recalls things perfectly during the day, but overnight he loses his short-term memory and can't remember anything from the day before and recent past."

"That would explain why I don't recognize this place," I said.

"Paul and I met in Hawaii last year and were engaged in Boulder, Colorado, a month ago. He flew out here last week and we're getting married." She held out her ring.

Detective Quintana wrinkled his nose like

he had smelled a dead fish. "May I see some identification now, Mr. Jacobson?"

"Your wallet should be in the nightstand, Paul."

I scurried into the bedroom to see what I could find. One bedside table only held a lamp and murder mystery, but the other had a note which read, "You're going to become a married man again today, you old poop. Don't do anything stupid when you wake up."

It was my handwriting. Too bad I hadn't seen it and followed directions. So here I was in Venice, California, waking up next to an attractive woman I didn't remember who seemed willing to get hitched to an old coot like me. What a strange world.

I located my wallet and returned to the living room to show my ID card to Detective Quintana.

"This shows an address in Kaneohe, Hawaii," he said.

"That's the retirement home in Hawaii where Paul and I met. Since then he went to live with his son in Colorado."

Quintana's mustache twitched. "Please give me the phone number here."

Marion wrote it down for him, and Quintana dropped a card on the end table. "If you think of anything else you should tell

26

me, call this number."

With that, he strode to the door and let himself out.

"Intense fellow," I said.

"I guess you have to be that way in his line of work. Now what were you doing this morning, Paul?"

"I woke up not knowing what the hell was going on and decided to take a little stroll. Wasn't planning on finding a dead body in a canal."

"You seem to have a knack for this kind of thing. You've attracted the attention of the police before."

"Don't remember anything like that, but I would appreciate a little more background on my recent past and our marriage plans."

Marion gave me a hug.

My heart raced. Something felt right about marrying her.

"Our ceremony takes place at two P.M. today at Saint Andrew's Church here in Venice. We'll have a reception in the court-yard after the service. It's the church my daughter and her family attend."

"And this family of yours. All I know is that the car in the garage is registered to a George Kanter."

"That's my son-in-law. He's married to my daughter, Andrea. They have two children, Austin who is thirteen and Rachel who is eighteen and taking summer classes at UCLA."

"I went to UCLA."

"We'll have to visit the campus together sometime."

"It's been a few years. Do we have any honeymoon plans?"

Her eyes lit up. "Yes. You arranged for an Alaskan cruise two weeks from tomorrow. Now, there's something I want you to do to help with your memory problem."

"Besides having a brain transplant?"

She swatted me on the arm. "You used to keep a journal. I think you should resume that practice. Every night before you go to bed, write down the day's activities. You can leave a note to remind yourself to read your diary first thing in the morning. Then you'll be armed with an account of your most recent adventures."

"Sounds like something I should do, especially since I'll be waking up next to an attractive woman each morning."

She blushed and squeezed my hand. "Your journal will help, and I'll have to keep reminding you as well." She gave me a kiss.

Damn. That would be hard to forget.

"So with that in mind, I have a wedding present for you," Marion said.

She retrieved a wrapped package and handed it to me.

"Shall I open it now?"

"Go right ahead."

First inspecting the silver paper imprinted with bells, I then tore it open like a kid on Christmas morning. Inside was a leather-bound book.

"Open it," Marion said.

I lifted the cover and found a picture of Marion and a handwritten note that read, "To my husband. Since you'll wake up almost every morning not remembering who I am, this is a reminder for you. We now live in Venice, California, with my daughter Andrea and her family. You can keep a running diary in this book as a reminder of your current life. Love, Marion."

"What's this about almost every morning?" I asked.

Marion gave me a Cheshire-cat grin. "There is one circumstance when you remember things the next day."

"And that is?"

"It'll be a little surprise for you. I'll make sure that you wake up tomorrow with a memory of today."

She refused to elaborate further, so I decided I'd just wait and see what mysterious remedy for my faulty memory existed. This was all so confusing that one more unresolved question wouldn't matter.

"Now," Marion said, "there's one thing we need to take care of. Your pills."

"But I hate taking pills."

She wagged her right index finger at me. "Paul, I have your pills all set up for you to take each day, once in the morning and once in the evening. They're supposed to help your memory."

"Doesn't look like they're doing any good. I remember diddly from yesterday."

Marion smiled. "They keep you from having further problems. Now are you going to be brave and take them?" She pointed to three rocks disguised as pills, resting on the table.

I felt like a little kid. "Do I hafta?" I surreptitiously covered the pills with a napkin.

She wagged her finger at me again. "Yes. You are under doctor's orders to take your medication twice a day. So quit trying to hide the pills."

I removed the napkin. "Damn. I thought I had you fooled."

She crossed her arms and stared at me.

"All right," I said.

I couldn't disappoint her, so somehow I managed to swallow the horse pills without choking to death.

She dusted her hands together. "With that taken care of we can begin our preparations for the ceremony. I need some time to myself, and your family is taking you out to breakfast."

"My family is here?"

"Yes. Denny, Allison and Jennifer will be by shortly."

She adjourned to the bedroom to do her wedding preparation thing, and I sat down in an easy chair to figure out my strange existence. I felt excited to be marrying this young chick, but uncertain about finding myself in a new place. And I looked forward to seeing my family. I needed to wrap my feeble brain around all these events. With a sigh, I decided to go with the flow. I'd follow what was set in motion and see where it led me.

True to Marion's word that my family was in town, thirty minutes later someone knocked on the door, and upon my opening it, a young girl bounded in to give me a hug. "Grandpa, this is your big day."

I stood back at arms' length and stared at her. "You look like an older version of my granddaughter, Jennifer."

She stomped her foot. "Grandpa, I'm twelve now."

"I last remember you being six."

She tisked. "That's why you need to start keeping a journal again. So you can remember what's happened."

"Marion gave me a book to write in."

"Then leave yourself a note and put it by your bed at night. Every morning you can review your journal before you go anywhere."

"You're the second person to give me that advice today. It would have been helpful this morning. I didn't know where I was and wandered around. I found a canal with a dead body in it."

"What?" Jennifer's eyes grew to the size of silver dollars. Then she put her hands on her hips. "You aren't involved in a murder investigation again, are you?"

"I don't know what happened. I just found a man floating in the canal. Met a Detective Quintana who questioned me."

"Grandpa, this is so cool. Maybe you can assist this detective. You've helped track down murderers before."

"Me? I'm just a retired auto-parts store owner. And besides, who's to say that the body wasn't an accidental death. And even if it was a murder, I don't know how to investigate crimes."

She scrunched up her eyebrows and stared

at me. "You helped solve a zillion cases both in Hawaii and Colorado."

I shrugged. "That all must have been lost somewhere in my mis-wired brain cells. I don't remember anything like that."

Now she smiled again. "And I can always help you like I did in Colorado. There, I charged you a stuffed animal for every crime I helped you solve. It will be my wedding present to you. I'll assist you any way I can, and I won't even charge you any stuffed animals for my services."

"That's mighty kind of you. But I don't think I'll need any help. I'm not involved other than finding a body."

She gave me another hug. "I don't know, Grandpa. You seem to find a way of being implicated in crimes."

CHAPTER 3

"Now, Grandpa, I want a tour of your new house," Jennifer said.

"I'll show you around. We both can learn what it's like since it's all new to me as well."

While Marion was in the bathroom, Jennifer and I entered the bedroom. Jennifer pointed to a bag on the floor. "There's the carry-on that you packed in Boulder."

A corner of a picture frame stuck out of the bag. "I guess I haven't finished unpacking it yet."

"You have some souvenirs, Grandpa. Let me show you." She removed a framed butterfly collection and an autographed picture of a stark, institutional building.

I stared at the two items she held. "What the hell kind of mementos are these?"

"Oh, Grandpa. These are presents from the two detectives that you helped. The butterfly collection came from Hawaii, and the other is a picture of the jail where you almost got locked up."

"I sure don't remember any of that."

"Here. Let me put these on your dresser." She set them up and stepped back. "Now you're officially moved in."

Jennifer skipped back to the bag. "Let's see what else you have in here." She sorted through and removed several pictures. "Grandpa, here's a picture of me and another of you."

"I'll keep the one of you, but you can have the one of me."

"Cool. You'll have to autograph it for me."

I found a pen and was ready to sign it when I had an idea. "Jennifer, here's a trick I taught myself when I was younger." I transferred the pen to my left hand and scrawled my signature. "Although I'm right-handed, I learned how to write left-handed as well."

"Cool. It looks different but it's readable."

"Yeah. I had my right hand in a cast in high school after I fell out of a tree. That's when I taught myself to write left-handed. You should try it."

She grabbed the pen and tried writing on a piece of paper, ending up with an undeci-pherable scrawl.

"It just takes some practice." I wrote a sentence below what she had tried and signed it with a flourish.

On our way to breakfast Jennifer said, "I want to see the canals."

Denny replied, "We can see the main canal right from Venice Boulevard." He pulled to a stop on a bridge, and Jennifer looked out the window. "Do you know why they're called canals, Jennifer?"

"No, why?"

"Because we can all see them," Denny replied.

Jennifer groaned. "That was a really bad one, Dad."

"He inherited that talent from me," I said. "But, in addition, all dads have to go to bad-joke camp."

Jennifer ignored my comment and looked out the window. "Is this where you found the body, Grandpa?"

"What body?" Denny and Allison asked in unison.

"Oh, just a floater I happened upon during a stroll this morning."

"Dad, you're not getting involved in a murder again, are you?" Denny said.

"Why do people keep referring to 'again'?"

"Because you have a history of getting in trouble with the police."

"That couldn't be me. I'm a law-abiding

citizen."

"But you have a way of finding dead bodies," Jennifer said. "Now point out to me where you found this one."

I leaned across to look out her window. "Over toward that white bridge."

"Cool."

After returning from gobbling an omelet, I read a number of short stories, resisted the urge to take a nap, and then traded in my Bermuda shorts for my dark-blue trousers, a white shirt and a throat-constricting tie. That's probably what did in my brain cells. Too much oxygen cut off by wearing a tie in my store all those years.

I admired myself in the mirror. Not bad for an old gentleman. I still had all my own hair so I didn't need to resort to a substitute contribution from some furry animal. In addition I retained my original teeth and stood firmly upright on my creaky but solid legs. I patted my stomach. No paunch. I couldn't have weighed much more than when I was a mere pup in college.

Marion had already left for a hair appointment, and she would then go straight to the church to change into her wedding getup there. I had a little free time on my hands, and then my family was due to retrieve me for a quick snack before the big event. I guess they wanted to make sure I didn't pass out at the altar from hunger. I could faint from fright instead.

My wife Rhonda and I had tied the knot in a small church in Long Beach many years ago. We had had a happy marriage with only a smattering of fights, usually due to my hair-trigger temper. But we always made up the same day. That was something I had learned. Don't let an argument simmer overnight.

But her once vigorous body had been attacked by cancer. I remembered sitting by her hospital bed and holding her hand the day she died. She looked over toward me and in a raspy voice said, "Paul, you find someone else after I'm gone. You're too good a man to be by yourself." Tears had welled in my eyes, and I squeezed her hand. Then her eyelids closed, and she drifted off.

But after she was gone, the opportunity had never materialized up to the time my memory went on the fritz. After that, who knew? What if I had hooked up with some other old broad along the way? What if I were about to become a polygamist? Nah. I was sure that no one else besides Marion had agreed to put up with me.

I could imagine Rhonda looking down,

chuckling and blowing a kiss to wish the best for Marion and me.

Still I found it amazing that Marion had signed on for a recycled putz like me. With my memory I wasn't the easiest person to live with. It would be tough for her when I woke up every morning wondering who the hell she was. Still, there seemed to be some special connection between us. Before today, I couldn't remember Marion from the dish drainer, yet I felt warmth in my chest when I thought about her now. I just hoped it wasn't a pending heart attack. Hell, if my old ticker had lasted this long, it probably would get me through the wedding. Wedding. I started to break out in a sweat. I was turning in my bachelorhood again.

Denny, Allison and Jennifer showed up in their rental car to whisk me off to a sushi bar for a prenuptial feeding frenzy. My son Denny maintained the family tradition by wolfing down a plate of raw denizens of the deep, while Allison had a small portion and Jennifer picked the raw fish pieces out to savor independent of the rice and seaweed. With my stomach in turmoil due to the upcoming event I limited my intake to some salmon, tuna, crab, eel, squid and octopus. All right, in my nervous state I guess I kept up with Denny by consuming my fair share of seafood.

Then we raced off to get me to the church on time. After we hopped out of the car, Allison straightened my tie. "You look very handsome, Paul."

"What am I getting myself into?" I asked. "What am I doing to Marion? She's being stuck with an old relic whose memory is as solid as liver pate."

Allison patted my arm. "I think Marion is delighted that you asked her for her hand in marriage."

"Sure. I get her hand, but she's stuck with my memory."

My family headed inside to take seats while I waited in the lobby. I paced the floor for a few minutes, stopped, took a deep breath and when I discovered I wasn't going to pass out, I surveyed my surroundings. The white walls and Spanish-style windows were reminiscent of the mission buildings that lined California. Then the minister, a tall man in flowing white robes, directed me to the vestibule to wait for my command performance.

I opened the door and found a small room. As my eyes adjusted from the bright sunshine outside, I saw a table full of presents and a man nearly my age holding one of them.

"What the hell are you doing?" I asked in my most inquisitive tone.

"I . . . I . . . I," he said as he stepped backward, tripping and falling. His flailing arms struck a table and two silver candleholders tottered. The man and one of the candleholders crashed to the floor.

I grabbed the other candleholder and steadied it.

The man lay quietly on the floor with a candleholder on his chest. I removed it and set it aside as I bent down to examine him. He didn't seem to be breathing.

"Hey," I shouted. "We need some help."

No one came.

I burst through the back door into an adjoining small office. A woman sat at a desk.

"Call an ambulance," I screamed. "A man is hurt in the vestibule."

Her eyes widened. "What happened?"

"He fell over and isn't breathing."

She reached for the phone and punched in the three digits.

While she spoke on the telephone, I raced out as fast as my old legs would take me. I entered the congregation room where thirty people were seated. "Is there a doctor here?" I asked, trying to keep my voice firm but calm.

A man in a dark suit near the back stood up and approached me. "I'm a pediatrician."

"That's going to have to do. There's an injured man in the vestibule. Come with me."

Inside the small room, the doctor bent down to examine the fallen man. He began administering CPR.

Moments later I heard a siren. Then two men burst into the room. One placed an oxygen mask over the face of the injured man.

"He's not responding," one of the paramedics said.

"That's because he's dead," the doctor replied.

Then a police officer strode into the room. "I received a report of an accident." He bent down to examine the body. "Strange head wound."

"He fell," I said to be helpful.

The paramedics placed the body on a stretcher and took it off to their waiting vehicle. The policeman surveyed the room and then noticed the candleholder which he stooped over to examine without touching it.

He reached for a cell phone on his belt and placed a call. Then he turned toward me. "You're the one who witnessed what happened?"

"That's right. I came into the room, surprised the man, and he fell over, hitting his head."

The policeman regarded me carefully, his gray eyes boring in on me. "Was anyone else in the room?"

"No, just him and me."

"Do you know him?"

"No, never saw him before."

"I'll need to ask you to remain here until the detective arrives."

"I'll be happy to stay at the church, but I'm getting married in a few minutes."

He looked at me again. "Show me some identification."

I pulled out my wallet and handed over my ID card.

"This has an address in Hawaii."

"I've just moved to Venice and will be living with my wife who is expecting me to show up for a ceremony momentarily."

He wrote some notes on a pad and handed my ID card back.

"Just don't leave after the ceremony."

"We're having a reception here, so I'll be around."

I hustled out to take my place at the front of the church. Denny stood beside me.

"What was the delay?" he asked.

"I'll explain afterwards," I said with a gasp. I was breathing heavily, both from the accident I had just witnessed and the ceremony I was about to undertake.

As Marion had mentioned to me, her son-in-law George and grandson Austin also stood with us. George was in his early fifties, tan from the California sun and approximately Denny's height at six foot even. Austin was a little older than Jennifer, with the sulky look of a new teenager.

Then down the aisle came Jennifer followed by an older girl, who I guessed was Marion's granddaughter, and finally Marion's daughter Andrea.

Jennifer winked at me as she took her place.

Marion was accompanied by the minister who "gave her away" and then assumed his place for the ceremony.

She looked radiant in her simple pale-blue dress and matching blue netted hat.

The minister began. I half expected him to say, "Do you two old goats take each other . . . ?" But the service proceeded with him describing the bond between a man and a woman. I agreed with this. Then he launched into the importance of the marriage vow to love, honor and cherish. Again

I heard nothing to object to. When we reached the part of in sickness and in health, 'til death do us part, I flinched, wondering how long that might be for an over-the-hill guy like me. It could be minutes or years. Oh, well. If Marion was prepared to sign up for it, so was I.

I kissed the bride and felt her warm lips against mine. My old ticker started thumping lickety-split. Here I was, hitched again. It felt right even though she was almost a stranger to me. The music played and we marched up the aisle and out of the church. Outside, I realized that in my panic, I hadn't even noticed what the inside of the church looked like. At least I knew what the bride looked like. Damn attractive.

As we gathered in the courtyard to be congratulated, I spotted Detective Quintana who I had met by the canal that morning. He worked his way up to me and said, "I need to speak with you, Mr. Jacobson."

"This isn't a very convenient time, Detective. My bride deserves my attention."

His dark eyes bore in on me. "I won't take much of your time. Come with me."

I sensed that I didn't really have a choice, so I followed him to a Sunday school room adjoining the courtyard.

We found two adult-sized chairs and sat

down. He pulled his chair up to face me with our knees practically touching.

"I understand you were in the room when Harold Koenig died."

"I don't know Harold Koenig, but if that was the man who fell and hit his head, yes, I was there."

"Describe exactly what happened."

I went through the whole rigmarole again.

Just then Marion entered the room. "I've been looking for you, Paul. Our guests are waiting for us."

"See, Detective, I told you this wasn't a convenient time."

"Mrs. Jacobson, I need to speak with your husband for just a few more minutes."

"Is this about the man he found in the canal this morning?" she asked.

"No, this is a different matter. It concerns Harold Koenig."

"What about Harold?" she asked.

Quintana regarded Marion. "Do you know him?"

"Why, yes. We were friends. We even went on a few dates. That is, until Paul and I got engaged." She squeezed my hand. "Paul, you met Harold at the party we went to last night."

Quintana eyed me. "I thought you said you didn't know him, Mr. Jacobson."

46

"I don't recall meeting him."

Marion smiled. "Paul wouldn't remember because of his short-term memory loss. I need to rejoin the reception. Don't take too long, Paul."

With that she left the room.

Quintana pulled out a small box. "I need to collect your fingerprints."

"Something you're concerned about, Detective?"

"Just part of my investigation into Mr. Koenig's death."

I volunteered my fingertips and Detective Quintana soon had ten neat prints on a card.

"I look like I've been playing with finger paints." I admired my fingers.

"It'll wash off. Now, I need to ask you not to leave the state in the near future."

"But I have a honeymoon coming up in two weeks."

He raised his eyebrows. "If you have short-term memory loss, how do you know that?"

"Because I discussed it with Marion earlier and I remember things fine during the day."

Quintana stood up. "One other thing. The man who you found this morning in the canal has been identified as Frederick Vansworthy. Name mean anything to you?"

"Nope. Never heard it before."

"Any speculation on how his body ended up in the canal?"

"None whatsoever."

He stared at me with his keen eyes. "We suspect he was murdered."

I blinked. "Murdered?"

"Yes. Anything you care to say?"

"Who do you think killed him?"

"I was hoping you might shed some light on that, Mr. Jacobson."

"No. I have nothing to add."

He eyed me again. "We'll be speaking again, Mr. Jacobson."

"You know where to find me, at least until my honeymoon cruise."

With that, Quintana departed.

I sat there thinking. Quintana had dropped some hints, but I couldn't have had anything to do with Vansworthy's death. Unfortunately, I couldn't remember one way or the other.

Returning to the festivities, I noticed both Jennifer and Austin, Marion's grandson, grazing at a table full of food.

"Save something for me to eat," I said.

"Hi, Grandpa. Have some cheese." Jennifer reached for a yellow slab and cut off a piece and plopped it into her mouth. "Ewww." Her face scrunched up in disgust.

I laughed. "That wasn't cheese. You just ate a big bite of butter."

I filled up a plate with goodies as Jennifer skipped off with Austin trailing behind her, still looking sullen. What a contrast. Jennifer bounced around like a pogo stick. Austin had his hands thrust into his pockets and slunk off like he was my age and had the weight of the world on his shoulders.

Marion was speaking with a man when I approached her. "Paul, meet Clint Brock. He's an art dealer here in Venice."

I stared at the Cary Grant look-alike and held out my hand. "Pleased to meet you." I received a firm handshake.

Clint Brock was in his forties, dapper dresser with neatly trimmed hair.

"I was just mentioning to Clint that there was an accident just before the ceremony. I never did hear the particulars, Paul."

"Really a strange event. When I entered the room, I seemed to startle your friend Harold Koenig. Then it was all like a slow-motion movie. I can picture it vividly. He fell and two candleholders toppled over. I grabbed one of them to steady it, and the other fell on Mr. Koenig. I moved that one off him. Apparently he hit his head. The combination of the fall and shock must have done him in."

"That's a shame," Brock said. He looked truly worried. "And for you with your ceremony about to take place."

"Not the kind of thing to calm the nerves of an old geezer like me."

"Marion was telling me that you have memory problems, but you seem to recall the details of Koenig's accident very clearly," Brock said.

"Yeah. I have this strange type of short-term memory loss. I remember things fine during the day, but once I fall asleep, I forget everything that happened to me before going to sleep. But I can still recall events from my more-distant past."

"Interesting. So if we had met yesterday, you wouldn't remember me."

"Not one iota. You'd be a complete stranger to me."

"That makes things difficult."

"You can say that again. That's why I'm very privileged that Marion agreed to hitch up with me."

She patted my arm and smiled. "I consider it an honor."

Brock excused himself and disappeared into the building.

I turned to Marion. "Does the name Frederick Vansworthy mean anything to you?"

"Why, yes. He's an art dealer and an

acquaintance of my son-in-law, George. He attended the party last night. You even spoke with him. Why do you ask?"

"Detective Quintana informed me that Vansworthy was the man I saw in the canal this morning."

Marion put her hand to her mouth. "Oh, dear. You and Frederick Vansworthy had a very heated argument at the party last night."

CHAPTER 4

I flinched at hearing that I had argued with Vansworthy the night before he turned up dead. "When Detective Quintana hears that, he'll be all over me like sweat on a marathon runner. I'll be his number-one suspect. He can't be thinking too highly of me anyway, since I appeared at the scene of two deaths within one day."

"But you didn't have anything to do with either," Marion said. "I was with you all last night, so you couldn't have done anything to Frederick Vansworthy between the time he was alive at the party and when his body showed up in the canal."

"Yeah, but you're my wife now so Quintana won't believe you."

"And poor Harold. That was obviously an accident. He had a bad heart so I'm sure surprise at seeing you and the fall could have led to a heart attack."

"Some medical types will be inspecting

his body to find out what happened."

Just then the wedding photographer approached and asked Marion to join him in the garden for a few bride pictures. I excused myself and wandered off to have another snack. Had to keep the old body nourished. I'd need all my strength to be able to perform on my wedding night.

After stuffing my face with some meatballs, baby hot dogs in thick brown syrup and a strawberry or two, I noticed Marion's grandson Austin off in the corner sulking. I ambled toward him and saw a black eye.

"What happened to you?" I asked.

"I ran into a hard object." He avoided eye contact and slunk away.

I wondered what was going on. A few minutes later I spotted Jennifer. Her perky demeanor had changed. She had a scowl on her puss.

"What's up," I said. "I saw Austin has a black eye."

"That jerk." Her eyes flared.

"Uh-oh. I detect some altercation between the two of you."

"That little toad tried to paw me. I let him have it. Pow." She punched her right fist into her left hand.

"I think you taught him a lesson," I said. "I need to have a little chat with him concerning his behavior."

"He should be locked up." Jennifer stomped off.

This was serious misconduct and required swift action. I wandered through the crowd until I caught a glimpse of Austin sitting on a cement bench by himself. I stood in front of him.

"You're going to receive more than black eyes if you don't learn to treat women right."

He scowled at me. "She was asking for it."

"I don't think so. The evidence on your face would indicate you weren't invited to touch her."

"Leave me alone."

"No. You need to apologize. We're one family now, and your behavior is unacceptable."

"You going to make me?" He still didn't make eye contact.

"Yes." I grabbed him by the collar and lifted him up.

He let out a yelp.

"I may be an old codger, but in our family we treat people with respect." I steered him back toward the reception.

He flailed his arms, but I had him off balance and kept moving.

We found Jennifer, and I called out to her. "Austin has something to say to you."

He tried to slink away, but I pulled him back.

Jennifer came up six inches from his face. "You looking for another black eye?"

"Jennifer, the violence is over. Austin?"

They glared at each other.

Finally, Austin averted his gaze. When he looked up again he said, "I'm sorry."

"See, that wasn't so tough," I said.

"I'm only forgiving you because of my grandpa's wedding," Jennifer said.

He let out a sigh of relief. "It won't happen again."

I think he was convinced that Jennifer had been ready to pop him in the eye again.

"Now why don't you two try to get along for the rest of the reception?"

"Okay," Jennifer said. She waved her fist at Austin. "But no more funny business."

He flinched, but stood up straighter. "Okay."

They headed off to graze some more at the snack table.

I rejoined my bride who had been immortalized in dozens of photographs while I was trying to render family unity.

"Where have you been?" Marion asked.

"I had a peacekeeping mission. I had to

prevent bloodshed between our two families."

"It was something to do with Austin, wasn't it?"

"Yes. How did you guess?"

"He's been a handful lately. Andrea doesn't know what to do with him."

"A little tanning on the backside wouldn't hurt."

"She doesn't believe in that."

"I don't know. There's something to be said for old-fashioned corporal punishment."

"You don't really believe that, do you?"

I smiled. "I go along with a good threat, though. Austin needs to understand the simple cause and effect of actions he takes. Between a black eye and a little friendly persuasion I think he got the message."

The band struck up a slow number, and I took Marion's hand to lead her out to dance. We made several passes around the patio, and I managed not to mangle her feet. Several other couples joined us. I held her close and felt proud that she had agreed to be my wife.

Later, suffering from too much liquid refreshment, I two-stepped off to the little boys' room and then felt much better. On my way back to the festivities, I spied Austin off in a corner of the courtyard smashing baby tomatoes against the church wall.

"What the heck are you doing?" I asked.

His head jerked up. "Playing a game." He scowled at me.

"Well, it isn't improving the value of church property. Go into the bathroom and get some wet paper towels to wipe this mess up."

He didn't move. "You gonna make me?"

The kid had obviously forgotten what had happened the last time he used that line. "Maybe I should ask Jennifer to come persuade you."

His eyes widened and he looked around wildly.

"Now, get cracking," I said.

He gave an exasperated sigh. "Okay. Okay."

He disappeared inside the restroom. Moments later he reappeared with a handful of towels and scuffed his feet as he returned to the scene of the damage he'd inflicted on the wall. As I stood over him with my arms crossed, he began scrubbing.

"What are you so unhappy about today?" I asked.

He sneered at me. "I want to be at the beach with my friends. My mom made me come here."

"Your friends can wait. This is an important event for your grandmother. She's pleased that you're here."

He looked surprised. "But I'm stuck with a bunch of old people."

I laughed. "I know how you feel. I hate being around old people."

"But you are one."

"True. That's why I like a group like today that has kids and adults as well as those who aren't spring chickens. One other thing for you to consider, Austin. You can learn things from old fogies like your grandmother and me. I wouldn't write off the old coots. You might pick up a pointer or two."

"Like how to scrub walls."

I chuckled. "Like how to avoid cleaning walls if you don't smash juicy vegetables onto them in the first place."

He kept scouring until he had the mess cleaned up.

"Now go throw away all the towels and we can return to the party."

Austin completed his task, and we strolled back to the gathering. I put my arm on his shoulder and whispered in his ear. "You might as well get used to having me around since I'll be living above your garage."

Marion saw us and asked, "Where have you two been?"

I winked at Austin. "We've been having a man-to-man talk."

Austin blinked but didn't scowl and then headed over to the grazing table. I watched him for a moment and noticed that he was avoiding the tomatoes.

"Austin seems very subdued," Marion said.

"He'd rather be somewhere else. Pretty normal reaction for a kid his age. Me, I'm perfectly content to be here with my new bride." I planted a smacker on Marion's lips.

Later that afternoon we returned to our honeymoon cottage, and I dispensed with the tie.

"We need to go over to George and Andrea's house now," Marion informed me.

"We being kicked out of the apartment?"

Marion swatted me. "No, silly. We're going to open presents."

"Then I guess my presence is required."

She made a motion to swat me again, but I ducked.

As we went out the door, the gray tabby cat I'd seen that morning appeared and rubbed against my leg. I reached down and chucked her under the chin.

"That's amazing, Paul. Cleo isn't friendly

with anyone except family members. She must have accepted you as part of the family already."

"I think she's sizing me up to use my leg as a scratching post."

Marion laughed. "It isn't that at all. She likes you, just as I do." She gave me a hug.

"I appreciate that. I need all the friends I can get."

We assembled in George and Andrea's living room to open gifts. Jennifer and Austin sat on the floor while the rest of us resorted to chairs with soft cushions and firm backrests. I watched Jennifer. She had the eager expression of Christmas morning. Austin had given up his sullen look and appeared to be a real kid again.

"Where'd all the presents come from?" I asked.

"I carted a trunk load back from the church," George said.

"And we have a collection we received in the mail," Andrea added.

"Let's get started," Jennifer said, clapping her hands.

Marion began opening presents while Andrea wrote down on a notepad what had come from whom.

We received a number of silver trays and pitchers, some kitchenware, a matching pair of fuzzy robes and then Marion announced, "Paul, here's a package sent by our friend Meyer Ohana from Kaneohe, Hawaii."

"Who's he?" I asked.

"Grandpa, Meyer was your best friend when you lived in the retirement home in Hawaii. He's a retired judge and lawyer."

"But I hate lawyers," I said.

"He's different," Jennifer said. "You like him."

Marion opened the box and displayed a set of monkeypod bowls. "There's also an envelope in here addressed to you, Paul." She handed it to me.

I opened it to find a card that read, "Congratulations, jerk. It's about time you made an honest woman of Marion." It was signed "Henry Palmer."

"What the hell is this?" I said, handing the card to Marion.

She laughed. "This is from Henry, your other tablemate at the Kina Nani retirement home. Henry always insulted everyone. You must really rate to receive a card from him."

"If you say so."

We finished opening the rest of the packages, and I surveyed the carnage. "Not a bad haul for two old newlyweds."

"Where are we going to put all these things?" Marion said.

"I'll help you carry them to your place," Jennifer said.

After we lugged the paraphernalia up to our apartment, Jennifer stayed to chat with Marion and me.

"Grandpa, are you in trouble with the police over the body you found in the canal?"

"Detective Quintana has been nosing around asking questions."

"You need to do some investigation on your own. I helped you when you were accused of crimes in Boulder."

"I'll take all the help I can get. So far Quintana's dropped hints but hasn't said anything about pressing charges."

"But when he finds out that you and Vansworthy argued, he'll be back," Marion said. "That's why you need an attorney."

"I acted as your lawyer in Boulder," Jennifer said.

"Then I'll rely on you again, if I need to," I said.

"Good," Jennifer said. "I'll make sure you stay out of jail."

That night after all the festivities, I sat down to document the day's activities in my journal. I felt a mix of excitement and concern. Imagine me at my age having a brand-new bride who seemed delighted to be stuck with me. My whole body tingled at the thought of what would happen later. But then my chest constricted at the thought of the two deaths I had encountered during the day. I had a whole new life here as a recycled married man, but couldn't avoid the cloud hanging over my head from my proximity to a murder and an accident. I'd have to learn more about this Vansworthy character — that was for sure. I could look into that starting tomorrow. But in the meantime . . . I closed my journal.

Marion came over and took my hand.

"What happens now?" I asked nonchalantly.

She swatted me on the arm. "Don't give me that innocent act. It's time for us to consummate our marriage."

"That sounds like fun. I hope I can live up to your expectations."

"I'll see to it that you do."

She snuggled up next to me and a little-used part of my anatomy came alive. "I'll be damned. Something's happening."

We kissed, and soon clothes began flying around like kites on a spring day.

Then we were in bed, and my hands began exploring interesting parts of Marion. One thing led to another, and soon we were hooked up and making the sheets hum. I upheld the family honor without suffering a heart attack, and afterwards I lay there feeling like the luckiest guy in the world.

"Not bad for someone your age," Marion said.

"Not bad? I'm grateful that everything went in the right place and worked."

The next morning I woke up and saw Marion sleeping next to me. I remembered who she was and replayed in my mind the words used by the minister to hitch us the day before. I shook her awake.

"Something amazing happened. I can remember everything from yesterday."

She yawned. "Do you remember me telling you that most days you can't recall anything from the day before?"

"Yes."

"Well, you've now experienced the exception."

I scratched my head. "Was it something I ate?"

"No, but there is one specific thing that activates your memory overnight."

"Must be getting married."

"Not directly, but in this case it contributed."

"You don't mean . . ."

"Now you're on the right track."

"Our little excursion between the sheets last night?"

"Exactly."

"Damn. I'd suggest a repeat performance, but I don't want to press my luck."

"You can press it whenever you want."

"My intentions might be better than my ability to execute."

"We'll have to see how it works out," Marion said. "The one caution. You only seem to remember things for one day and then it wears off. So enjoy your memories of yesterday, today."

"I'll do that. I recall a wonderful ceremony, a beautiful bride and an exciting end to the day." I didn't bring up that I also remembered a dead body in the canal and a friend of Marion's falling over and dying.

Marion said, "I hope I didn't keep you awake during the night."

"No. I slept right through after you knocked me out."

"I tossed and turned and woke up several times. I don't seem to be able to sleep through the night anymore."

"Well, you didn't bother me. I guess I'm lucky. Once I zonked out, I slept for the whole night."

"I used to be that way, but in the last several years I've turned into a light sleeper," Marion said with a frown.

"Before I retired, I went through a period like that. Usually I was worrying about problems at work. Once I became a retired gentleman, I learned how to sleep through the night again."

Marion smiled. "But that won't work for me. I'm not a retired gentleman."

"I'll say. You're one hot retired gentle-woman. Have you tried sleeping pills?"

"Yes, but they don't do any good for me."

"I feel the same way. In fact you can stop forcing me to stuff pills down my throat like you did yesterday." Then I remembered something from the morning before. "Yesterday when I got up and wandered around, you seemed to be sleeping pretty well."

Marion smiled. "For some reason, I seem to sleep fine when it gets light."

With a stomach full of pancakes and bacon cooked by my lovely wife, I settled in for my first morning as a second-time husband, opening the *Los Angeles Times* to an article about scams being perpetrated on geriatrics like me. Couldn't be too careful when you reached my height in geezer-land.

My perusing examples of roofing, insurance and mail fraud was interrupted by a knock on the door.

"Who'd be interfering with a pair of newlyweds after their first night of marital bliss?" I asked.

"I'm washing the dishes," Marion said. "You can do the honors."

I lifted my aging but still-active body off the couch and moseyed to the door. Upon opening it, I spied my good buddy Detective Quintana who I easily recognized because of my sex-induced super memory.

"Detective, please come in to our humble abode."

His mustache twitched at me. "We need to talk."

I motioned toward the couch. "Can I offer you a beverage: coffee, tea, hemlock?"

He didn't smile. "Nothing." He sat down with his mustache continuing to twitch. "I want to review some information about the two deaths you reported yesterday."

"Yes?"

"First, the body of Frederick Vansworthy, found in the canal."

"Go on."

"There's one thing that puzzles me, Mr. Jacobson. I have a report that you had a heated argument with Mr. Vansworthy the night before he turned up murdered. Care to share your recollection about the dispute?"

"Unfortunately, I don't remember the events of that evening."

"Pretty selective memory."

"I don't seem to remember things overnight."

He stared at me. "Then how did you recognize me this morning?"

CHAPTER 5

I didn't want to go off into the effect of sex on my leaky brain cells so I merely said, "I guess it's because you're such a memorable character, Detective."

He peered at me like he was trying to suck any good brain cells out through my eye sockets. "I've interviewed two people who overheard you and Mr. Vansworthy arguing about the treatment of the aging population."

"That's entirely possible, since I'm part of that aging population."

He flipped open a small notepad. "And I quote, 'If you think older citizens should receive declining Social Security payments after reaching age eighty, maybe you could help the situation by dying early.'"

My heart started beating like I was going to cash in the old chips. Damn. I couldn't remember saying that, but if the guy had pissed me off, it was entirely possible that I would have made a dumb comment like that.

Marion came over. "Yes, Paul said something along those lines, but only because Frederick Vansworthy was acting like a jerk."

I smiled at Marion. "See, Detective. My bride has a good memory and gave you a plausible explanation for what happened."

Quintana drummed his fingers on his notepad. "Still, it's very interesting that the next day Vansworthy turns up dead and is discovered by, of all people, you, Mr. Jacobson."

I gulped. "Yeah. That was strange."

"And another thing. The matter of the death of Harold Koenig. You're alone with him and he's found dead with a head wound. Did you hit him, Mr. Jacobson?"

Marion gasped.

"Why would you ask that?" I said.

He gave me his fierce stare again. "Your fingerprints were found on a dented candleholder that had the victim's blood on it."

I thought back to the event, thankful for the sexual assist the night before. "No, he fell over and hit his head on his own. The candleholder toppled over and landed on him. I can't speak to how it received a dent." Then a thought occurred to me. "But it would have been logical to have my fingerprints because I removed it from on top of him. As for blood, when I set it down it could have been brushed against blood from his head wound."

"Possible. But, once again, Mr. Jacobson, you had a motive. Mr. Koenig was reported to be interested in your wife."

Marion cleared her throat. "But I wasn't interested in Harold, Detective. And Paul married me so Harold was out of the picture."

"Maybe Mr. Jacobson wanted him permanently out of the picture."

"Give me a break, Detective. Harold Koenig's death was an accident. He was surprised to see me, tripped and hit his head. No deep dark plot behind it."

Quintana held up two fingers. "Within one day, two deaths. One a confirmed murder of Mr. Vansworthy and the other the death of Harold Koenig under suspicious circumstances. Both reported by you, Mr. Jacobson. Both with motives linking you."

I flinched. "How was Vansworthy killed?"

"I thought you might be able to shed some light on that, Mr. Jacobson."

"But I didn't kill anyone."

"You're this close to moving from a person of interest to a full suspect." Quintana held his thumb and index finger half an inch

71

apart. "Judges and juries in Los Angeles are more lenient when the murderer confesses and acts contrite than when he pretends to be innocent."

"But I am innocent."

"We'll see, Mr. Jacobson. We'll see. Any final words for me?"

"Yes. Koenig's death was an accident. And go find who really killed Vansworthy."

Quintana's mustache twitched and he stood up. "Think this over, Mr. Jacobson." Then he turned and let himself out.

I looked at Marion. "Quintana's convinced I'm the Hillside Strangler."

"We'll find a way to clear your good name." She gave me a pat on the arm. "But I think you need a good lawyer."

"I don't want any slimy lawyer. I can take care of this myself."

She regarded me thoughtfully. "You should reconsider that position, but let's see what happens. Now, we need to dress for church."

"Church?"

"Yes. There's a ten-o'clock service at Saint Andrew's. I've been attending with my family."

"Being in church twice in two days. Will they invite me back after what happened with Harold Koenig there yesterday?"

Marion smiled. "Of course. We'll have a calm service today with nothing like that event."

We crammed into George's white Camry with Austin sitting between Marion and me in the backseat. It was a good thing that Marion's granddaughter Rachel was back in her dorm room for the summer session at UCLA or we never would have all fit.

"I've got my eye on you," I whispered into Austin's ear.

He flinched.

Then Marion put her arm around him. "Don't worry. Paul's bark is worse than his bite."

I leaned toward Austin and said under my breath, "Woof."

He jumped.

Austin just needed a little reminding.

We parked on a side street off Venice Boulevard, and I admired the church of my previous day's activities. I'd been so pre-occupied with the upcoming ceremony that I hadn't really paid attention to what the outside of the building looked like. What a perfect setting. A two-story white structure with red tile roof, bell tower — a modern Spanish mission, adorned with palm trees and emerald-green grass.

A man in a gray suit and a red carnation in the buttonhole greeted us at the door and handed us programs. We slid into a stained hardwood pew midway back. Now I had time to inspect the place. Yesterday had been the panic from the Harold Koenig death followed by the further terror of getting hitched. I took a deep breath and scanned the side of the church where small square stained-glass windows shone red, green, blue and white from the morning sun. I craned my neck upward to see larger, arched stained glass windows. Straight above, dark wood beams formed supports for the roof. Ahead, a white cloth covered the altar and large candleholders stood on each side. I'd had enough of candleholders. Music boomed out, and I turned around and noticed a large pipe organ in the balcony.

Not a bad place to have tied the knot.

I survived the sitting and standing for singing and responsive readings, a sermon (on helping your neighbor) that didn't put me to sleep, and the donation of five dollars from my Social Security earnings. Near the end of the service the minister announced that they were looking for volunteers to help in the office.

Marion squeezed my arm and whispered

in my ear. "I've been helping two days a week. You should join me."

"I could handle that. Where do I sign up?"

After the service, Marion led me to the office. "I'm here as your latest recruit," I said.

"I'm Marisa Young," a perky woman in her fifties said, reaching out to shake my hand. "We're having an indoctrination meeting in fifteen minutes."

"I don't know about being indoctrinated," I said, "but I'm willing to be trained."

She smiled at me. "That's just church talk, you know."

Out in the courtyard, refreshments were being served. I grabbed a cookie and a cup of punch and surveyed the crowd. Groups of middle-aged matrons and men in suits munched away while a smattering of kids bobbed and weaved through the crowd. Off to the side I spotted another group — poorly dressed, men with shaggy beards, women in torn long dresses.

I ambled up to Marion. "What's with the members who look like street people?" I asked.

"Oh, those are street people. This church has an active program to support and help the homeless."

I looked again at the motley crew. They

seemed to be enjoying the refreshments, but stayed off by themselves. There, but for the grace of money saved and Social Security, went me.

I noticed that the clean-cut church members weren't mingling with the scruffy ones. "They may be invited to church," I said to Marion, "but they aren't welcomed with open arms."

"What do you mean?" she said.

"Just look. They have their own little enclave over there, but it's obvious no one else is talking with them."

"You're right. I've never made the connection."

"Well, I'm going to do something about that."

I ambled over and spotted one bearded man who seemed to be leading a lively conversation. I tapped him on the shoulder. "I hope I'm not infringing, but I wanted to come over and introduce myself. My name is Paul Jacobson." I held out my hand.

A smile appeared on the man's weathered lips. "I'll be damned. You must be new here. I'm Harley Marcraft." He gave my hand a vigorous shake.

"You're right, Harley. I moved here recently and just remarried. That's my wife over there." I pointed to Marion who was now talking with the man she had spoken to after our wedding yesterday.

Harley chuckled. "Aren't you a little long in the tooth to be a newlywed?"

"Nah. I'm just getting started. An old fart like me is always ready for new challenges. So how long have you been coming to this church?"

"Over the last year. Good place to find something to eat on Sunday mornings."

"So you pick up brunch here. Where do you usually hang out?"

"Mainly down by the beach. Great place to sleep, out under the stars."

"And with the warm Southern Californian weather that should work out most of the time. What do you do when a rainstorm moves in?"

"That's another good thing with this church. When the weather turns to crap, they open a room for us to sleep in."

"Sounds like you have all your bases covered."

"You better watch your wife so she doesn't take up with Clint Brock," Harley said, pointing to the man speaking with Marion.

I remembered my discussion with him the day before. "He's an art dealer."

Another hirsute guy sidled up to us and shouted at me. "Art dealer! Are you tied in with those scumbags?"

"Hold your water," I said. "I've met him, but that's it."

The guy became more agitated and grabbed my shirt collar. "You're one of them! I can tell!"

"Get your hands off me!" I ordered, raising my voice and whacking his hand away from my shirt.

"Asshole!" he yelled back.

Now I was really heated. "Go crawl off into a closet somewhere and disappear!"

The guy's eyes grew wide, he sputtered, turned on his heels and marched away.

"What's with him?" I said to Harley. "I'm only trying to be friendly, and he comes up and acts like a jerk."

"Don't mind him. He's been kind of testy lately. He may not appreciate it, but I'm glad you stopped over to say hello."

"If we're coming to the same church, I figured we should meet. If you'll excuse me, I'll rejoin my bride."

Marion was still speaking to Clint Brock. I scrutinized his face and matched it to the one I had seen the day before. Amazing how my memory could imitate a normal person's with a little injection of marital nighttime escapades.

Marion frowned as I joined her. "Paul,

what was all that shouting about?"

"Strange. I went over to speak with some of the street people. Met a nice guy named Harley Marcraft, but this other wild man came up and yelled at me. I knew I should hold my temper, but he riled me up so I shouted back."

"No harm done."

"Yeah, you're right. I'll probably never see him again, not that I'd recognize him anyway."

"Your short-term memory problem?" Brock asked.

"That's right. Tomorrow, this fine day will all be blotto."

Someone tapped Brock on the shoulder, and he turned to join another conversation.

"That homeless guy really acted nuts. I made a comment concerning your buddy Clint Brock, and he went ballistic. Seems he's not fond of art dealers."

"Probably had a bad experience on the street."

"Must have. Other than that encounter, I'm beginning to like your family's church."

"I certainly have fond memories of being here yesterday," Marion said.

"I'm still amazed that you consented to go through a ceremony with an old poop like me."

"I only married you so you'd add some excitement to my life."

"Well, I'll try to live up to that whenever possible."

Marion looked at her watch. "Now, you're due for the office indoctrination. Marisa runs a tight ship so you better not keep her waiting."

"After all the years managing my own store, I'm now assigned to be an assistant clerk in a pathetic, two-bit nonprofit outfit."

"I thought you liked the church."

"I do. I just feel like bitching."

"Go." Marion pointed toward the building.

"Yes, ma'am." I saluted and headed into the church.

I returned to the office and survived the indoctrination, learning where staplers, stationary and paper clips were stashed and avoided any paper cuts or other vagaries of the low-budget, nonprofit office world. I signed up to help assemble a mailing on Monday. Not that I would remember what to do then, but it obviously made Marisa happy to see me nod my head at her instructions. She proposed several other ways I could assist, but I adamantly avoided committing to anything that might entail touching a computer.

Afterward I sat by myself contemplating my navel. I felt the uncertainty of this new life of mine. Here I was in a place I didn't know, preparing to pitch in at a church that was new to me and living with a brand new wife. That last part made me feel good all over. Marion was quite a woman. I'd have to look to her to steer me as I forgot things from day to day. I'd pitch in to do my best whether assisting in the church office or helping around our apartment.

When I returned to Marion I said, "Now your job is to remind me to go to the church office tomorrow at ten."

"Agreed. Andrea can give you a ride if you like."

"It's not too far. I can walk over if you remind me where it is."

Back at our honeymoon shack, I received a call from Jennifer.

"Grandpa, we're picking you up in thirty minutes."

"You kidnapping me?"

"No. We're taking you to the La Brea Tar Pits."

"You planning to tar and feather me?"

"Oh, Grandpa. We're going to see the old bones."

"Fine. I'll fit right in."

Marion decided to stay to organize our

wealth of gifts, so I had a kitchen pass to head off with my family on my first full day of marriage.

In the backseat of Denny's rental car, Jennifer leaned over. "Tell me more about the body you found in the canal."

"All I know is that he was an art dealer named Frederick Vansworthy. We apparently met at a party Friday night and I argued with him."

Jennifer pursed her lips. "And you're in trouble because of that."

"Exactly."

"I overheard that argument," Denny said from the driver's seat. "The guy was acting like an idiot."

"That's what Marion told the detective as well," I said. "He still wants to haul me in."

"Sounds like you need a lawyer, Dad."

"No way. Jennifer can help me."

She smiled. "Just like I helped you in Boulder. We're a great investigating team, Grandpa. Maybe the murder has something to do with stolen art or forged paintings, the victim being an art dealer."

"I have no clue," I said.

"You'd better find out more about the victim, Grandpa. That way you can help track down the real killer."

"I wish it was that easy."

"As I told you, my wedding present is to help you clear your name, pro bono."

"Uh-oh. You sound like a lawyer."

"No. Jennifer Jacobson, private investigator." She thumped her chest. "When I return to Colorado, I'll do research for you on the Internet. We'll find out more concerning one Frederick Vansworthy."

With that decided we arrived at our destination without being run over by any smog-impaired, freeway-incensed, gun-toting Los Angelenos.

First we visited the Page Museum and mingled with the saber-toothed cats, short-faced bears, mastodons, mammoths and Shasta ground sloths.

"Some of these animals are even older than I am," I told my family.

Jennifer glared at me. "Grandpa, you don't even compare."

"I don't know. I've been referred to as an old fossil from time to time."

As we exited the building, I saw a man handing out flyers. Jennifer skipped over to obtain one and then brought it over for us to read. In bold print it said, "Save Our Surfside. Please help us protect the beach environment of Southern California."

I moseyed over to the brochure man who stood there in jeans and a white T-shirt.

"How come you're trying to save the ocean shores here at the tar pits?"

He smiled. "We're canvassing all the major tourist attractions."

"What are you going to save the beaches from?"

"Exploitation and overdevelopment. We want the shoreline to be returned to a natural state without all the commercialization and overuse."

"Seems like it's a little late to put that genie back in the bottle."

"It's never too late. At one time we had no national parks or forests."

"What do you propose — dynamite all the buildings along the beach?"

"No. Nothing that extreme. We want to amend the California Coastal Act of Nineteen Seventy-six to place a moratorium on adding multiple-story buildings within two hundred yards of the beaches in Los Angeles."

"What if people want to improve their homes or businesses?"

"That's fine as long as they follow the proposed height restrictions."

"I can buy that."

"Would you care to sign our petition?"

"Let me take a look." I read through the notice and decided it was innocuous enough.

He handed me a pen, and I filled in my name and signed.

"Anyone else in your party care to add a signature?" he asked.

"I'm the only California resident in the crowd."

"Would you be willing to make a donation?"

"Don't press your luck."

"Come on, Dad," Denny said. "We want to show Jennifer the outdoor pits."

"Heck. I'm ready now. Had to do my environmental duty."

Denny steered me toward the path, and I took one last look at the guy handing out brochures. That would be a hell of a way to spend a nice day, but he seemed perfectly content accosting people.

We wandered along, viewing various pits of goo where the bones had been pulled out. I could just imagine some huge hairy creature being stuck in tar and slowly sinking while it let out bellows or yowls or screams. Not a pleasant way to go.

Jennifer seemed pleased with her cultural experience as we headed back to Venice Beach. "Tonight's the big night," she said.

"I thought that was last night — my wedding night."

"That too. But tonight we're going on a grunion hunt. You're coming too, Grandpa."

"Grunion? Is that anything like a snipe hunt where you leave someone out in the woods or tar pit on their own?"

"No. Grunion are little silver fish that you catch by hand. Tonight is a grunion run and we can catch some."

On the way home as I sat in the car contemplating my new life in Los Angeles, I had a mixed feeling of awe and confusion. It made my tummy warm to be with my family during their visit, and Jennifer invigorated anyone including an old ancient like me. After all the years I had spent in the LA area as a young first-time married man and then raising Denny, now I had returned. Back then we had to navigate city streets versus the now-crowded freeways. Still I suffered the strange repercussions of my weirdly wired brain with the last six years or so having disappeared into the dust bin.

Oh, well. With my new bride, I'd have to enjoy things as they came: a new place to live . . . and a bevy of dead bodies. Crapola. I had to figure out what was going on with the murder. Then I could truly relax as a retired guy in the jungles of Venice Beach. And now I was signed up to catch grunion.

I'd jump in and do that with the young whippersnappers. Hell. I'd caught a few fish in my time.

And true to Jennifer's word, that night we all assembled. George, Andrea, Austin, Denny, Allison, Jennifer, Marion and yours truly with buckets in hand and armed with flashlights headed down to the beach.

"What's the protocol?" I asked.

George cleared his throat. "The grunion come in at high tide which is ten o'clock — in fifteen minutes. They wiggle into the sand and you can grab them when they're laying and fertilizing eggs."

"We're going to interrupt their sex lives?" I said.

"There are hundreds of thousands of them when they run. A few won't be missed."

"I don't know. I wouldn't appreciate being put in a bucket in the heat of the moment."

As we marched out onto the sand, we found several hundred of our closest neighbors also with buckets in hand.

"Seems like a popular event," I said.

"Fairly typical crowd," George said. "The unpredictable part is how many grunion will show up. On some runs we've seen the beach covered with silver. Other times, nothing."

"You'd think the grunion would find a more private place to have sex," I said.

We waited with George checking his watch and giving a countdown on expected time of arrival.

Jennifer and Austin were friends again and yakked about surfing, iPods and other current events.

Then my old eyes spotted flashes of silver in the sand. "Look. Over there."

Slivers of silver wriggled in the sand as thousands of tiny fish stuck their tails downward to enjoy a moment of bliss. The mass of bucket carriers converged on the dancing silver fork handles, grabbing and lifting.

After a moment of hesitation, I joined the foray, eagerly extracting the wiggling fish and dropping them in my pail with a thump.

Finally, Andrea suggested that we head back home for a fish fry. We gathered our pails and headed toward the street.

"Uh-oh, I left my sandals on the beach," Jennifer said.

"You better watch it or you'll end up with a memory like mine," I said. "I'll walk back with you."

We retraced our steps, and Jennifer found

her footwear on the sand. As we returned to the street a man in uniform approached us.

"Good evening, Officer," I said.

He didn't smile at me. "May I see your fishing license?"

"Fishing license?"

"Yes. You need a fishing license to catch grunion."

My mouth dropped open, and then I regained my composure. "I've never heard of such a thing. Just to grab grunion?"

"That's the law. May I see some identification?"

I reached in my back pocket, extracted my wallet and showed him my ID.

"This has an address in Hawaii."

"I know. I need to update it. I'm living in Venice now."

He wrote out a ticket. Unfortunately, I remembered my new address and being a law-abiding citizen, I gave it to him. He tore off a copy for me.

"You should make an exemption for my grandpa. He's eighty-five years old."

"No. Anyone over sixteen needs a fishing license. How old are you?"

Jennifer stamped her foot. "I'm twelve."

He turned and strolled off to accost the next victim.

"It's like shooting fish in a barrel for the

game warden tonight," I said. "I feel like one of the grunion we caught."

We rejoined the family group and I displayed my new souvenir.

"I've never heard of that," George said.

"Well, there's a fish and game warden who is going to exceed his quota tonight. Let's get out of here before he stops anyone else in our group."

As we headed home, rain began to fall.

"What's this?" I asked. "I didn't think it rained in Los Angeles in the summer."

"Not very often," Marion said. "But we do have occasional storms blowing in."

Back at the ranch Andrea put a large skillet on the stovetop and began rolling the grunion in flour. In moments the little fish were sizzling in the pan. When offered one, I bit down on the crunchy bones and small amount of flesh that tasted like flour and seawater. Oh, well. I had my fishing violation as a souvenir of the evening's activities.

The rain was coming down like bobcats and prairie dogs by this time. I was glad we still weren't out on the beach grabbing sex-crazed silver fish. I sat down to write my escapades, knowing I wouldn't be up to a memory jolt that night in bed with my new bride.

The next morning I woke up, shocked to find a woman sleeping next to me, but fortunately found a note on top of a journal resting on my nightstand. It read: "You're now a happily married man again, you old fogy. Read this diary before you wander off and do anything dumb." With that pointed reminder, I sat down and learned about the life of Paul Jacobson, murder suspect and grunion scofflaw. I may have been dealt a crapola memory, but at least I still had good eyesight to read my memoirs. What a life I led.

When my bride emerged from the blankets, she reminded me that I had church duty at ten. I dressed in my official helper slacks, put on a clean polo shirt and tennis shoes, stuffed my tummy with a bowl of puffed air disguised as puffed rice and with Marion's explicit directions, ambled off to Saint Andrew's to do the stationery shuffle.

Along the way I noticed the puddles in the street and recalled what I had written in my journal about the rainstorm the night before. I avoided getting lost and arrived without mishap. Marion had given me excellent directions. I admired the white bell tower before moseying into the church office. Marisa Young, the office manager, introduced herself to me, obviously warned by Marion, and welcomed me. Although I had read her name in my journal, she didn't look the least bit familiar. I had also read that I had been indoctrinated, but had no clue what that prepared me to do.

Oh, well. It would give Marisa a little more challenge to have a memory-impaired assistant. My first assignment was to collate a five-sheet monthly church newsletter. As I worked I scanned through the pages, seeing a picture of a group of parishioners at a picnic, a list of the names of the new church officers and a statement that the church planned to continue to finance homeless assistance. After deftly compiling three hundred newsletters, I asked, "What do you want me to do with the completed work of art?"

"There should be some empty cardboard boxes in the storage closet. Just go in and grab a couple." She pointed toward a door.

I strolled over and opened the door. A man's body tumbled out and landed right on my tennis shoes.

CHAPTER 6

Marisa Young screamed at the sight of a hairy, rumpled, badly dressed middle-aged man lying dead on the rug of the Saint Andrew's church office.

Coagulated blood from his head left reddish-brown marks on my previously clean shoes. I stepped back in shock.

Marisa gasped. "It's . . . it's Muddy Murphy."

"Whoever he is, call nine-one-one," I shouted.

Marisa reached for the office phone with a shaky hand and punched buttons. She had visibly paled, and I hoped she wouldn't pass out. I couldn't deal with two bodies on the floor.

I dropped into a chair, my old ticker exceeding the suggested beats per minute. No sense having two men dying on the same morning.

After a few deep breaths, my heart rate

returned to only twice normal.

The paramedics arrived shortly and began working on the scruffy man, but I could tell that it was too late for him. They might have been able to do some good if Marisa or I had keeled over, though.

Marisa stood in the background, wringing her hands as all the activity progressed. Then a short guy in a suit arrived and took over. He examined the body and asked, "Who found this man?"

I raised my hand from the chair where I sat. "Me."

He stared at me with his dark mustache twitching. "Well, well. If it isn't Mr. Jacobson."

"You know me?"

"Why, yes. We've become well acquainted over the last several days."

"And you are?"

"Detective Quintana."

The name clicked from my journal. "Oh, yes. I've read about you."

He let out a breath. "Tell me what happened this time, Mr. Jacobson."

"It's pretty simple. I opened the door to the storage closet, and this body tumbled out."

He looked downward. "You seem to have some blood on your shoes."

"Must have happened when the body fell."

"Anyone else around at the time?"

"Just the two of us," Marisa said. "We've been short of volunteers lately."

I could imagine Marisa's problem if people kept dying in this church.

An assistant medical examiner arrived to check the body followed by a crime-scene investigator and photographer to take pictures and sniff around. The investigator, who had donned rubber gloves, lifted a candleholder out of the storage room and began dusting it for fingerprints.

Quintana asked me to wait in the small adjoining kitchen while he questioned Marisa. Then after fifteen minutes he came in to speak with me.

"When did you arrive at the church this morning, Mr. Jacobson?"

"An hour ago."

"And before that?"

"I walked over from my apartment."

"Can you account for the eight hours before that?"

"I was asleep, woke up, peed and ate breakfast."

"I need to collect a sample of the blood from your shoes."

"Help yourself. It's from the body when it fell out of the storage closet."

Quintana extracted a kit from his pocket, removed a cotton swab and dabbed at my shoes before dropping the evidence in a brown paper bag.

After the crew removed the body, I sat down in a chair next to Marisa, who was still shaking. "You recognized the victim."

Marisa rested her head in her hands. "Yes. Muddy Murphy."

"He looked like a street person."

"He had taken to sleeping on the beach, but he was a renowned artist."

"Dressed like that?"

"Muddy never paid much attention to his clothes. He's been a regular in Venice for many years, painting, selling his artwork and hanging out in cafés along the boardwalk."

"But if he was a popular artist, he probably could support himself and not have to sleep on the beach," I said.

"I'm sure Muddy made a sizeable income. For some reason he chose the homeless lifestyle. He was a regular for Sunday services here. Always showed up with other homeless people. He attended just yesterday."

I thought back to what I had read that morning in my journal. I had spoken with some of the street people after the service on Sunday. The only name I'd noted was Harley Marcraft. Then I had a heated exchange with some wild man. Oh, hell. What if that had been Muddy Murphy? Detective Quintana would be all over my behind.

"So he was here yesterday for the morning service. But he didn't look like he had been dead that long. He must have been killed last night. Any reason why he would have been here last night?"

"Because it rained," Marisa said.

"I don't understand."

"Whenever the weather is bad, we open the meeting room so it can be used as a homeless shelter. When the storm came through last night, I stopped over around eleven and unlocked the door so people could sleep out of the rain."

"Did you see Muddy then?"

"I didn't pay that much attention. But a big crowd arrived."

"So any one of the homeless people could have killed Muddy."

"I don't think they're violent."

"Did you leave the door unlocked?"

"Of course. I wanted to make sure any stragglers would have shelter."

"But anyone else could have entered as well."

Marisa put her hand to her mouth. "Oh, dear. That's possible."

"Well, enough of that. Anything else I can do to help?"

"No. I think I'll close the office for the day. I'm pretty shaken."

"I understand. I guess I'll meander on home then."

I waited for Marisa to lock up.

"Can I give you a ride?" she asked.

"No, thanks. I think I'll take a little walk. The old legs can use the exercise."

I retraced my path and returned to my honeymoon cottage. My apartment was empty so I went to the back door of the main house and knocked.

A middle-aged woman who I assumed was Andrea came to the door. "Your wife and I are having coffee. Come on in."

Marion sat at the kitchen table. "What are you doing back so soon? I thought Marisa would work you most of the day."

"We were disrupted by finding a body in the storage closet."

Marion and Andrea both gasped.

"A man named Muddy Murphy was murdered and stuffed in the closet."

"I know Muddy," Andrea said. "He's a famous artist."

"He didn't look very famous. I understand he even sleeps on the beach."

"That's the favorite hangout for homeless

people," Andrea said.

"I can't imagine anyone choosing to sleep on the beach," I said.

"I don't know. Many of the homeless people in Venice have been offered shelter but refuse it."

"It does seem strange that both an art dealer and an artist were murdered within a few days," Marion said.

"Yes, from reviewing my journal this morning that concerns me. Particularly since Detective Quintana is hot on my tail because I found both bodies."

"But you had nothing to do with either." Marion patted my arm.

"Thanks for your vote of confidence, but the detective doesn't seem to share it. And there's one other problem."

"What's that?" Marion asked.

"I have a sneaking suspicion Muddy Murphy is the same guy I shouted at yesterday when I went over to talk to the homeless crowd after the church service."

Marion put her hand to her mouth. "Oh, dear. I overheard that. I see the problem."

"Yeah. If that's the case, Detective Quintana will be all over me like flies at a picnic. It will be one more little piece to make me look guilty as hell. So, Andrea, tell me more about this Muddy Murphy character."

"That's an interesting story." Andrea looked up thoughtfully. "He was quite successful but then started arguing with the art dealers along Abbot Kinney Boulevard. Muddy felt they were exploiting him so he refused to paint anymore. Then he decided to hang out with the homeless community."

"What the heck is Abbot Kinney Boulevard?"

"It's the street named after the founder of Venice, who in Nineteen Oh-five dreamed of a cultural center for Los Angeles amid a myriad of canals. Unfortunately, the only surviving parts of the dream were a small section of canals and an emerging yuppie street with art stores and cafés."

"I think I'll check it out. Anyone care to join me?"

"Sure," Marion said. "It's only a short walk, and I don't want you getting in any more trouble."

While I waited for Marion to change into her walking shoes, I plopped down in an easy chair with my mind in a state of turmoil. My stomach felt tight, and I hoped I wasn't developing an ulcer. Thoughts of dead men swirled in my soggy brain. Having read that morning about two deaths and then discovering another man in the closet at the church set the hairs on my arms at attention like I had wandered into an electrical storm. What was going on around here? I needed to gain a handle on all these strange events. Obviously something in the art community had spun out of control. With Detective Quintana turning up every time I happened upon a body, I needed to figure out a way to clear my name. First step, understand more regarding art dealers.

Marion reappeared, and we strolled a few blocks up Venice Boulevard and turned left onto a street lined with palm trees. New brickwork facades mingled with shops under construction and stores needing a twenty-first-century face-lift. After peeking through the windows of several antique stores, we stopped in front of a gallery with an all-white interior complemented by jet-black tables, displaying distorted pink pottery and shiny silver sculptures that resembled human arms cut off at the shoulder and wrist. On the walls hung paintings with liberal splotches of color and photographs of multiple hazy images that, in my day, would have been the work of a dysfunctional camera.

"If we were independently wealthy, I'd want to buy a few of those vases," Marion said, placing a finger to her chin.

"If we were independently wealthy, I think I wouldn't."

Marion poked me in the ribs. "Don't be such a cynic. Isn't there something here that interests you?"

"Only the woman standing next to me."

She gave my arm a squeeze.

After gawking through a few more windows, we picked a gallery that seemed to have more paintings than sculpture and entered through the arched doorway to the sound of chimes.

A skinny man in a dark suit with equally skinny tie and pencil-thin mustache slithered up to us, rubbing his hands together. "May I be of assistance?"

"Do you have any Muddy Murphy paintings?" I asked.

"Why, yes. Come this way. We have two of his works on display."

He led us to a mounted canvas approximately four feet wide by two feet tall. Patches of red, orange, green, yellow and blue blobs formed a blend that made me feel seasick.

"Mr. Murphy produced many fine works. I personally purchased this extraordinary specimen. It's from his fantasy period."

"I wonder what he was fantasizing." I said.

The man pursed his lips. "We don't know. Mr. Murphy never shared his views concerning his work. Here is another from his more realistic period. Notice the composition and the unique blend of pigment."

I stared at a group of people sitting at a café. Kind of impressionistic dabs of bright color formed their clothes, but all of the faces were blank canvas.

"Guess he didn't go in for facial features," I said. "How much does this one go for?"

He cleared his throat. "Eleven thousand dollars. But I am prepared to discount it ten percent today."

I whistled. "Seems pretty steep for a local artist who forgot to paint the faces."

He stuck out his lower lip. "Mr. Murphy was a renowned Venice artist who passed away recently, and the value of his paintings has risen dramatically."

I stared at the price gouger. "Word circulates quickly here. He only died this morning."

The man shrugged. "In any case, artwork increases in value when popular artists pass on. Which of the two works interests you most?"

"We'll need to think some more . . . out of curiosity, are there any art dealers who have significant holdings of Muddy Murphy's work?" Marion asked.

"There are three. Vance Theobault, Clint Brock and Frederick Vansworthy."

I would have spit out my teeth if I didn't have all my permanent ones. "Frederick Vansworthy? He's dead."

He put his hands on his hips. "There was a rumor to that effect. I believe he and Mr. Theobault had some sort of partnership."

"I know Clint Brock," Marion said. "Paul, you met him at our wedding and at church on Sunday."

"I remember reading the name in my journal."

"I can arrange for us to speak with him. That might be useful."

"We'll have to do that." I turned toward my new slimy acquaintance. "This Vance Theobault. Does he have a gallery around here?"

"Yes. On Windward Circle. Now, regarding the Muddy Murphy works?"

"I think we'll take a rain check. But thanks for the discount offer. We'll keep you in mind when we decide to add to our collection."

The man slapped a business card into my hand as we headed toward the door.

Outside Marion grabbed my arm. "What did you mean by that last comment?"

104

"Well, I have a picture of a jail on my dresser. Those god-awful paintings would fit right in."

"I guess I didn't marry an art connoisseur."

"Not for that kind of art. I appreciate a good landscape or picture of posies but don't go in for blobs of paint or blank faces. I'm more interested in the art dealers. Something's fishy there. Particularly if they profit from Muddy Murphy's death by the paintings increasing in value."

Marion stopped and looked at me thoughtfully. "As I mentioned, I can arrange a meeting with Clint Brock, but I've never met Vance Theobault."

"Maybe we can pay him a surprise visit. Do you know where Windward Circle is?"

"It's within walking distance."

"Lead on. If you're not pooped, I have some more exploration left in my old legs. Besides I'm on a roll with this art-dealer business."

Marion guided us several blocks until we came to a traffic circle. We strolled around the outside of the circle, checking store fronts until we spotted the name of Theobault Gallery on a two-story brick building. Inside we found a large stark room with only half a dozen paintings on the wall.

A man stood off to the side on a cell phone. At the back sat a brightly-frocked, blond receptionist, ensconced behind a mahogany desk.

Not wanting to disturb the man, who seem to be in a heated conversation, we approached the gal.

"Is Mr. Theobault in?" I inquired.

"Yes. Who may I say is calling?"

"Mr. and Mrs. Jacobson."

She raised her perky chin toward me, obviously expecting more explanation.

I gave her my wealthy, erudite, connoisseur smile.

She sighed, reached for a phone, pushed a button and spoke in a low voice. She listened for a moment and then turned her gaze in our direction.

"You may go inside." She pointed to the adjoining closed door.

We entered and found a man standing behind a mahogany desk even larger than the one in the reception area. He had a solid chin and neatly trimmed brown hair, and he wore an expensive-looking shiny gray suit.

"Mr. and Mrs. Jacobson. Please take a seat on the couch." He motioned toward a brown leather sofa. Lining the walls were framed pictures of Theobault shaking hands with dignitaries.

We sank down into the soft cushions, and Theobault pulled a chair toward us. He sat down and crossed his legs.

"How may I be of assistance?"

I realized I hadn't thought through this step, but I started improvising. "We recently viewed some works of Muddy Murphy's in a gallery nearby and were informed that you were one of the few dealers who had significant holdings of his paintings."

"That's correct. I pride myself on the depth and quality of my Murphy collection."

Marion got in the swing of things. "We were trying to find out where we could view a larger selection of his paintings."

He smiled, showing even white teeth. "I may be able to arrange that as I do maintain a considerable inventory of Mr. Murphy's work."

At that moment, the phone rang. He excused himself and picked it up. "No, I'll come out there." He smiled at us again. "I need to sign some papers a courier has delivered. Please wait here, and I'll be back in a few minutes. May I have Emily get you some coffee?"

We both shook our heads.

He strode to the door, exited and shut it

behind him.

I immediately jumped up, as much as my unbending could be considered a jump, and began inspecting the photographs on the wall. Marion joined me.

"Here's Theobault with Ronald Reagan," Marion said.

"Yeah, and one with Gerald Ford. He makes the rounds."

I found an adjoining door and opened it to find a room full of paintings stacked against a wall. I turned on the light switch to see the collection more clearly.

Marion ducked inside and thumbed through a number of the pictures. "He wasn't kidding. Look at all these Muddy Murphy paintings."

"I hope he remembered to paint the faces this time."

"Quite a collection."

I regarded the paintings. "So it's no skin off his back that Muddy isn't in the land of the living anymore. He has his stack of paintings to sell and since Muddy isn't around to paint new ones, Theobault benefits from the higher posthumous prices."

We heard the door handle turn. I flicked off the light, and we scrambled out of the storeroom just as Theobault returned.

"I'm sorry for the interruption. A lot is

happening right now."

"I can imagine," I said. "I heard that you had some sort of partnership with Frederick Vansworthy."

His smile evaporated faster than a drop of water on a hot griddle. "Why are you referring to Frederick?" He stared at me with dark focused eyes. "And why are you really here?"

Uh-oh. It was obvious I had hit a sensitive spot. Rather than backing off, I plunged right into the middle of the poop. "Seems to me it's kind of strange that Frederick Vansworthy and Muddy Murphy would both meet their demise within a period of a few days."

Theobault's cheeks turned red, and he let out a hiss like steam escaping a boiling kettle. "Out." He pointed to the door. "Get out, both of you."

He pushed us toward the door, grabbed the handle and not too gently dispatched us into the reception area as he slammed the door behind us.

I smiled at the receptionist. "Seems that your boss has a bit of a temper."

She grimaced. "He's been very testy lately. And now he's upset over some papers a courier just brought him to sign."

"Yeah, it must be tough with all the

Muddy Murphy paintings he has to peddle."

Her smile returned. "Oh, no. We've had numerous requests today. They're very popular."

I thought I'd try one more avenue. "Say, Emily, do you know Frederick Vansworthy?"

She raised her well-lined eyebrows. "Yes. He and Mr. Theobault worked together."

"I thought art dealers tended to work on their own," Marion said.

"Mr. Theobault and Mr. Vansworthy go way back. They set up an informal partnership, although there was some kind of problem lately."

"Did you know that Mr. Vansworthy is dead?" I asked.

She put her hand to her cheek. "No. He visited just last week. That's terrible."

"Dead as a doornail, or rather a water-soaked seagull. He was murdered."

She gasped. "He was such a gentleman. Always took a minute to talk with me before his meetings with Mr. Theobault. I love speaking with people who come in here. Mr. Theobault says I yak too much but that's just the way I am." She gave us a wide smile.

"You mentioned some issue between them recently," Marion said.

She leaned toward us and in a conspiratorial tone said, "They had an argument two weeks ago, but seemed to patch things up when they met last week." She looked at her watch. "Oh, my goodness. I didn't realize what time it was. If you'll excuse me, I need to complete a letter for Mr. Theobault."

We said good-bye and took a quick spin around the gallery looking at artwork that didn't turn me on. The salesman we'd seen earlier approached us. The guy had bushy eyebrows and a crooked nose. "May I help you?" he asked.

"No, thanks," Marion said. "We're just browsing."

We completed a pass around the gallery and headed out the door.

"What did you make of all that?" I asked Marion.

She pressed her lips together for a moment then said, "You obviously hit a nerve when you mentioned Vansworthy. Theobault acted very suspicious and almost violent."

"Yeah. There must be something going on in the art community that links the deaths of Frederick Vansworthy and Muddy Murphy."

"When we get home, I'll call Clint Brock to set up a meeting. He may give us some insight into the situation."

We strolled back to the old homestead,

my young bride and me amid all the summer teenagers on skateboards with their music plugged into their ears and their jewelry dangling from ears, noses and assorted body locations.

I hadn't even had a chance to rest my feet when there was a knock on our door. I opened it to find Detective Quintana in his dark suit with his mustache twitching like a hyperactive caterpillar.

"Mr. Jacobson, I need to ask you to accompany me to police headquarters."

"Am I receiving some kind of police appreciation award?"

"No. Are you going to cooperate?"

"Why not?" I turned. "Marion, the detective wants to take me for a ride. Hold down the fort for me."

"Paul, do we need to find a lawyer?"

"I don't want any stinking lawyer. I can handle this myself."

She wrinkled her forehead. "I don't know."

"I'll call if there's any problem." I faced Quintana. "Okay, Detective, let's go. I'm ready for a guided tour of your world-renowned police station."

We left and he escorted me to his Crown Victoria parked in the alley.

"You need to clean your car, Detective. It looks like a seagull used it for a restroom."

Quintana grunted at me and pushed me into the car.

After he locked me in the backseat, I asked, "What's the big deal, Detective?"

"I need to ask you some further questions. I thought having a room to ourselves would be appropriate."

He wasn't in a loquacious mood so we continued the journey in silence, arriving in front of a two-story red-brick building with letters that read: Los Angeles Police Department Pacific Station. In the front stood a flagpole with an American flag on top and the California flag dancing in the breeze beneath it. Other than several large trees in front, it looked like a prison — no windows, no pretty flower garden, just stark institutional architecture.

Quintana led me inside, past a female desk sergeant who looked like she was ready to wrestle me to the mat and snap on cuffs at the slightest misstep. Down a corridor with no pictures on the walls, Quintana strode, with me keeping up the best I could, to a small room where we entered and sat on either side of a 1970s gray metal table. I smelled sweat and didn't know if it was mine or left over from a generation of overanxious suspects.

I looked around the room. Bare walls, one

door, a one-way mirror and bright overhead fluorescent lighting with one tube flickering, which produced an annoying background hum.

"This is a cozy place," I said.

Quintana glared at me and then read me my rights, probably preparing to trap me into saying something incriminating. "Mr. Jacobson, you've been on the scene of three recent deaths."

"Yes. I remember Muddy Murphy from this morning and I've read in my journal about the others."

"We found fingerprints on a candleholder in the storage closet where you discovered the bludgeoned body of Mr. Murphy. We suspect that it was the murder weapon. Care to venture a guess as to how *your* fingerprints got on that candleholder?"

CHAPTER 7

I flinched at hearing that my fingerprints were on a suspected murder weapon. "I have no clue how my fingerprints ended up on the candleholder."

"It's very interesting that your fingerprints were also on the candleholder found next to the body of Mr. Harold Koenig two days ago as well. You're a walking, one-man crime wave."

"But for someone my age, walking is a victory." I thought back to my journal. "Wait a minute. I read this morning in my diary that the candleholder fell off a table and I picked it up." Then it struck me. "I also touched the other candleholder to keep it from falling over. Could that have been the one you found in the storeroom?"

"Interesting theory. For someone with a bad memory, you're recalling a lot of detail."

"My memory is pretty darn good during

the day. It's just overnight that it goes blank."

Quintana stared at me like he was trying to extract the fluids out of my eyeballs. "And I discovered that you had a confrontation with Mr. Murphy yesterday at the very church where he was found murdered. Interesting that a witness overheard you shouting at him about a closet and then the next morning he's found bludgeoned to death in a closet."

Damnation. So my suspicion was correct. I had argued with Muddy Murphy, not knowing who he was at the time.

"He was testy toward art dealers. I didn't even know I was arguing with the illustrious Muddy Murphy at the time."

"Was it when you killed him that you realized who he was?"

"I had nothing to do with his death. Afterwards, I pieced together who he was."

"So are you ready to confess, Mr. Jacobson?"

"Confess to what? I happened to come on the scene of two murders and the accidental death of Harold Koenig. That's it."

"Peculiar sequence of events. An argument the night before the first victim was murdered, a confrontation with the second just as he died and a shouting match with

116

the third the day before his death."

"I'm a peace-loving old codger who happens to speak his mind."

"Or do you have an anger-management problem that turns violent?"

"I think you're barking up the wrong sycamore, Detective. If I were you I'd investigate the art community here in Venice. Something's going on there. I bet you could find a link between the deaths of Frederick Vansworthy and Muddy Murphy. You should start with Vance Theobault. That guy's mighty suspicious."

"Is that why you were in his gallery today?"

Uh-oh. "Have you been following me, Detective?"

"You allude to deaths in the art world but are seen nosing around with art dealers. To say nothing of inquiring into Muddy Murphy paintings. Seems to me you are awfully curious regarding your victim's artwork."

"Now you're starting to piss me off. He wasn't my victim and, yes, I've been nosing around. I don't see you arresting anyone, and you keep bugging me. I felt it my obligation to find out more to protect my good name. It turns out Vance Theobault and Frederick Vansworthy had some sort of partnership. You better check that out, Detective."

Quintana regarded me with his forehead-piercing stare. "Getting kind of heated over this, Mr. Jacobson?"

"Damn straight. Go catch the real killer. What have you found out about the link between Theobault and Vansworthy?"

"I don't have to tell you anything, Mr. Jacobson."

"I know that. Just indulge the curiosity of an old geezer."

He looked at me for a moment. "I'm aware of their relationship. We're certainly looking into that. But right now I'm more concerned with you, Mr. Jacobson."

"I appreciate the personal attention, but I think you're off in the weeds if you consider me your prime suspect." I thought back to my conversation with Marisa Young. "Here's something for you, Detective. The office manager at the church told me that she unlocked the church last evening so the homeless people could have shelter from the rain. Muddy Murphy probably came in then. Someone could have snuck in anytime during the night and whacked Muddy over the head."

"Interesting that you know so much about it."

"Check it out, Detective. I had nothing to

do with it."

"We'll see, Mr. Jacobson. Any further information you'd like to share?"

"No. You've sucked me dry. Now I'd like to return to see my bride."

"I'll arrange a ride for you."

With that he left the room. I had to wait a good half hour before a uniformed policeman entered to say he would drive me back to my humble abode.

"What happened?" Marion said, looking up from a *Smithsonian* as I stumbled back into our honeymoon shanty.

"Just a little police harassment to see if I'd confess to something I didn't do. We need to find out more. Call your pal Clint Brock."

Marion picked up the telephone and was able to set up an appointment for the next morning.

"While you were gone, Denny phoned to remind us that they're taking us out to dinner tonight."

So that evening my family showed up, and we took off in Denny's rental car with Jennifer squeezed in between Marion and me in the backseat.

"I went surfing today, Grandpa. I had

some great rides."

"Well, I'm glad to see you survived. You'd never get me out in the ocean."

"Oh, Grandpa. It was a beautiful day with three-foot-high waves — just the right size for me. I met a whole crowd of surfers, and they were very friendly. The water's cooler than in Hawaii, though. I had to wear a wet suit."

"I'll stick with my landlubber suit. How can my own offspring enjoy the ocean so much?"

"We've talked about this before. You need to learn to have a positive attitude when you think of the ocean. It's just beautiful water as far as the eye can see."

"I detest the ocean. I can't swim worth snot, and I don't like the idea of other wiggling and chewing things in there with me."

Marion smiled at me. "Yes, Paul. The ocean and lawyers."

"I hate both of them."

Jennifer rolled her eyes. "I know. And you hate taking pills."

"That too."

We arrived at McCallisters and I proceeded to get my revenge by eating a selection of sea creatures. As one more shrimp bit the dust, I described our encounter that day with Vance Theobault and my subsequent experience at police headquarters.

"Cool," Jennifer said. "Was it anything like the police station in Boulder?"

"Can't say since I don't remember that one, but I suppose most police interrogation rooms are pretty much the same."

Jennifer frowned. "It's too bad. You have all these exciting adventures but can't remember them."

"Maybe that explains why I'm still alive. If I recalled what happened to me, it might cause my old ticker to give up the ghost."

"Oh, Grandpa. You still have lots of years left."

Marion looked over at me. "If he can stay away from murderers."

"That's right. I may start disliking denizens of the land as much as denizens of the deep. Speaking of which, Jennifer, I need you to do some research on your computer for me when you get home."

"Okeydokey. When we talked yesterday, I offered to help you. What do you want me to find for you?"

"Here are three names for you to check out: Vance Theobault, Frederick Vansworthy and Clint Brock. Shall I write them down for you?"

Jennifer tapped her right temple. "Nope. I have them locked up here."

"It's good that somebody in this family has a good memory."

"I have a photographic memory, just like you do during the day, Grandpa."

"But don't you even need me to spell the names for you?"

Jennifer rolled her eyes. "I'm a good speller."

"That's my granddaughter. So see what you can uncover. Together we'll circle the wagons and fend off the attacks of Detective Quintana."

Back home that night I felt the weight of the world on my shoulders. Still, I had to count my blessings. I was still alive and kicking; my son, daughter-in-law and granddaughter were here visiting; and Marion hadn't reneged on her wedding vows. What a woman. To put up with my sieve-like memory required being a saint. Oh, well. I'd keep on trucking and do the best I could in my altered mental state. As I looked out my plantation window, I could rest assured that Scarlett was right. Tomorrow would be another day.

The next morning I woke up wondering where the hell I was. I felt like a lost child, trying to figure out what place I was in and how I had ended up there. A kind woman lying next to me in bed explained my marital situation and told me to read the journal on the nightstand. I duly followed her instructions and to my amazement, that cleared up some of the mystery of Paul Jacobson and his errant brain cells.

With my life in a semblance of order, Marion sat down at the table while I cooked a stack of buttermilk pancakes. At least I remembered how to flip flapjacks. After stuffing my yap and cleaning up, I contemplated the day ahead — trying to find a way to keep out of jail and to figure out who had done what to whom in the Venice art community.

"We have an appointment this morning," Marion reminded me. "I set up a meeting at one of the local art galleries for you."

"I'm glad you're here to point me in the right direction, otherwise I don't know where I'd end up."

We strolled over to Clint Brock's art gallery on Venice Boulevard. Along the way I said to Marion, "In reviewing my journal, I learned several things. First, Muddy Murphy probably spent the night at the church when he was murdered because he was getting out of the rain with the other homeless people. Second, someone could have entered the church in the middle of the night and killed him."

"Assuming it wasn't some argument with another homeless person, we need to find out why someone wanted to murder him."

"Something is going on with these art dealers. Vansworthy might have been caught in some kind of vendetta, and Muddy Murphy must have been tangled up in something as well."

"But you don't know of a motive for sure," Marion said.

"Not yet. That's why I need to learn more about this whole art-dealer world."

We arrived at Brock's gallery and entered a remodeled red-brick warehouse that now looked like a museum. Colorful paintings lined the walls, and large stone and metal sculptures stood on pedestals, evenly spaced on a polished hardwood floor. Eyeing a series of sculpted stone heads, I felt like I had landed on an Easter Island for pygmies.

"Quite a place," I said to Marion.

"I've meant to visit Clint's gallery. I've heard so much about it." She pointed to a silver sculpture suspended from the ceiling. "What do you think of that?"

"It's either an advertisement for United Airlines or a captured CIA spy device."

The place was unnaturally quiet and our

footsteps echoed as we walked across the floor. I smelled the aroma of brewing coffee and shivered in the overly air-conditioned atmosphere.

A pleasant young woman in black jacket and skirt, complemented by dangly gold earrings, greeted us and directed us to a room in the back. We entered and a man I assumed was Clint Brock came out from behind a glass-covered desk to welcome us. He wore dark slacks and a white turtleneck. He gave me a firm handshake and then clasped Marion's hands in both of his. I thought back to the description I had written of him in my journal. He definitely had that Cary Grant persona, complete with solid chin and generous smile.

"Thank you for making time to see us, Clint," Marion said.

"It's my pleasure. You're long overdue to visit my gallery. Let me give you a tour."

He led us back into the main room and began describing the Michelsons, Rachlieus and Beauchamps lining the walls. I stared at the weird collection of paint blobs, skewed lines and crosshatched patterns, not recognizing a worldly object or scene in the lot.

"And your Muddy Murphys?" I asked.

"Over here." He pointed to two large

paintings that covered most of a side wall. One looked like horse heads emerging from garbage cans, and the other displayed a group of filmy bodies floating over something that might have been rows of corn.

I squinted at the horse heads. "I'm obviously not communing with this painting."

Clint laughed. "Muddy Murphy grows on you. He painted in a very broad and eclectic range of styles. These are from his composite period where he mixed touches of realism with an air of fantasy." He pointed to the painting of the rows of corn. "Notice the blending of colors, the firm brushstrokes and the balance that focuses your attention to the left center."

"Did he ever paint real pictures?" I asked.

Clint's eyes sparkled. "Obviously you are a traditionalist, Mr. Jacobson. Muddy's early works were in a style similar to Andrew Wyeth's but then he began experimenting and that was when the value of — and interest in — his artwork soared. He has become one of the most popular artists in the California school over the last five years."

I scratched my head. "Maybe his school let kids pass to the next grade, but I can't make much of this type of art."

"I can assure you that if you continue to

view Muddy's works, you'll become a fan of his."

I didn't share his optimism.

Clint led us back into his office and showed us to chairs facing his desk.

"I understand prices for his paintings have increased since his untimely demise," I said.

"That's correct. With no future supply, there is increased demand for the existing work."

"We were told that you were one of the three primary dealers in Mr. Murphy's work," Marion said.

"Yes. I have a number of his paintings in my offsite warehouse and the adjoining storage room." He pointed to a door off the side of his office.

I watched Brock's face carefully. "What about these two other dealers, Vansworthy and Theobault?"

No change in expression. "Yes. They have been my friendly competitors."

"I can't imagine that it was too friendly. When you're all competing for business, they must be a threat to you."

I detected a small downturn at the corners of his mouth. "Obviously any time two or more people are seeking sales from the same base of customers, there will be some tension, but we each have separate portfolios of work. You must realize, Mr. Jacobson, that, in our world, personal preference dictates the client's final decision. My holdings are only as good as the match to the interests of my clientele. Having competitors may divert some sales, but it also directs people to me if my competitor's selection is not as good as mine."

"And the breadth of choice these others offer of Muddy Murphy's work. How do they compare to yours?"

He now gave me a broad smile. "A fair portfolio, but not as complete as I can offer."

Marion jumped in. "Mr. Theobault seemed to have quite a few Muddy Murphy paintings."

"Yes. He provides an adequate portfolio. But he didn't start collecting Murphys as soon as I did. He lacks coverage of the eclectic early stages of his work."

"And old Vansworthy kicked the bucket. What happened to his collection?"

A glint appeared in Brock's eyes. "I imagine Theobault will pick it up. They had a partnership."

"Aren't you worried that that will give Theobault a better collection than yours with the two businesses now combined?"

Clint gave a dismissive wave. "We're down

to two major sources that people can buy from. I'll earn my fair share."

I thought for a moment. "Then Theobault may have benefited from the death of Vansworthy."

Brock also paused. "He did. There was tension in their partnership, and now Theobault will possess the whole portfolio."

"Doesn't it seem suspicious that Vansworthy was murdered and then Theobault benefits?" Marion asked.

"An astute observation," Brock said. "I'm sure the police are looking into that motive."

"So Vansworthy bites the dust, and you and Theobault have one less competitor. What I still don't understand is how Muddy Murphy's paintings jumped in value so quickly after his death."

"It's very simple, Mr. Jacobson. When a tragedy like this occurs, word gets out immediately in the art community. People who have contemplated buying a Murphy work suddenly realize that the supply is limited. Rather than waiting, they're willing to pay a premium before someone else steps in."

I thought back to what I had read in my journal. "But I understand Murphy had given up painting."

"He had, but there was no telling that he

wouldn't pick up his brush again at any time. His death punctuates the finality of his creative stream."

I felt like he was describing the demise of a popcorn machine rather than the death of a human being.

"I still don't comprehend why he stopped painting," Marion said. "If he was so popular and able to command high prices, why would he give it up?"

Clint sighed. "The idiosyncrasy of the artistic mind. Muddy Murphy was a genius and like many geniuses, a little unbalanced. He developed a paranoia toward art dealers, myself included, and refused to contribute any more works for sale. It was his decision, and he stuck to it."

Marion turned toward Brock. "At the church last Sunday, you and I were talking when Paul had a shouting match with a street person. You must have overheard that."

"I did."

"That was Muddy Murphy," Marion said.

"It was," Brock replied. "An example of how unhinged he had become."

I grimaced at the reminder of my link to Muddy and his ultimate demise.

"But if he loved painting, how could he just give it up like that?" Marion asked.

"Putting the economics and personal issues aside, I would think an artist would be driven to keep working."

"Some people suspect that he was still secretly painting. I, for one, think he was spiteful enough to quit."

"So he stops painting cold turkey to piss off you, Theobault and Vansworthy," I said. "Pretty extreme."

Brock grit his teeth. "Look at how he lived. He could have chosen the lifestyle of a wealthy man with an upscale apartment or mansion and all its trappings. Yet he decided to sleep on the streets and hang out with the local bums. Not your typical approach to being an acclaimed artist." Brock clenched his fists.

I stared at him, noticing the chink in the armor of his composure. "Did you try to talk him into painting again?"

"Several of us made the attempt, to no avail. He had made his mind up and could be extremely stubborn."

"So who could have benefited from the deaths of both Muddy Murphy and Vansworthy?"

Brock paused for a moment, regaining his pleasant demeanor. "That's easy. Theobault. Why so much interest in this whole affair, Mr. Jacobson?"

"I'm just a nosy old coot. Since I'm now a Venice resident, I'm trying to understand our local culture."

"In that case you might enjoy an exhibit opening on Saturday." Clint handed each of us a three-by-eight-inch card. On one side were two color pictures of wild and splashy abstract paintings with the words "Brock Gallery presents paintings by Muddy Murphy." I turned it over. This side elaborated: "Brock Gallery presents the paintings of Venice's renowned artist Muddy Murphy. Please join us from 6 to 8 P.M. Saturday, July 29. Refreshments and the music of the Kiernan Quartet."

Marion looked at me. "Sounds like something we'd enjoy attending. Thank you, Clint."

"Now, if you'll excuse me, I need to leave for an appointment in Beverly Hills."

We shook hands, and Marion and I found ourselves escorted out of the office. We took one last spin around the gallery as I kept my hand on my wallet. I viewed one more atrocity, a sculpture that reminded me of snakes tied in knots, and then we headed out to the street.

"What did you think of that?" Marion asked.

I rubbed my chin. "He acted like a pretty

smooth operator. But something bothers me. He obviously had some negative feelings about Muddy Murphy, yet he stands to profit from Muddy's death. And having an exhibit the Saturday after Muddy's death . . ."

"That's obviously been planned for some time with the color cards already printed. But you're right. He did have a reaction when we talked of Muddy Murphy. That was the one time he exhibited a lot of emotion."

"The Vansworthy and Theobault connection is very suspicious. I wonder if my good buddy Detective Quintana has found out anything concerning the relationship between those two?"

"If he has, he'd never share it with us."

"That's the damn problem. I'm in the middle of this thing and it's like pulling hen's teeth to track down any useful information. This art-dealer outfit doesn't pass the sniff test, but I can't piece it together yet. How well do you know Brock?"

"He's just a social acquaintance."

"Do you trust him?" I asked.

She looked at me thoughtfully. "I don't know. I've never had any problem with him, but I've never witnessed his business dealings."

■ ■ ■ ■

Back at the old bungalow, Marion disappeared into the powder room and I plunked my aging frame down in a kitchen chair to contemplate if I'd have something to eat or try to resolve the other pang in my gut over the art-dealer world. I decided to munch on an apple while I analyzed what we had learned from Clint Brock. He seemed like a nice-enough fellow, but I had been fooled before. Way back when, I thought a lawyer was helping me and he turned out to be collecting information for litigation and proceeded to sue me, causing me months of hassle and expense, before the whole damn thing was tossed out of court. Had never trusted lawyers since.

Was Brock genuine or two-faced like this lawyer from my past? I couldn't tell yet. I'd have to keep sniffing around and see what would crawl out from under the rocks I turned over.

My ruminations were interrupted by a knock on the door.

"Come on in," I shouted.

Andrea strolled in. "I have a message for you."

"A long lost relative willing me a fortune?"

"No, but the next best thing. Jennifer couldn't reach you so she called me and asked me to invite you to watch her surf today. She'll be by the breakwater in front of the plaza in thirty minutes."

Marion reappeared.

"Well, I better mosey over there. Marion, you up for another stroll?"

"No, Paul. I need to write thank-you notes for our wedding presents. You can find it on your own. Go to the path along the beachfront and head north past the paddle-tennis courts and Muscle Beach."

I flexed my biceps. "I should be able to find it if they don't rope me into modeling first."

Marion picked up the newspaper and swatted me. "Get out of here."

"Yes, ma'am."

CHAPTER 8

I followed Marion's instructions, gawking at crowds of people dressed or undressed in every conceivable type of outfit. As I wandered along the boardwalk, I looked up to see a building that looked like the Doge's Palace: arches over windows with balustrades below, intersecting diamond patterns in brown on an off-white surface. Above the roof fluttered half a dozen flags including those of the United States, United Kingdom and Italy.

I peered at one of the windows and did a double take at the sight of a woman framed there. She looked like a younger version of Marion. On closer inspection I saw it was a painted image and not a real person. Damn. Artists sure went wild in this town.

I found a plaza with an enthusiastic group of young men playing basketball on a blue court. As I moved toward the beach, I spotted a skating area with people of all sizes and shapes twirling around and just beyond, a graffiti wall with spray-can-armed minor criminals doing their thing. I noticed off to the side a small building that looked like a concession stand on steroids that had a blue sign hanging from the roof that read "Police." Over a large window, a yellow banner had been attached that said, "Now Hiring! Join." How would Detective Quintana react if I submitted an application?

The wide open plaza was full of people. Off to the north a row of twenty-foot-tall palm trees swayed in single file like troops preparing to invade Santa Monica. Lumbering above the trees appeared a metal sculpture that looked like the letter "K" designed by an artist who drank a little too much bubbly. I was sure the Venice Beach art dealers would wax poetic on the beauty of the gawd-awful rusted and weathered structure.

The graffiti wall was a piece of work. Two cement cones, each the size of an Apollo space capsule, stood atop supporting concrete wall slabs, projecting out underneath. Then the *pièce de résistance*. A nearby seven-foot-high cement wall that stretched twenty yards across the sand amid a clump of palm trees. Every wall, cone, trash can and palm tree in the immediate vicinity was blanketed from ground level to ten feet up with dabs, streaks, logos, script, zig-zags, and initials in every imaginable color of the rainbow and then some.

I shook my head. Spray-can maniacs would have a field day here. And they were. A group of young men sprayed and dabbed to their hearts content, defacing old art with their new creations. No women engaged. I guessed they were too smart.

I surveyed one section of the wall that had what appeared to be dancing white ghosts amid a background of black and red ghouls. Next to this rested a garbage can embellished with initials and warped smiley faces in blue and green. One of the cones displayed large white letters "PPT" over a background of schizophrenic pink waves. Someone had scaled to the top of the cone to paint "ADDE 626." I'm sure that was significant to some weirdo.

As I continued to stroll through the warped artists' paradise, I watched a hirsute young man in paint-spattered jeans complete yellow letters outlined in black that read "HITNRUN." That summed it all up. Hit the wall with the spray can and take off before the sight gave you the runs.

I meandered down to the beach and sat down on the sand, enjoying the heat of the sun on my old joints. Out in the ocean, waves broke, and half a dozen surfers sat on boards waiting for their perfect waves. I could have nodded off with the sound of waves breaking and the gentle ocean breeze running through my hair but didn't want my memory to do the Jacobson white-out.

"Hi, Grandpa," came a shout behind me.

I turned to see a young girl decked out in a black wet suit, struggling toward me carrying a large surfboard.

"You look like a seal trying to carry a tree," I said.

"I'll make it. It's not much farther." She dropped the board next to me and plopped down on the sand.

"So you're going to show these Californians how a Coloradan surfs?"

"You bet, Grandpa. Watch me catch some good rides. These waves are perfect for me."

"The only waves perfect for me are the ones who are in the Navy. You'll never get me out in that water."

Jennifer clicked her tongue. "Grandpa, I don't know what to do with you. You live near the beach now. You need to change your ways and learn to appreciate the wonders of the ocean."

"Not likely at my age. But I'll be happy to watch you surf while you enjoy the seven seas. You go play porpoise, and I'll fight the sand fleas."

Jennifer looked around and pointed. "You should go over to that pile of rocks. That'd be a good place to watch me. It's higher up and closer to where I'll be surfing."

"You're right. From there I'll be able to see you fine. It's a good thing my eyesight is much better than my memory."

We both stood up. Jennifer lifted the front of her surfboard and dragged it the remaining distance to the water.

I traversed a spit of sand to reach the rock jetty. At the end of the jetty, two fishermen balanced on an uneven rock surface with their poles pointing seaward. An old cracked concrete pipe emerged from the sand and led out toward the water. When waves crashed into the jetty, water shot out of a hole in the side of the pipe.

I watched as waves splashed up, hitting hard in certain parts of the jetty and sending plumes skyward. A young boy laughed as he enjoyed the free shower from the spray descending from five feet above his head.

Turning toward the small bay protected by the jetty, I spotted Jennifer as she paddled out, gracefully alternating arms stroking in the water. She joined the clump of surfers and turned her board around to be ready for a wave. Then she began to stroke like mad, and a wave carried her forward, but she missed the break, coming to a standstill. I found a rock to sit on as she turned her board and headed back out. On her second attempt, she caught the wave, steadied herself, stood up and rode almost to shore.

I clapped my hands. My own offspring out doing that in the water. Life never ceased to amaze me.

After watching her catch half a dozen waves, my butt started getting numb so I shifted to another rock. I happened to look down and among the broken shells and drift junk saw a briefcase wedged between the rocks. I turned my head toward shore. No one else around. Just the surfers in the water, the two fishermen way at the end with backs to me and some kids playing in the sand several hundred yards away. I grabbed the handle and tugged to remove it from the rocks.

I examined the smooth leather and tried to unlatch it. Locked. And without the combination or a pry bar, it would stay that way. I hefted it and determined that it contained something heavy. I could have put it back or . . . maybe the police substation served as a lost and found.

After watching Jennifer catch several more waves, I backtracked along the jetty and crossed the sand to the building I had passed earlier. Two black-and-white police cruisers were parked outside and a long line of people now stood in front of a sliding window.

"What's the occasion?" I asked a woman in shorts with a police insignia on her shirt and a clipboard in her hand.

"Permits for street vendors are being renewed."

"I'm not seeking permission for anything and don't want to stand in that long line, but I found a briefcase left out on the jetty that I thought I should turn in here."

"We're pretty busy right now. Leave it inside that doorway." She pointed to a yellow door ajar to the left side of the line.

I tucked it away where she had indicated and returned to the beach. Shortly, the rest of my tribe, Denny and Allison, showed up.

"We need to retrieve Jennifer," Denny said. "Time to return the rental equipment and head back to Colorado."

After Jennifer rode a wave, Denny caught her attention and she paddled in to shore.

"Pack up," Denny shouted.

"Ah, Dad. One more wave?"

"No. We have a flight to catch."

We all headed up to the motel where they were staying just off the plaza. While Jennifer showered, I sat out on the balcony and looked down on the crowd of beach revelers. I could see the panorama of the basketball court, skating area, graffiti wall and the numerous street vendors doing their thing.

I could have sat there forever and not been bored, but finally Denny tapped me on the shoulder. "Jennifer's changed, and we're ready to leave."

I helped them lug their suitcases down to the car, parked in the basement of the motel.

"We can give you a ride back to your house on our way," Denny said.

"I'll take you up on that. I'm pleased I got to see all of you once more before you sail off into the sunset."

At my place we exchanged hugs, and Jennifer held on the longest. "I'm so glad you and Marion are married, Grandpa. I'd love to stay here, surf and see you every day. I'm going to miss you."

"I'll miss you, too. Write to me once in a while."

"I'll also call when I find out something about the names you gave me. I just wish you'd learn to use the Internet, Grandpa."

"I'm too old for that, but I know how to use paper and pen and the telephone just fine."

Jennifer's eyes lit up. "I know what I can

do. I'll send e-mail messages to Austin. He can either print them out for you or you can read them on his computer."

"Whatever. As long as I don't have to mess with any of those electronic contraptions."

I waved as my offspring drove off. Now I could continue with my new life as a newly-wed in the wilds of Venice Beach.

I climbed the stairs to my honeymoon roost, feeling a touch of sadness because my family was on their way back to Colorado. Marion wasn't home, so I could indulge myself by saying "woe is me" for a while. In the morning I would remember squat anyway. At least I never had to worry about staying in the same funk for more than a day.

Being sorry for myself was interrupted an hour later by a knock on the door. A little guy overdressed in a suit and possessing a twitching mustache stood there.

"I'm not buying any magazines this month," I said.

He whipped out a police badge. "We need to speak, Mr. Jacobson."

I inspected the name. Sure enough it was my nemesis, Detective Quintana.

"Come on in and tell me what's upsetting you this time."

He strode inside like he owned the place.

From what I had read in my journal, he had been here enough times that maybe it felt to him like a second home.

Quintana leveled his gaze at me. "Did you leave a briefcase at our Venice Beach substation?"

"As a matter of fact, I did. Your people seemed kind of busy renewing vendor permits, and a nice lady officer told me to leave it inside the doorway."

He sighed. "It was unfortunate that our personnel were so lax. I had to check fingerprints on the handle which traced it to you. What were you doing with the briefcase?"

"I found it out on the rock jetty when I was watching my granddaughter surf. No one was around to claim it, so I decided to turn it in."

"Do you know what was inside?"

"I have no clue. It was locked."

"Enough plastic explosives to send the substation into orbit."

CHAPTER 9

I discovered that my mouth had dropped open at the revelation of explosives being in the briefcase I had found. My mind whirled with pictures of rock jetties or police stations going up in smoke.

"Mr. Jacobson, are you now a terrorist trying to blow up police property?"

"Hell, no. I just turned in the briefcase because I thought someone had lost it. Geez, I'm glad someone discovered what it was before it went off."

"We suspect that a group called Save Our Surfside was preparing to stage an ecoterrorist event. Name of the group ring any bells?"

I thought back to my diary. "Oh, crap."

"That's right, Mr. Jacobson. We traced your name to a petition circulated by this group."

"But I signed in support of height restrictions on buildings near the beach."

146

"We suspect that is a front for a more violent agenda. Very interesting that you signed as a supporter of the group and then left an explosive device at the police station by the beach."

"I have no part of that kind of agenda. I've never even given them a penny or supported them in any other way. Regarding the briefcase, I was trying to be helpful when I found it. I'm just an old relic doing what I think is right."

He regarded me thoughtfully. "In another hour that jetty will be teeming with people. There's a beach concert later this afternoon."

"I'll be damned."

"If it was truly imbedded in the jetty as you say and set to go off during the concert, hundreds of people could have been killed and injured. I don't know if you were trying to blow up the police substation or if you prevented hundreds of innocent people being killed and injured. I want you to come with me to show me exactly where you claim to have found the briefcase."

"I'll do you one better, Detective. I'll show you exactly where I did find it."

He led me to his unmarked car and locked me in the backseat. Damn police. They never trusted anyone.

We parked in front of the police substation. All the vendor permits must have been issued because there was no longer a line. The beach was packed with families on blankets settling in for the concert. We wove our way through boxes of burgers and coolers of soft drinks to the jetty. After climbing over several rocks, I oriented myself and pointed to the crevice where I had found the briefcase, aka an improvised explosive device.

Quintana inspected the rocks and reached down to extract a crumpled ball of paper, which he proceeded to unfold. "Interesting," he said.

"Something helpful?"

"Could be. I need to make some calls from the substation. I'm not convinced of your innocence, but I know where to find you."

"And here I was enjoying your company so much, Detective."

"Don't give me that crap. You still have some murders to account for."

"Thank you for not arresting me, Detective. I'll take it from here."

Quintana shot off like a bat out of Hades.

I let out a deep breath as I felt a sense of relief. Once again I had stepped in some doo-doo, but had escaped Detective Quintana hauling my butt off to jail. I needed to keep on my toes around Venice Beach. Too much crime was infringing upon my newly married life. I had a lot of pieces to fit together and seemed to have more uncertainty occurring than resolution. I'd have to keep my old eyes open and see what I could figure out.

I decided to stick around to take in the concert. I had attended outside concerts in amphitheaters and in parks in my younger days but never where crashing breakers would complement the *1812 Overture.* I watched as the orchestra, sitting on folding chairs on a large tarp that served as a platform, tuned up. The musicians wore tan shorts and aloha shirts rather than the tuxedos and long black dresses of concert hall performances. One of the trombone players had a yellow flower attached to his slide.

I thought I'd keep an eye on the spot where I had found the briefcase, so I posted myself on a rock where I could watch the proceedings and any suspicious activity.

As the orchestra launched into Debussy's *La Mer* I noticed a man in worn jeans peeking in the rocks where the briefcase had been left. He shot upright with his long black hair flapping behind him. He looked wildly around then stuck his head back in the rocks.

I climbed off my rocky perch and approached two uniformed policeman who stood on the edge of the audience.

"Gentlemen," I said. "There's a suspicious character looking in the rocks over there." I pointed toward the man who was still frantically inspecting the space between rocks. "I think he's checking to see if his briefcase of explosives is still there, which it isn't."

One of the officers narrowed his gaze at me. "How do you know that? George, go haul in that guy on the rocks." Then he turned toward me. "You come with me."

"I'm the guy who found it earlier. Detective Quintana has already grilled me."

"I don't want to hear any lip." He grabbed my arm and steered me toward the police substation. I considered shouting, "Police brutality!" but decided that wouldn't help my situation any, so in my most sincere voice I said, "But I'll miss the concert."

"You'll be able to return shortly if things check out."

I gave a resigned sigh and joined him on the forced march to the police building, which I had passed by enough times for one day.

I was directed to a chair against the wall

where a huge cop watched over me like I was about to steal his grandmother's dentures. The nervous man I had seen scouring the rock jetty sat in a chair across the room. A policeman with crossed arms guarded him. We made an interesting pair of criminal suspects.

Oh, well. So much for the concert.

Then Detective Quintana showed up. He strolled right over to me with his mustache twitching in double time. "I leave you alone for a few minutes and you get in trouble again, Mr. Jacobson."

"All I did was call attention to that suspicious guy." I pointed across the room to the man huddled in his chair.

"And what raised your suspicion?"

"He was nosing around the rocks where I found the briefcase earlier. Like he was checking to make sure it was still there."

"Trying to deflect attention away from yourself again, Mr. Jacobson?"

"Right. As if I enjoy encounters of the police kind. Check that guy out and then you'll know if there is anything to my hunch."

Quintana went over and questioned the suspect and then fingerprinted him. Maybe the fingerprints would match something on the briefcase other than my prints deposited on the handle when I picked it up.

After a while Quintana sauntered back over to me.

"May I return to the concert now?" I asked.

Quintana's mustache twitched once and he stared at me.

"We're done with you for the time being."

"Can you share what you learned from that guy?"

"No."

"Mighty talkative today, Detective."

"Get out of here." He pointed toward the door.

Only too happy to oblige, I scampered away as fast as my old legs would carry me.

Outside I let out a sigh of relief having once more escaped the clutches of Detective Quintana. After the cramped police building, I reveled in the afternoon sun and open space of the beach.

Returning to the concert, I heard the grand finale which wasn't the *1812 Overture* with briefcase-bomb accompaniment but instead was Dvorak's *New World Symphony*. How appropriate. My whole life was a new world every day.

I sat on a rock pondering what the briefcase bomb was intended for. An ecoterrorist plot from the folks whose petition I had signed? A disgruntled concertgoer? Someone who didn't like rock jetties? And why had the guy returned to check it out? Did he think something had gone wrong with it? Did he get cold feet? Did he realize he had left his favorite briefcase?

I had no clue. I'd have to wait until Detective Quintana was in a more loquacious mood. I meandered back toward the boardwalk, watching the families packing up their baskets and blankets. The graffiti artists, roller skaters and basketball players were still at it. I stopped at Muscle Beach to watch a group of men and women flash their well-oiled biceps. Man, some of those broads looked like they could wrestle a horse to the mat. What had happened to dainty female beauty?

I continued my journey and stopped at the paddle-tennis courts to watch a game in progress. Climbing onto the bleachers, I sat next to a scruffy guy who sported a long gray beard. One of the players hit a solid passing shot, and my companion shouted, "Nice shot, Louie."

I turned toward him. "Sounds like you know the players here."

He smiled. "Yes, indeed. I hang around here all the time. This is one of my favorite forms of entertainment." He looked more carefully at me. "Hey, don't I know you?"

I shrugged. "I don't recognize you, but I have short-term memory loss so we might have met before."

He squinted at me. "I've seen you somewhere." Then he snapped his fingers. "That's it. At Saint Andrew's Church."

The name clicked. "I've been to that church."

"Yeah, I remember. You were there after the Sunday service. You came up and introduced yourself to me."

I thought back to my journal. "I remember reading a name — Harley Marcraft."

"That's me." He thumped his chest and held out a large paw.

I shook his hand. "Paul Jacobson."

"That's right. But I haven't seen you here at the paddle-tennis courts before."

"First time I've stopped by. Tell me, how is this game played?"

"It's like tennis except you have only one serve, and the service area extends to the double line near the baseline."

I watched as the players whapped the tennis ball with their paddles. "How come the ball makes that flat sound when they hit it?"

Harley laughed. "They puncture regular tennis balls with a nail to deflate them."

"No kidding."

"Yup. That's the way this game works."

"Seems like you've got this all cased out."

"Yeah. I know these guys pretty well. Look at Louie's partner, Ned. He hits the ball well, but is too inconsistent. He'll wind up and smack this next return of serve, and odds are he'll miss it long."

I watched and sure enough Ned walloped the ball two feet outside the baseline.

"How'd you know that?"

"I've been watching these guys for years. Know 'em like the back of my hand."

"You live around here?" I asked.

"I sure do. I have the largest suite along this whole beach."

I looked at him carefully. His clothes were crumpled and old. "You putting me on?"

Harley laughed. "I sleep on the beach. My bedroom stretches for miles."

"I used to like camping out, but I can't imagine sleeping on the beach every night."

Harley shrugged. "Don't have any family and felt too cooped up in an apartment. I can pick a different spot every night, snuggle down with a blanket in the soft sand, look at the stars, listen to the waves. There's nothing better."

"Isn't it dangerous?"

He waved his hand dismissively. "I know everyone around here. Sure, I been beat up once, but I didn't have anything worth taking. Not any more risk than driving on one of those damn freeways."

"What happens when it rains?"

"We don't have much bad weather here. For a light shower, I wrap up in my blanket. If a storm comes in, I head to Saint Andrew's Church. They have a room where we can sleep."

"My wife and I tied the knot there last Saturday."

"That's right. You told me you had given up your independence."

"Yeah. I moved here and am now a happily hitched old geezer."

He slapped me on the back. "If she ever kicks you out, you can come join me on the beach."

"I'm not planning on that."

"You never can tell. I was happily married once, but my old lady ran off with an insurance salesman. Damn unpredictable broads . . . nice forehand, Frank."

I turned my head to watch a point with one team hitting a high lob and then tracking down the resulting overhead smash. I started thinking. "Say, Harley, when we spoke at the church last Sunday, there was a guy who came up to me, who I understand was Muddy Murphy."

156

"I remember. You got into a shouting match with him."

"Yeah. Apparently so."

Harley looked at me askance. "You have a temper, old man."

"Sometimes it gets the best of me."

"Damn shame what happened to Muddy."

"You mean being murdered?"

"That and what led up to it." Harley scratched his stomach.

He now had my full attention. "What was that?"

"Muddy got crosswise with the local art-dealer community. They were taking advantage of him so he up and quit painting to show them. They got him in the end."

"What do you mean?"

"I'm sure one of them knocked him off. Those bastards will do anything to increase the value of the paintings they sell."

"I understand that the prices of his paintings have gone up since he died, but why would someone run the risk of murdering him versus just letting him die of natural causes?"

Harley shrugged. "I haven't a clue."

"Did he ever mention any particular art dealer to you?"

"No. He cussed all of them. I'd listen to him complain when he and I shared the same section of beach."

"I'm still trying to get a handle on this lifestyle of yours, sleeping on the beach."

"It's simple. Every month, I collect my Social Security check which keeps me in food, don't have to worry about anyone stealing my belongings because I don't have any, know everyone here along the boardwalk, spend time outdoors with the ocean breezes blowing the smog away. What more could I ask for?"

"I always pictured homeless people as really struggling."

He frowned. "Most are that way. Combination of desperation and mental disorder. Muddy and I were the lucky ones. We chose to be homeless. You'd never find me living inside again."

"I don't know. I'm kind of partial to my soft bed."

"You have a wife. Me, I have no permanent relationship, so the beach is a perfect home." He slapped me on the back. "As I said, if the old lady ever throws you out, come team up with me."

CHAPTER 10

As I ambled home, my head swirled with all that was happening to me. I felt like one of those hamsters stuck in a wheel, running and not getting anywhere. I mulled over what I had heard. One of the art dealers must have murdered Muddy Murphy. With Vansworthy out of the picture, the prime suspects would be Brock and Theobault. It appeared that Theobault also benefited from the demise of Vansworthy. If Quintana arrested one of these guys, he'd be off my back. Then I'd be free to go on our Alaskan honeymoon cruise. I had to keep plugging away at trying to figure out what had gone down in the Venice Beach art world. What other choice did I have anyway?

Back in our apartment Marion was waiting for me.

"I was starting to worry," she said.

"I had another adventure with Detective Quintana and spoke with an interesting street character named Harley Marcraft. He said if you ever kicked me out I could come join him living on the beach."

"No chance of that. I'm not giving you up."

"Well, that's good news. In spite of how enthusiastic Harley is about sleeping on the beach, I prefer being in a bed next to you."

Marion gave my arm a squeeze. "You have a letter from our friend Meyer Ohana. To remind you, Meyer is the retired judge and lawyer whom you met at the retirement home in Hawaii. You and he sat at the same table in the dining room and became best chums."

"That's amazing. I was on good terms with a lawyer?"

"Yes. You two were very good buddies. You spent a lot of time together."

"Well, I need all the friends possible. Let's see what he says."

I opened the letter. Meyer congratulated me again on marrying Marion and said that with his macular degeneration he now had a girl who came in to read to him several times a week, but she was going on vacation for two weeks. He reminded me how I used to read to him. That gave me an idea.

"Do we have Meyer's telephone number?" I asked Marion.

"Yes, it should be in my address book." She found the book and handed it to me.

I punched in the digits. A woman answered and I asked to speak to Meyer Ohana. In a few moments, a man's voice came on the line.

"Hey, you old fart, this is Paul."

"You're the only one in the world who would greet me that way. How's the old married man?"

"Old is the operative word. My beautiful bride and I are reveling in marital bliss. I heartily recommend the institution of marriage."

"It's nice to hear your voice."

"I suppose it's good to hear your voice too, except I don't recognize it."

"Same old memory. I thought as a newlywed, you'd have your memory jogged every night."

"I guess last night was my off night. Your letter said that your reading companion is going on vacation and that I used to read to you."

"You're correct on both counts."

"I thought I'd see if you'd like me to read to you over the phone."

There was a pause on the line. "That would be wonderful."

"Hold on a second while I find a book."

I retrieved a hardcover from the bedroom and picked up the phone again. "I enjoy a good story, but novels don't work for me. You can imagine how frustrating that would be for me when I can't remember anything from the day before. But with short stories, I read a story each sitting, can enjoy it and then it doesn't matter if I reread the same story the next day because it's all new to me anyway."

"You lead such a unique life, Paul."

"So here's what I can offer you. I have a collection of stories by O. Henry."

"It's interesting that you selected O. Henry as the author to read to me," Meyer said.

"Why's that?"

"Do you know anything about him?"

"Only that I read some of his stories in high school. My English teacher Miss Mathers practically wet her pants over him."

Meyer chuckled. "Well, he was one of the leading short-story writers at the turn of the nineteenth into twentieth century. He was a very prolific writer. I also read some of his works in high school in the thirties."

"We both have good memories for things back then. Too bad my klutzy brain doesn't hold things now. So why the interest in O. Henry?"

"His real name was William Sidney Porter and there was one unusual thing about him."

"I hope you're not going to say he was an honest lawyer."

"Worse than that. He worked as a teller for a bank and ended up involved in some suspicious activity that smacked of fraud. He even spent time in prison."

"I hope that doesn't happen to me. I have a police detective breathing down my neck and I detest jails."

Meyer clicked his tongue. "Same old Paul. You have a way of attracting women and detectives. Have you run across any more dead bodies lately?"

"Yeah — three."

"What! You're kidding. Something must be happening in that seaside resort."

"Looks like some trouble in the art community, and I got stuck in the middle — up to my neck."

"I assume you're resisting hiring an attorney?"

"Yes. No bloodsucking lawyers for me, present company exempted."

Meyer laughed. "Attorneys can help people like you who are falsely accused of crimes. Someday, you'll overcome your dislike of lawyers."

"Nah. It's too much fun having an enemy. If I didn't have lawyers to dislike, how could I keep being such a curmudgeon? But I have a question for you."

"You're seeking some free legal advice?"

"Yeah, I'm wondering — if the police aren't aware of some crucial motive in a murder, how do I bring this to their attention when I'm a suspect?"

"A good detective will listen. Just give him a call and pass on the information."

"I think the detective involved is competent, but he sure is on my tail all the time."

"No different than when you were in Hawaii. Just level with him."

"I guess you're right."

"And maybe the detective will start changing his opinion of you."

"That's too much to expect. But I do need to keep a step ahead of the law. Detective Quintana is very persistent. I'm sure something fishy is going on here with some of the art dealers in Venice. An art dealer and an artist were murdered, and I'm trying to figure out why the victims were killed."

"And obviously you're a suspect."

"Yeah. Somehow Detective Quintana thinks I'm a better person of interest than the art dealers. I need to find a way to get him on the right track."

"Sounds like you need to uncover a motive. You have no reason to be accused."

I paused. "Actually, there is. It's my rotten temper. I have a way of arguing with people before they're found dead. Makes me appear suspicious."

Meyer cleared his throat. "You're no different than when we lived in the retirement home together. On the surface you always come across as this gruff old codger. Underneath you're a gentleman."

"Tell that to the detective. He acts like I'm part of the Manson gang. Now are we going to yak all day or do you want me to read you a story?"

"Go ahead. Pick one out."

I thumbed through the table of contents and selected a title that sounded interesting. "Given what we've just discussed, here's a tale called 'The Cop and the Anthem.' "

I proceeded to read the story of Soapy, who does everything he can to get arrested so he can spend the winter months in the comfort of jail. He eats at a restaurant and tries to leave without paying, breaks a window, steals an umbrella, harasses a woman, commits disorderly conduct, but nothing achieves his objective of being arrested.

At this point in the story, I paused. "So

what do you think, old man? Will Soapy achieve his goal of being arrested or not?"

"I'll have to think it over. I'm not sure yet."

"Let's put some meat in the game. How about a friendly wager on the matter?"

"Are you proposing some cross-state-lines gambling?"

"Nothing like that. Just a small wager to make it more interesting."

"What do you have in mind?"

"I have a hankering for some chocolate. Let's set the stakes at a box of chocolates."

Meyer chuckled. "All right, a box of chocolates it will be."

"And I'll even let you choose your position," I said magnanimously.

"Hmmm. In that case I bet that Soapy doesn't end up in jail."

"And I'll hold the position that he's incarcerated."

"Done."

I picked the book up again and began reading how Soapy keeps trying unsuccessfully to get arrested. Then he passes a church and is inspired by the sound of an anthem played by the organist. He has an epiphany and decides right then and there to quit being a bum and seek employment the next day. At that moment a policeman arrests Soapy for loitering and sends him to jail for three months.

I could hear Meyer sigh over the phone when I finished reading. "It reminds me of some cases I had when I was a municipal judge. There is always a certain element that views jail as free room and board."

"I look at it differently. I'm trying to stay out of jail, and my detective buddy is always hinting at his intent to give me a new home. I don't want to end up behind bars."

"Well, it's obvious you're approaching this entirely the wrong way, Paul. If you were more eager to go to jail, like Soapy, you'd have a better chance of staying free."

"Not with Detective Quintana. If I let up one iota, he'll have me spread-eagled on the floor of some dungeon."

Meyer laughed. "You always have this very graphic way of describing things."

"Just the reality of my life and encounters with crime and law enforcement. A time-worn veteran like me should be free to sail off to Alaska with my bride, but Quintana has a different agenda."

"Paul, you should be flattered that he would consider you able, at your age, of committing those crimes."

"There's no way I'm glad he's breathing down my neck."

"You'll work your way out of this like you did before."

"I sure hope so. I'm too old to decorate a cell. Now to our wager. I can already taste that chocolate. You're not going to welsh on our bet, are you?"

"No, Paul. I'll pay up. We have a van picking us up tomorrow for an excursion to the shopping center. I'll see what I can find, although I can't guarantee exactly what gets selected given my poor eyesight."

"Just as long as it has chocolate. It can be dark chocolate, milk chocolate, chocolate mints . . ."

"What if I send chocolate-covered ants?"

"Doesn't matter. Chocolate is chocolate. Just don't substitute something like carob or dates. It has to be chocolate."

"Okay, you'll be receiving a present. And thanks again for the story."

"Tell you what. I'll put a note in my journal to give you a call again to read another one. As long as the young chick who's been reading to you has deserted you, I'll be happy to fill in."

"I welcome the companionship."

"Does this time of day work for you?"

"Paul, I'm in a care home. All I do is listen to the television, take naps and eat, so any time is fine."

"You make it sound so exciting."

"Without you around, my life has become very boring."

"Well, I'll try to spice it up a little. I'll keep you apprised of my run-ins with the law and read more exciting O. Henry stories to you."

"I don't want you running up a large phone bill."

"I'll check with my accountant, but I'm sure I can swing it."

After hanging up I said to Marion, "I'm going to write this in my diary, but also remind me to call Meyer periodically to read to him."

"That's nice of you."

"Sounds like he's stuck on his lonesome, so it's the least I can do to help. But I hope I'm not overextending our telephone bill with the long call to Hawaii. That must have been expensive."

"Not to worry. The plan we're on is only three cents a minute so your call probably cost less than two dollars."

"And here I thought I had spent my whole fortune and would have to sleep on the beach."

I settled into the easy chair in the living room, wondering at the strange existence of those long-in-tooth like Meyer and me. Each of us had our own defects — his eyesight and my scrambled brain. We each were dealing with our own situations in our own ways. I could help Meyer by reading to him and he could give me some ideas to augment my inconsistent mental wiring. What a world. I could feel sorry for myself or do something about my situation. I decided to keep playing my hand in the poker game of life.

I had just picked up the O. Henry book to continue reading short stories to myself when I heard a knock on the door. "Who'd be coming to visit us?" I said as I shuffled to the door.

A young boy stood there holding a box.

"You collecting for the Boy Scouts?" I asked.

He wrinkled his nose like he had smelled a dead rat.

Marion emerged from the bedroom and said, "Hi, Austin. What brings you here?"

"Mom asked me to bring this pie over."

"Well, come on in," I said. "Let's see what we have to feast on."

He stepped inside like he was treading on hot coals.

"How's band camp?" Marion asked.

"Okay."

Marion moved over and gave him a hug. "Now I'll let you two gentlemen talk for a minute. I have a hot iron that needs attention."

Marion returned to the bedroom.

I regarded Austin's scowl and eyes that never moved above rug level. "So your mother drafted you to run this errand. Not something you particularly wanted to do."

Austin scuffed his right foot on the kitchen floor.

"Look at me," I said.

His chin popped up, and suddenly his eyes grew wide.

"I'm not going to bite you. Let me tell you a story. When I was your age, my mother made me visit a woman who had been my second-grade teacher. I'd say, 'Oh, Mom. Do I have to?' and she'd reply, 'Yes. Now go.' This was painful duty even though this teacher had helped me learn to read. Then I discovered that her husband had a collection of toy soldiers that he let me play with. Instead of being a burden, I started looking forward to my visits to Mr. and Mrs. Jensen."

Furrows appeared in his brow. "How come you remember all that? I thought you had a bad memory."

I chuckled. "Good. You have been paying

attention. It's like this, Austin. Overnight my memory does a reset like the clock on a microwave when the power goes out. Most days I couldn't tell you what I did the day before. But my memory still holds for things that happened to me years ago. Also, I have pretty good recollection during the day. You want to test me?"

His scowl had disappeared completely and was now replaced with a quizzical expression. "Test you?"

"Sure. You write down a string of twenty digits and show it to me." I went over to the counter and retrieved a pencil and piece of paper. "Make them random. No simple patterns such as one, two, three . . ."

He bit his lip and scribbled.

When he had completed writing, I took the piece of paper, studied it for a moment and handed it back to him.

"Now follow to see if I remember correctly." I proceeded to reel off the twenty digits.

He looked up at me with his mouth open. "How'd you do that?"

"Just a quirk of my strange brain. I may forget things overnight, but during the day I still have an excellent memory. I was born with this ability, but you can train yourself to remember numbers as well. Now, while you're here, do you want a piece of your mom's pie?"

His eyes lit up. "Sure."

I cut a piece for each of us, and we sat down at the table. I watched Austin as he munched away, his attention never leaving the pie.

"You look like you have the weight of the world on your shoulders," I said.

His face popped up for a moment, then his gaze dropped back to reexamine the cherry pie.

"You know, Austin, I was once your age and even had a son your age at one time. The one thing I know is that when you've got a problem, it's good to find someone to talk to. Anything you want to tell me?"

"It's nothing anyone can help with."

"I can't say for sure, but it probably has something to do with girls, other guys or growing up."

He jolted upright. "How'd you know?"

"I just took a wild guess. Look. I'm an old poop, probably won't be around that much longer, but sometimes I can lend a little perspective from my many years of doing my share of dumb things. If you ever want someone to listen to you, I'm here."

He nodded his head.

"The good thing is that since I forget

overnight, your secrets are safe with me."

He gave me a wan smile. "I'll think it over."

"You do that. Now, do you want another piece of pie or are you going to lick that fork to death?"

We each had a second helping and halfway through his, Austin tapped his fork on the plate. "Do you know anything about homeless people?"

"I met some who live around here."

He bit his lip. "Some guys I know from school talk a lot . . ." He gulped. "They think it would be cool to beat up a homeless person . . . and they want me to join them."

"And what do you think of the idea?"

"I think it sucks."

"Good. You and I agree on that."

"But I'm the only one who feels that way. The others are all in agreement and will call me a wimp if I disagree."

"How many boys are in the group?"

"Six besides me."

"Maybe some of the others feel the same way you do but are afraid to voice their opinions."

"I don't know. They all seem to support the idea."

I watched Austin carefully. "Or is there a

ringleader who's goading the others on?"

"Well, Pierce is the one who came up with the idea and keeps discussing it. He definitely is eager to do this."

"Maybe, just maybe, some of the others aren't that enthusiastic but don't want to step down in front of the whole group. Have you ever discussed it with any of them one-on-one without Pierce around?"

He shook his head.

"You might poke at that a little," I said. "I'd venture a guess that you might not be the only one questioning the wisdom of Pierce's idea."

Austin squinted at me. "You really think so?"

"Yes. Take it from me as I've been around the block a few too many times. When I was a young whelp, I hung out with a crowd of boys in my neighborhood. We played baseball, kicked cans and made up stories together. But one day the biggest kid, Lenny, got it into his thick skull that we should catch a stray tomcat and torture it."

Austin gasped.

"Lenny was your typical bully, and no one wanted to stand up to him. We all reluctantly agreed to the scheme, thinking we'd look like sissies if we backed out. Fortunately, my best friend Harry and I finally leveled with each other that we thought Lenny's idea was as good as a sardine sundae. Together we confronted Lenny and discovered that no one else in the gang wanted to follow Lenny's suggestion."

"What happened?"

"Lenny stomped off calling us all turds and tried to catch a cat on his own." I chuckled at the memory. "Damn feline clawed him up one side and down the other. I heard many years later that Lenny died in the Battle of the Bulge. Lenny was your garden-variety psychopath and probably enjoyed the opportunity to kill Germans until one took care of him."

Austin wiped his face with his arm and stood up. "Thanks for the pie."

"Well, thank you for bringing it over. Stop by anytime, and we can have another snack and chat."

Austin headed to the door with a lighter step than when he entered, clearly not the result of eating two pieces of pie.

After he left, Marion emerged from the bedroom. "I know I shouldn't have eavesdropped, but I heard your conversation with Austin." She placed her arms around my neck and planted a juicy smacker on my cheek. "You said just the right things to him."

I shrugged. "He's basically a good kid. Just struggling through the growing-up process and facing issues that boys his age have struggled with for eons."

"He ponders things a great deal and will take in what you told him."

"Now it will be up to him to resolve this situation."

"I'm a grandmother and find it hard not to jump in," Marion said. "Don't you think we should intervene?"

"Austin will struggle with this, but I believe he has the gumption to confront this bully. If we interfere, he'll never have a chance to test himself."

"But what if the kids actually hurt a homeless person?"

"I hope I'm right, but I don't think Austin will let that happen."

CHAPTER 11

The next day after reading in my journal how inexpensive phone calls could be, I decided to contact Jennifer.

After she answered the phone, I said, "I need you to do some research for me on your Internet thingy."

"I've already started, Grandpa. I checked out the art dealers you mentioned to me: Theobault, Brock and Vansworthy."

"What a memory."

"Elephants and Jennifer never forget. And guess what I discovered?"

"That they have a secret cabal to take over the Venice Beach graffiti wall?"

"Now be serious, Grandpa. This is important."

"Yes, ma'am."

"I came across a long article from the *Los Angeles Times* that appeared five years ago. It describes the leading galleries and art dealers of Venice Beach. In addition to the three you mentioned, two other names appeared: Pieter Rouen and James Farquart."

"Those are new ones for me. They haven't shown up in anything I've read in my journal."

"And here's why. They used to be successful art dealers who were driven out of business by ruthless competition."

I thought for a moment. "So they might have some interesting views regarding the two surviving art dealers."

"Exactly. I've tracked down contact information for you. Rouen and Farquart both moved to other parts of the country."

I reached for a pencil and notepad. "Okay, fire away, and I'll write down the information."

"Grandpa, I'll make it easier for you. I'll e-mail everything I have to Austin, and he can print it out for you."

"What makes you think Austin will cooperate?"

"I had a talk with him before I left Venice Beach. We reached an understanding."

I thought back to what I had read in my journal. "You must mean he didn't want another black eye."

Jennifer giggled. "Something like that. He's coming around. After my little reminder and the conversation you had with him, he improved for the better. He won't be messing with me again."

"I see. You gave him a wake-up call to rejoin the human race."

"Oh, Grandpa. Austin's not so bad. We became friends by the time I left."

"In any case, go ahead and send the material to Austin, and I'll go pick it up."

"Okeydokey. It's on its way."

I imagined little pieces of paper flying over my head and recombining in Austin's computer. Oh, well. I was too old to understand this computer crap anyway.

After I got off the phone, Marion said, "We have a trip planned today."

"Where to?"

"I'm going to abduct you for a journey to Catalina."

"Twenty-six miles across the sea."

"That's right."

"I don't think I'm up to the swim."

She swatted me with the newspaper. "We're flying on a seaplane from San Pedro. You won't be anywhere near the water."

"That's a relief."

With my day duly scheduled for me, I changed into my Catalina wandering clothes and we headed off for our plane ride.

The little red seaplane looked like it had

seen better days. At least it floated so if the engine failed while in flight . . .

We arrived in Avalon harbor, and the plane coasted into a dock where we disembarked.

Marion looked at her watch. "We need to meet back here at three P.M. for the return flight so I have you all to myself today."

"That sounds like a good plan for us newlyweds."

I noticed a place to rent bicycles.

"Let's show all these young kids wandering around how to do things," I said. "How about a bike ride?"

Marion wrinkled her forehead. "Are you sure you're up to it?"

"Give me a break. I'm old but fit." I patted my stomach. "I don't feel a day over seventy. We'll explore this whole island."

I paid the bike ransom, and we hopped or, more realistically, struggled aboard. We both started pedaling and drew stares from the crowd, lining the streets. There probably wasn't another bicyclist over forty, and there we were — two vintage models. We headed along the bay, past the casino and came to a dead end.

"Okay," I said. "Let's head the other way."

We cycled through town like on the Tour de France, senior style. My legs felt fine from all the walking I had been doing, and Marion held her own as well. We pedaled up a hill on the other end of town and in ten minutes came to another dead end. We stopped and looked down toward the harbor.

"What's with this town?" I said. "I thought we could cycle around the island."

I accosted one of the local inhabitants and asked, "Where can you ride besides this short stretch in town?"

The woman swept back a strand of hair from her forehead and laughed. "That's it. Beyond the fence is private property."

"I'll be damned. I rented a bike so we can ride back and forth on a one-mile stretch."

"That's right."

We headed back to the shop and returned the bikes.

"With the size of this place, we can explore it on foot," I said.

Marion put her arm through mine and we strolled along the waterfront. We watched the other tourists as people ducked in and out of shops.

I spotted an art gallery. "Let's go inside so I can do some research."

A skinny man in black slacks and a white shirt greeted us. "May I help you?"

"You have anything by Muddy Murphy?" I asked.

He frowned. "I'm sorry. We don't. He's handled by only a few art dealers, primarily in the Venice Beach and Beverly Hills area."

"What's the link between Venice and Beverly Hills?"

"The artist you mentioned is from Venice. Financing often comes from Beverly Hills."

That clicked with what I had read in my journal. I would have to check it out at the gallery open house.

We had fish and chips at a small waterfront café and enjoyed watching the sailboats enter and leave the harbor. When Marion excused herself to visit the powder room, I contemplated my predicament. So here I was with Detective Quintana on my tail. It made me break out in a sweat every time the thought of the murders popped into my mind. Still, I had to stay focused and keep plugging away to learn more regarding these art dealers. With Vansworthy and Muddy Murphy dead, the chief suspects were Theobault and Brock. I went back over what I had read in my diary. Theobault had gone ballistic when Marion and I confronted him. Obviously we struck a nerve. Brock had been cordial, but I didn't trust the son of a bitch. It was a coin toss between those two. I'd have to collect more information to ferret out who the bad guy was or if the two of them were in cahoots. I'd have to snoop around some more and have my computer expert, Jennifer, do some additional research for me. With more data assembled, then I'd have something to show to Detective Quintana to direct him the right way so he'd have something better to do than bug me. That would be refreshing. Then I could move on with my life, however much time was left, and take my bride on our honeymoon cruise.

My musings were interrupted by my beautiful wife who reminded me it was time to ride back to the mainland on the seaplane.

As we took off I watched the sea below us and listened to the rattling of the plane. My stomach tightened at the thought of flying over twenty-six miles of ocean. Control your thoughts, I told myself. I took a deep breath and decided to gut it out. I had to uphold appearances for my bride.

The remainder of the return flight was uneventful other than the airplane feeling like it would shake apart at any moment. I watched boats down below, thankful that we were staying in the air. The main thing was that I escaped any close encounters of the ocean variety.

Late that afternoon, I moseyed down the stairs and over to the main house. After taking a moment to listen to birds chirping in the trees, I knocked on the door, and Andrea greeted me.

"Hi, Paul. What brings you over?"

"Jennifer sent something to Austin's computer that I need to read. Is he around?"

"Come on in. Austin is back from band camp and up in his room. Second door on the right."

I climbed the stairs, nearly tripping over a gray tabby cat that didn't seem inclined to interrupt its nap, and found Austin's door open.

"Hi, sport," I said. "I understand Jennifer sent you something for me."

He looked up and gave me a smile rather than the sullen nod I had read about in my journal.

"Yup. There's an e-mail message waiting from her. Let me open it up."

I pictured him using a can opener to pry the lid off a coffee can and reach inside to remove a scroll. Instead words popped up on his computer TV screen.

"Can you print everything she sent?"

"Sure." With his hand, he shifted and clicked a little object half the size of a glasses case, and suddenly paper started spewing out of a box sitting next to the computer. I shook my head in amazement.

While sheets continued to churn out, I looked around his room. Austin had several pictures of musicians holding guitars. There was one of a young man in jeans with no shirt and wild curly hair holding a microphone.

"Who's that?" I said, pointing to the picture.

"Jim Morrison of the Doors."

I wouldn't have known him if he had been Joe Schmo of the Windows. I looked at a poster of two men in dark suits, dark glasses, dark ties and dark hats. The title read, "The Blues Brothers."

"Hey, I remember that movie," I said.

"I thought you had memory problems," Austin said.

"I saw that movie before my memory went in the crapper. That was something, those guys charging around Chicago like two pissants."

Austin laughed. "You talk funny."

"Yeah. That's the way someone over the hill like me is."

Just then the gray cat sauntered into the

room and jumped up onto a counter which contained a tank with a school of goldfish.

"Does your cat try to catch the fish?" I asked.

"No. She's just curious."

"Must be a watch cat," I added.

Austin crinkled his nose at me. "Did you know that a goldfish has an attention span of three seconds?"

"Kind of like my faulty memory. Where'd you learn that interesting fact?"

He shrugged. "Something I picked up when I was doing research for my science-fair project. I was breeding goldfish."

"Just as long as you don't breed discontent."

He shook his head. "Jennifer warned me about your dumb jokes."

"Hell. It's a way a late-fall-chicken like me can entertain himself."

"I thought you entertained yourself by finding dead bodies."

"Touché." I gave Austin's hair a quick ruffle.

He stood up and went over and shut the door to his room. "Can I talk to you in private?"

"Sure." I sat down on his bed. "Whatcha have in mind?"

"It's about Pierce wanting to beat up a

homeless person."

"Although I don't remember our conversation, I wrote something down in my journal."

"Journal?"

"Yeah. Since day to day I can't remember squat, I write down — every night — what happens in my strange life and review it the next morning. That's the world of Paul Jacobson, memory minimalist."

"So anything I told you won't be secret."

"Sure it is. I just have to write it down to remember."

He sighed. "I guess it doesn't really matter anyway."

"You don't look real happy. What's going on?"

Austin took a deep breath. "You said I might not be the only one who questioned beating up a homeless person. You were both right and wrong."

Now I was puzzled. "How so?"

"Last night I talked to one of my friends, Jason, and he admitted that he didn't want to go along with it. Then I called Pete, another guy in the gang. He also said he didn't want to hurt anyone. This morning when we all met at the beach before I went off to band camp, I approached Pierce and told him it was wrong to beat up an innocent person."

"Good for you." I slapped him on the back.

He gulped. "It didn't work out as I expected. I turned to Jason and he looked away. I pointed to Pete and asked if he agreed with me. He wouldn't look at me either. Neither of them stood up for me!"

"Uh-oh. Groupthink."

"Huh?"

"They were afraid to express their real views in public. Even though they agreed with you, they were intimidated and wouldn't stand up in the larger group."

"Something like that. Anyway, Pierce called me a wussy and said they should beat me up along with a homeless person."

"I tried one more time with Jason and Pete, but they wouldn't say anything."

"So you have a situation where at least three of you disagree with Pierce's misdirected course of action, but you can't convince the others to stand up for what they really believe."

"That's why I brought it up. I don't know what to do now."

I thought for a moment. "Three of you are sane and one is a screwball. How do the others really feel?"

"The other three always go along with

what Pierce suggests. But Ralph can't really agree with Pierce. He claims to be a pacifist."

"So deep down at least four of seven would vote against it . . ."

"Vote." Austin's eyes opened wide. "What if we had a secret ballot? I bet the other three would take my side then."

I chuckled. "See, you did come up with a solution."

Austin punched his right fist into his left hand. "Yeah. I know just what I'm going to do."

I collected the sheets of paper, thanked Austin for printing the material from Jennifer and headed back to my place. After reading through the article, I had the impression that these art dealers were all eager to slash one another's throats. I tried the two phone numbers Jennifer had tracked down for the vanquished ex-Venice art dealers, but only got messages on answering machines.

As I sat down to relax, I felt a sense of pride on behalf of Austin. The kid was coming around. From what I had read in my journal, he had been a bit of a mess when I first met him, but now he was getting his act together. I sighed. If I could only get my act together and figure out what these art dealers were up to. Between Austin and Jennifer I had loads of help, but I hadn't been able to decipher the enigma yet. Oh, well. I'd keep after it. Either I'd solve what was what or Detective Quintana would chain my butt up in a dungeon somewhere.

Deciding it was time for my late-afternoon constitutional, I grabbed a baseball hat to protect my wavy locks, gave Marion a peck on the cheek and headed out into the wilds of Venice. As I explored around, I happened to look up and on a second-story balcony saw two mannequins dressed up in Blues Brothers outfits. A few blocks later on the side of a scruffy apartment building I spied a three-story-high replica of that same picture in Austin's room, the guy from the Doors, this time next to two windows. Venice Beach had this thing about art in all its weird forms. Where else could you find murals every couple of blocks?

When I had worn myself out and returned home, I found Marion banging drawers in the kitchen.

"What's all the noise?" I asked.

She looked at me like she wanted to close one of my hands in the drawer she was slamming shut. "I can't find my reading glasses."

I stared at my bride. "Well, at least they're

not on your head. Let me help."

We explored every surface and drawer in the whole place. Then I looked under the couch cushions and beneath the couch itself.

"There aren't that many spots I could have left them," Marion said, spitting out the words.

"When do you last remember having them?"

"I was sitting in the easy chair in the living room reading and then went to fetch a glass of iced tea."

I dug into the cushions of the chair and then lifted up the chair's skirt. Nothing. "This is serious." I gave her a wink. "We can't have two people with bad memories in the same house. That's one more than the standard quota."

I entered the kitchen and opened the refrigerator. There next to the container of iced tea rested Marion's glasses. "Case solved," I said handing them over to her.

"My hero." I finally earned a smile rather than a glower. "How did you figure that out?"

"Geezer intuition. I just retraced your steps. If I could only have the same insight into these murders I'm being blamed for."

CHAPTER 12

I woke up in a place I didn't recognize. I looked around a small room. No one there. I saw a pair of brown Bermuda shorts and a well-worn T-shirt tossed over a chair. I tried them on. They fit. Finding two tennis shoes and socks, I put those on. Where the hell was I? I found a door and went down a set of stairs, out through a wooden gate to an alley and finally came to a larger cross street. Seemed to be a quiet neighborhood on a quiet morning. The sun shone down, warming my arms. Bees hummed in flowery hedges, and a gentle breeze rippled across my face. No one around. Finally after several blocks I spotted a guy in his fifties or so walking a dog.

"I hate to bother you, but where are we?"

"Pacific Avenue."

"I'm needing some further orientation. What community?"

"Why, Venice Beach."

"I'll be damned. I last remember living in Hawaii."

"You really are lost. Memory problems?"

"So it seems."

"Let me buy you a cup of coffee. Maybe sitting down will help."

"That's mighty kind."

"There's a little outdoor café around the corner."

I followed him and his Corgi to a table, and we both plopped down with the dog snuggled at his feet.

"My name is Al Bertrand. So what do you remember?"

"I know my name's Paul Jacobson. Pleased to meet you. I woke up in a strange apartment above a garage and then wandered around."

"I guess I'm fortunate. I have a solid memory. But if I did start having problems, I'm sure I'd still be able to find my way around here. I've lived in Venice for forty years."

"Seen a bit of change in that time, I imagine."

"Yes. Venice has had its ups and downs. Just look at that building across the street."

I stared at an apartment house with fresh white paint and shining metal balcony rails. "Seems to be newly renovated."

"That place used to be a run-down dump. This area is definitely improving."

It would have improved for me if I had some clue why I was here. Oh, well. I decided to go with the flow and enjoy a cup of java.

After we had sipped for a while, Al asked. "Memory coming back yet?"

"Nothing yet." I regarded my companion. "So, Al, what do you do for a living?"

"I'm an attorney. I primarily practice small-business law."

I flinched. "I'll be damned. A lawyer buying me a cup of coffee."

He chuckled. "You're not one of those who think all lawyers are scum, are you?"

"Well, I have to admit my experience with attorneys hasn't been that positive. One nearly ruined my auto-parts business many years ago."

He set his lips for a moment and then said, "I'm sorry to hear that. But many in my profession help clients who have problems, rather than cause problems." His eyes lit up. "And you're starting to remember things from the past."

"That's the crazy situation. I can remember fine from the distant past and from this morning, but can't pull anything out of my cranium from yesterday."

195

"If I can be of any help, let me know." He handed me a card which I put in my pocket. "There's a police substation at the plaza by the beach. You could seek further assistance there. I'd be happy to walk with you."

"Thanks, but I'll mosey there on my own, and you and your dog can make your rounds. Just point me toward the beach."

"Just two blocks that way, then turn right." He gestured down the street.

"Thanks for the coffee and conversation."

We shook hands, and I followed his directions to a wide beach with a cement path along the city side which I took to the right. I passed a large parking lot half full of cars, a bunch of shops and hot-dog stands. If I had wanted to, I could have bought any type of junk food or any cheap China-made souvenir. So this was the world-famous Venice Beach. Ahead a small set of bleachers stood near a fence behind which a group of people were whapping tennis balls with paddles.

Deciding to put off for a moment the visit to the police substation, I sat down to watch. Shortly, a bearded guy in grubby clothes sidled up to me. "How ya doin' today?"

I looked him up and down. "Not so hot. I don't know why I'm here."

He laughed. "On your spiritual journey?"

"No. Just trying to figure out why the hell I woke up in Venice Beach."

"That's happened to me a few times. A little too much vino, and I had no idea why I woke up where I did."

"But I don't drink much." I couldn't remember recently, but the last I recalled I only tippled the occasional glass of wine.

"That's serious." He raised his eyebrows. "You and I have talked before. Right here. I'm Harley Marcraft."

I eyed him. The name didn't click. "I'm Paul Jacobson. So I've been around this place before?"

"At least for the last week. I don't think I'd seen you before then."

Realizing I hadn't paid attention during my wanderings that morning, I asked, "Any clue where I live?"

"No." Then his eyes lit up. "But you were at Saint Andrew's Church." He snapped his fingers. "I met you after a service, and you told me you got married there."

"Married? I thought I was a single geezer." This was getting stranger all the time.

"Maybe someone at the church can help you. They're very friendly. You should talk to the people in the office there."

"It's worth a shot, although I don't remember the place at all. Where the hell is it?"

"Easy to find. At the parking lot, head away from the beach. The major street's Venice Boulevard. Half a mile on the left side you'll see a white Spanish-style building with a bell tower. That's Saint Andrew's. There's always someone in the office."

"I guess I can find that. Much obliged." We shook hands. Deciding I'd rather try the church than the police, I started off on my discovery mission. Along the way I passed kids with skateboards, a young man bouncing a basketball and a myriad of beachgoers. I passed over a bridge and caught a glimpse of a canal lined with hedges and half a dozen rowboats moored to the side. I paused and looked down. My heart started pounding. Damn. I didn't like bodies of water larger than a bathtub.

After twenty minutes I spotted a building that met the description Harley had given me. As I approached I noticed the bell tower and decided I had reached my destination. I opened a thick, carved wooden door and wandered inside to find an office. A pleasant woman looked up and smiled at me, showing even white teeth.

"I'm Paul Jacobson."

"I know. You help out here once in a while."

My head jerked involuntarily. "I do?"

"Yes. You look lost."

"I am. A friendly man directed me to the church since he claimed he had seen me here before. I don't know where I live."

She clicked her tongue at me. "Marion warned me that you have memory problems and might forget things. I'll give her a call."

"Who's Marion?"

"Your wife."

That hit me like a ton of crumbling mortar. My wife Rhonda had passed on. Had I remarried? What the hell was going on?

She picked up the phone, punched some buttons, spoke briefly and then explained that someone would be over to retrieve me in half an hour. She directed me to a chair to sit in until my ride arrived.

While waiting, I read a church magazine article that described the declining attendance in California churches. Maybe the trend would reverse as the population aged. If more people had memories like mine they'd spend more time in church.

A little later two women entered the office.

Both were fetching ladies, but I was

especially attracted to the older one, who appeared to be in her late seventies. Could this be my wife?

"Are you here to rescue me?" I asked. "And who's Marion?"

The older woman winked and gave me a gentle smile. "I'm Marion and this is my daughter Andrea. I guess I need to keep a better eye on you."

"Well, I don't mind keeping my eyes on you. Rumor has it that we're hitched."

She laughed. "That's true. Now, time to take you home."

On the way back I asked, "Do either of you know a man named Al Bertrand?"

"Why do you ask?" Marion said.

"Because he helped me on my ill-fated sojourn this morning. Even sprang to treat me to a cup of coffee."

"That was nice from a stranger."

"The name's familiar," Andrea said. "I think George may know him."

"Check it out for me if you would. It's nice to know there are Good Samaritans in the neighborhood." I extracted the business card from my pocket and looked at it. "He's a lawyer and has an office on Washington Boulevard."

"That's right," Andrea said. "He's assisted

George with some business dealings."

"I'll be damned. Can you believe it? A lawyer who helps people."

Marion patted my arm. "Not all lawyers are the villains you always make them out to be. You even have a friend in Hawaii who's a retired attorney and judge."

I shook my head. "Will wonders never cease?"

Back at the place where I had woken up earlier, Marion explained to me the details of my new life. "My daughter Andrea and I went to breakfast with some friends of hers so I let you sleep in. And obviously you didn't read your journal this morning."

"What journal?"

"The one on your nightstand."

I waddled into the bedroom. My pajama tops rested on the nightstand. Underneath I found a nice leather-bound diary which I proceeded to read.

Damn. What a life I led. I felt like a voyeur peeking into someone else's world. Could all these things be happening to me? I didn't know if I was a criminal or a victim.

I felt like a little lost boy . . . just like the time I had wandered off into the hills of San Mateo as a child of seven. At first I had a wonderful time listening to the chirping of birds and chasing squirrels, but then I discovered I didn't know my way back. I remembered that sinking feeling, much like I experienced now. Back then, fortunately, I came to a clearing and spotted a dirt road that led me back to civilization. Now, Marion was my road and guide, built into one. I counted my blessings for her assistance and decided to keep working to solve this art-dealer conundrum.

When I moseyed back to the living room, Marion was reading a newspaper. She looked up. "We need to do something in case you get lost again."

"Do you want to give me a homing pigeon or a long string?"

"No. But at least some directions. If you were really lost where would you look for information about yourself?"

"I'd check my wallet first."

"Okay. I'll write up a note you can keep in your wallet to call me. I'll include our phone number and address."

"Then all I have to remember is to look in my wallet."

She wrote the information on a piece of paper, trimmed it with a pair of shears and handed it to me to stash away in my billfold.

With that set, the odds of me finding my

way home increased a percentage point or two.

I cleared my throat. "Now this matter of the police breathing down my neck because of some murders. Anything new I should know?"

"You've kept your journal current. There's an art gallery showing the day after tomorrow that you want to attend. I'll have to trust you on your own as I promised to go with George and Andrea to a band camp concert Austin is in. He plays the trumpet."

"I'm musical too. I play the radio."

Marion glared at me, and then her face relaxed. "Oh, I was supposed to remind you to call our friend Meyer."

"Yeah, according to my journal, he lives in Hawaii and I read stories to him."

"He'd love to hear from you. Why don't you grab your short-story book and give him a call?"

"Why not?"

I retrieved the O. Henry collection and punched in the phone number that Marion showed me in an address book. I asked for Meyer Ohana, and when a man's voice came on the line I said, "Is this the poop who is older than dirt just like me?"

"Paul, you called again."

"Damn right. You can't get rid of me. I

found a note, and my bride reminded me to call you to read a short story. So I'm armed with my short-story collection and raring to relate an O. Henry adventure to you."

"By the way, I sent you something to pay off our wager."

"That's right. I whupped your butt in our little bet. Good thing I wrote it down in my journal."

"I should have conspired with Marion to eliminate that page of your diary. Then I could have neglected sending it, and you never would have known."

"True, but you're an honorable gentleman, and *you* would have known. I'm sure it would have played heavily on your conscience."

He snickered. "You have me pegged. I wouldn't shirk my obligations."

"I can almost taste that chocolate now. There's nothing as good as something sweet, won fair and square."

"My betting career is over, now that my debt is paid."

"And I won't even report you to the Retired Judges of Hawaii Anti-Gambling Committee."

"Remind me to never bet against you, Paul. With your ability to attract women and escape murder allegations I should have known better."

"I got lucky. If only my luck would change concerning Detective Quintana, I'd be set. Now, are we just going to chitchat, or shall I read you a story?"

"With an offer like that how can I refuse? I'm all ears."

"Any requests?"

"Pick out something colorful."

"Now let me find us a story to read." I thumbed through the table of contents. "Here's one called 'The Green Door.' How does that sound?"

"Fine. I'm ready."

I opened the book to the right page and read aloud the story of Rudolf Steiner who receives a card with the words "Green Door." Seeking an adventure, he enters an apartment building and finds a green door. He knocks and discovers an attractive woman who is starving. He helps her, feeling that the card led him to her. When he leaves he discovers that every door in the building is green and the card had been an advertisement for a theater called the Green Door.

When I finished I asked Meyer, "What did you think of that?"

"Interesting story. Paul, you're an adventurer just like Rudolf Steiner."

"It reminds me of what I read in my journal about my crazy life. This guy ended up in the wrong place at the right time. Only difference is that I seem to end up in the wrong place at the wrong time and find dead bodies instead of green doors."

"But you found Marion."

"Somehow. I don't remember how it happened, but I sure am grateful. Someone past his prime like me ending up with a chick like Marion is quite an accomplishment."

"You're an adventurer with a life of surprises."

"I still need to find a way to stay out of jail."

"You'll work out something, Paul."

"So tell me how your health issues are doing."

"Well, with my macular degeneration, I can't read anything, so that's why your reading to me is so much appreciated. I can barely see my plate at dinner. Once in a while I'm surprised to be eating what I think is a piece of zucchini and it turns out to be cucumber, but other than that I'm getting by. I listen to the TV, but the picture is a blur."

"Not much worth seeing anyway. It's all sex, violence and crime."

"Kind of like your life, Paul."

"Give me a break. In between the weird stuff, my life is pretty boring. Anyway, you should be able to find something worthwhile to watch . . . I mean listen to on TV."

"I take in the sound and try to imagine what's going on. Then there is the matter of my incontinence. The medication I'm on seems to help. I only have a few accidents."

"That must be a pisser."

"Well stated. I shouldn't keep you longer. Marion won't appreciate it if I take up all your time."

"No problem. She's the one who reminded me to ring you up. I'll give you a call again, Meyer."

After I hung up, I had the mixed feelings of excitement from a conversation with a good friend, with an element of sadness because I couldn't recall anything else about him other than what I had read in my journal. I thought about my condition and Meyer's. He could remember but couldn't control his peeing — couldn't even see well enough to read or watch TV. I was in great shape thanks to my regular walks, but my memory leaked like a dripping faucet. The luck of the draw. I guess I should have been grateful that all my major organs functioned well, except my brain. But what the hell, I had to feel sorry for myself once in a while.

I would get on with my crazy life for however long it played out, but for the moment I sat there letting all the events swirl around in my dysfunctional cranium.

Before I had a chance to improve my attitude, I heard a knock on the door. Marion answered it.

"Hello, Austin."

"Grandma, I have an e-mail message from Jennifer for her grandfather. I printed it out." He handed her several pages.

Austin trotted off, and Marion gave me the papers.

"I'll be damned. A message from my granddaughter."

I settled in an easy chair and started reading an article describing the relationships between the three leading art dealers in Venice: Clint Brock, Vance Theobault and Frederick Vansworthy. It was obviously written before Vansworthy met his Maker. It touted Vansworthy, the most recent on the art scene, who through his superior art-selection skills seemed poised to surpass the more senior Brock and Theobault. With that in mind, Theobault had struck a deal with Vansworthy that left Brock in the most precarious position.

I thought over what I had read in my journal. Here were motives for both

Theobault and Brock to put Vansworthy permanently out of the way. Theobault benefited from taking over the partnership, and Brock would have one less competitor.

And then the matter of Muddy Murphy was muddying the waters, so to speak. I wondered if the detective I had read about was making any progress.

Marion interrupted my muddling. "Paul, our honeymoon cruise is a little over a week off. I'm concerned because Detective Quintana told you not to leave the state."

"I hope this murder situation gets cleared up quickly. I'll have to see if I can help move it along. Apparently Quintana hasn't brought the perpetrator to justice yet. He's been too busy badgering me."

That afternoon I strolled down to the beach. My musing about art dealers and murdered artists led me to the graffiti wall, and I watched a man with wild, spiky red hair wield a collection of spray cans like a juggler. After he had covered an area approximately five feet by four feet with vivid geometrical shapes, I confronted him.

"Why do you do this?" I asked.

He spun around and gave me a toothy grin. "Because it's here. I can't resist adding my designs to the wall whenever I have the chance. Look at the color, the texture, the blending of hundreds of layers of paint."

"But doesn't someone else just come along and paint over your work?"

He shrugged. "It's the painting that matters. I do mine. Someone else does theirs. Then I come back again. It's like having an unlimited canvas." He swung his arms out to highlight the panorama of the whole wall.

I stared at a pattern that reminded me of a seasick sailor surrounded by boxes of exploding oatmeal. "Not really a career where you could support yourself."

"This is my therapy. I pick up cans and squirt paint to my heart's content. I come here and let my imagination run wild without getting into trouble like I used to."

"What do you mean?"

His face turned serious. "I'm a reformed environmental artist. I got in trouble by destroying trees when I lived in Boulder, Colorado."

"Hey. I have family in Boulder."

"It's a nice place, but they're very touchy when it comes to certain types of art. I even did a stint removing graffiti. That's where I came to appreciate the nuances of spray paint. By the way, my name is Pitman. Mallory Pitman."

I introduced myself and then had an idea. "Did you know Muddy Murphy?"

His eyes lit up like Christmas candles. "Yes. Now there was an original artist." Then he frowned. "Too bad he died."

"Yeah. He was murdered. I hear it may have been because he and some art dealers didn't see eye to eye."

"Those vultures." He threw a can of spray paint into the sand.

"You don't think highly of them?"

"No. They like to wring blood out of the local artists. They should be supporting up-and-coming artists, not beating us down."

"Sounds like you've had some bad experiences."

"That's why I restrict my art to the graffiti wall for now." He stepped back, extended his right thumb as a reference to where he was painting and squinted at his work. "I support myself as a waiter in the evening at the Renaissance Restaurant. Good tips."

"But art is still in your blood."

"As long as I have the graffiti wall, I'm content."

When I returned home, I said to Marion, "I met a graffiti artist who used to live in Boulder. Name of Mallory Pitman."

She looked at me askance. "You've obviously forgotten, but you had a run-in with him when you lived there with your family."

"Don't remember it."

"He sawed down trees in the yard of a friend of yours. You turned in Pitman to the police."

"He must have as bad a memory as I do. He didn't recognize me."

"I think it all happened at night so he may not have even seen you. I saw some of his work when I visited you in Boulder. It was on display at an exhibit on the Pearl Street Mall."

"I'll be damned. In any case, he knows the local art community. He might be a source of useful information. How'd you like to go out to dinner tonight?"

"You have something in mind?"

"Yeah. There's a restaurant I want to try —The Renaissance."

CHAPTER 13

Marion forced me to swallow three huge pills before she would accompany me to the restaurant. Then after a call to the local taxi monopoly and a short wait, our chariot driver arrived.

When the cab dropped us off at the restaurant, the first thing I noticed was a gilded entryway with a large chandelier overhead. Inside, the room had multiple identical chandeliers with the lights dimmed and a string quartet playing from an alcove. The aroma of sizzling steak permeated the air. I suddenly felt hungry.

"Pretty swanky," Marion said.

"Nothing but the best for my bride."

We were seated at a table with a crisp white tablecloth, gold utensils and crystal glasses. I unfurled a white napkin and placed it in my lap.

When our waiter appeared, I was pleased to see the red mop top of Mallory Pitman.

He didn't seem to recognize me, so I said, "We spoke at the graffiti wall earlier today."

He wrinkled his eyebrows and then smiled. "Oh, yeah. Now I remember."

"As a result of that conversation, I decided to try your fine establishment. You can tell your boss that you've brought in a new set of customers."

"Then I'll bring you the chef's hors d'oeuvres on the house."

He trotted off and soon returned with a plate of pâté, shrimp adorned with a béarnaise sauce and mushrooms filled with crab.

"Not bad," I said as I munched away at some of the pâté on a dark rye cracker.

We ordered glasses of Bordeaux, salads and juicy steaks. Afterwards I asked for a doggie bag for the steak scraps, and we completed the meal with crepes to die for.

Now fully sated, I signaled for Pitman to come over.

I leaned close to him. "When we spoke earlier today, you mentioned you lived in Boulder. I have a confession to make. I was the guy who turned you in for sawing down trees in people's yards."

His eyes grew large. "You're the one who stuck a stick in my back pretending it was a gun?"

"I don't remember the particulars, but my

wife reminded me of the event. I'm afraid I'm the one who interrupted your art career."

Rather than acting irritated, Pitman laughed. "I guess I deserved it. My limited local acclaim went to my head. The new scenery here has given me a better perspective on life."

"But don't you miss your artwork?" Marion asked.

He leaned close to us and spoke in a soft voice. "I've saved some money from tips and can soon afford to rent studio space. I'll start over from the right basis this time. When the creative desire strikes me, I'll pursue it in a more appropriate manner."

"I'm glad there are no hard feelings," I said. "In fact I wanted to ask you a favor."

"Sure."

I cleared my throat. "I'm trying to learn more about the art dealers in this community and could use the advice of someone, like yourself, who is versed in the art world. I'd be willing to pay a little stipend if you'd serve as an art consultant to me."

He gave me a large grin. "I'll tell you what. I'll be happy to advise you. And no charge."

"There's an open house at Clint Brock's

gallery Saturday night. Could you meet me there?"

"That's my night off and I planned to stop by anyway. I try to attend all these events. I'm developing contacts for when I start working again . . . I mean other than being a waiter."

I thanked him and left a sizable tip to move him closer to his dream of having his own studio.

In the cab on the way home, Marion and I held hands. I was excited by her touch, but felt a twinge of sadness, thinking of my friends and acquaintances who I would forget overnight.

"You seem pensive," Marion said. "A penny for your thoughts."

"Hell, I'd give a few hundred thousand dollars to have my memory back."

"That would be nice, but it isn't going to happen."

"Don't use reality to confuse me," I said. "I have to have something to gripe about."

Back at our place as we climbed the stairs, a gray tabby cat joined us.

"Hello, Cleo," Marion said.

I reached down and opened the doggie bag I'd brought.

Cleo busied herself munching the goodies left over from our feast.

"And I thought the scraps were for you, Paul."

"Nah. I thought I'd bring them for our watch cat."

The next morning after I reacquainted myself with the life and times of Paul Jacobson of the journal-reliant memory, I decided to wander down to the beach while Marion was off running errands. Along the way I passed a vacant lot with what looked like a convention for homeless people going on. Next to a building stood half a dozen shopping carts loaded with clothes and plastic bags. Sitting on the scraggly grass was a scruffy crowd of people in a random medley of ragged clothes.

One man waved to me. "Hey, I know you. Come on over."

I pointed to myself.

"Yeah, you're Paul Jacobson."

What the hell. I ambled over.

The man who had shouted to me lumbered up. He stood my height with a beard, wavy hair — not too dirty — and wore old baggy jeans complemented by a plaid shirt.

He grabbed my arm. "We talked over by the paddle-tennis courts."

217

"My memory's not so hot so I can't say for sure."

"That's right, you told me that before. I'm Harley Marcraft."

The name rang a bell with what I had read in my journal. "Yeah, we did speak."

He snapped his fingers. "We talked about Muddy Murphy."

Now he had my attention. "I am interested in Muddy Murphy."

The man threw his arms out toward the crowd of folks sprawled on the grass. "Here's Muddy's extended family."

"Some of you knew Muddy?" I asked.

Half a dozen heads nodded.

"Wow, Harley, you have quite a mob here."

He grimaced. "Unfortunately, our population has increased lately."

"Poor economic times?" I asked.

"No. It's the Los Angeles Police Department. They've been cracking down on the homeless in downtown LA. They let people pitch tents at night, but during the day they keep kicking people out of their territory."

"How does that affect you here in Venice Beach?"

"Simple. If the police hassle our colleagues in downtown, they just migrate out to the beach. Our people are not going away. We move on."

I scanned the crowd. One woman who I had noticed shaking her head continued to do so while mumbling to herself. I hoped she enjoyed the conversation with herself.

"It's surprising that Muddy lived on the street when he was a well-known artist."

"There are a number of us who choose to live here even though we could afford accommodations. Take Ralph for example." He pointed to a man in his thirties who nodded at me. "Tell him your story, Ralph."

Ralph stroked his bearded chin. "I used to be a stockbroker. Had a decent place in Santa Monica. Then one day I quit my job. I could have lived in my apartment but just let the lease expire and took to the streets."

"But you can't afford an apartment anymore, I bet."

He shook his head. "That's not the case. I left my portfolio intact and haven't touched it since. Probably worth a fair amount. I'm not interested in it. I found my friends here, and I don't have to put up with all the crap of being in an office anymore."

"I don't know," I said. "I'm kind of attached to sleeping in a bed."

"You get used to it. It's not so bad as long as the weather holds. But, hey, this is Southern California and it doesn't rain that much. And if a storm comes in we can go to Saint Andrew's and sleep on the floor of the meeting room."

"I did my fair share of camping when I was a young squirt," I said. "The old body now prefers sheets and a mattress. I'm curious. What kind of reactions do people give you when they see you on the street?"

"Three general types. First, most people won't make eye contact. They want to pretend homeless people don't exist. Then there are the do-gooders. They want to convince me to find a job and live in an apartment. They mean well but generally have no clue. The third category is the bad one. Those that like to beat up homeless people."

"Does that happen often?" I asked.

"Once a month or so a homeless person is found beat-up or dead. Recently a woman had her head bashed in down on Speedway. It was sad. She was harmless. Don't know why some people seem to get their jollies through violence. It's the negative side of the people who ignore us. This third group places no value on the life of a homeless person. But still this is the lifestyle I've chosen."

I turned toward Harley. "Not all these people are here by choice."

"No. Most have no alternative. The combination of poverty and mental illness is pervasive. Take Benny for example. He's the one standing against the wall."

I looked over. A man had his hand to his ear and his mouth moved a mile a minute.

"He's either on a cell phone or he's on his own wavelength," I said. "I can't tell if half the people I've seen today are on cell phones or nuts."

Harley laughed. "Benny has no cell phone. He doesn't need one. He's in constant communication with his departed wife, the CIA and an invisible UFO hovering over Santa Monica Bay. He has a party line that he thinks is the result of a chip being implanted in his brain by al-Qaeda."

"I don't have an implant. My problem is that someone snipped some of the wiring."

"You'd fit right in. You should join us."

"I don't think my new wife would approve. As I said, I'll leave the camping to you younger folks. So, any new theories on what happened to Muddy Murphy?"

My buddy scratched his head. "Theories range from sea monsters to art dealers doing him in. I still side with the view of art dealers. Muddy had pissed off enough wealthy people that someone decided to get him out of the way. These powerful types seem to do what they want and others suffer."

"And the value of his paintings shot up after he died."

"There you go. Greed probably led to his murder."

In the crowd, I spotted a young fellow who appeared to be in his early twenties. He seemed too clean-cut to belong. "What's that guy doing here?" I asked as I pointed.

"Why don't you go over and ask him?"

I moseyed over to the young man who whistled a happy tune while arranging things in his backpack. "What brings you to this gathering?" I asked.

He smiled, leaned close to me and whispered, "I'm not really homeless. I'm out of college for summer vacation, and I'm spending it here at the beach."

"So what gives?"

"I'm trying to see if I can get by all summer without spending any money."

"I gather the beach provides your sleeping accommodations."

"Exactly."

"How about food?"

"That's easy. I have a routine. For breakfast I visit one of several motels that provide free breakfast for their customers. I drop in, have a bowl of cereal, a bagel or sweet roll, orange juice and coffee. I can usually leave with a banana or apple and a muffin for lunch. One-stop shopping." He laughed.

"Doesn't anyone stop you?"

"As long as I look neat, no one questions me. I shave and wash off every morning in the outdoor shower on the plaza. I make sure my shirt is clean and my hair combed. Appearances are everything."

I shook my head in amazement. "That provides breakfast and lunch. What about dinner?"

"Several choices there. I hang around restaurants on Main Street. When people leave with doggie bags, I politely confront them and with an accent ask if they would help feed a down-and-out foreign student. Works at least twenty percent of the time so within an hour I have a meal. Usually pretty good food, too."

"What happens when the weather's bad?"

"That's pretty infrequent. Then I join the rest of the crowd here sleeping on the floor of the church up Venice Boulevard. Not a bad life."

"And you'd rather do this than have a summer job?"

He shrugged. "I worked construction in Ohio last summer. I decided to see a different part of the country this year. It's a good way to spend time at the beach and it prepares me for my anthropology major. This is like studying a tribe in the Amazon or on a Pacific island. You get to know them by living with them."

"Any of the real homeless types resent that?"

"No. I'm unobtrusive. I let them live their lives, and I go about my business. People here aren't trying to foist themselves off on others."

"Well, you've given me ideas on how to survive if my wife ever tosses me out."

"Just stay away from the dumpsters. That can make you sick."

As the young fellow strolled away to organize his backpack, I gave a doleful glance at Benny, still communicating with aliens over Santa Monica Bay. He and I shared scrambled brains. At least I could function, although I needed Marion and my journal to provide any continuity. In spite of my travail trying to stay out of the clutches of the law, I preferred my problems to his. I'd have to suck it up and keep figuring out the links in the chain of solving the Venice Beach murder spree.

I said good-bye to Harley who told me he was going to head down to the paddle-tennis courts in a few minutes. I decided to continue my trip to the beach on my own, mulling over, as I walked, the mixed bag of the people ignored and written off as homeless. Then I had a sudden need to visit a restroom. Fortunately, I found a facility on the plaza near Muscle Beach. It wasn't the type of place I wanted to frequent but walking home would take too long. Inside I had the place to myself, other than one man who obviously used the restroom for his personal grooming, at least as much as his rumpled demeanor required. I entered a stall and looked down at the toilet bowl that exhibited deep scratches. Oh, well. It gave new meaning to the phrase "shitting bricks."

CHAPTER 14

By the roller-skating area at the beach, a young twerp accosted me. When he realized I didn't recognize him, he explained he was Marion's grandson Austin. The name clicked from my diary, and I remembered reading about his difficulties and activities.

"I thought you had band camp," I said.

"I do but it doesn't start for an hour."

"How are things with your Pierce problem?" I asked.

His eyes lit up. "Better. I convinced the guys to hold a secret ballot on whether or not to beat up a homeless person, and my side won five to two. That idea you helped me come up with worked."

"I'm glad I was able to assist in some small way." I thought back to what I had read in my journal. "So you received one more vote than you expected."

"Yeah. Only one other guy sided with Pierce." Then his glum expression returned.

"But you still don't look that excited by the outcome," I said.

"I'm happy that we're not doing anything as a group, but Pierce is still determined to cause trouble on his own. After the vote he stomped off and said he'd do it himself since we all were a bunch of chickens. That guy is something else."

"At least he didn't try to draft the one other remaining holdout."

"No, but I'm concerned he'll hurt somebody. He has a real violent streak, and I don't know how to stop him."

"I have an idea. You want to take a stroll over to the paddle-tennis courts with me?"

"Sure."

As we walked along, a loud bang sounded behind us. I turned around to see a puff of smoke from the muffler of a motorcycle that had just come to a stop and also happened to notice a man in tan slacks, white shirt and a gray baseball cap half a block behind us. He saw me looking his way and ducked into a vendor's stand.

A few minutes later Austin stopped and bent down to tie the laces of one of his tennis shoes. I watched the crowd of beachgoers stroll by. As I turned, I caught sight of the same man I had seen before. He had paused and appeared to be inspecting a pair of sandals at a street vendor's stand.

Austin stood up and we continued on our way. As we approached the paddle-tennis courts, I said to Austin, "Keep your eyes peeled for a guy with a beard who yaks a lot."

Austin pointed out a bearded man sitting in the bleachers, waving his hands and talking to a young woman.

"That's him."

We sidled up to them. "Harley, I have something to discuss with you," I said.

"Fire away."

"This is my wife's grandson, Austin."

Harley stretched out a large worn hand, and Austin shook it.

"Austin has learned something of importance that concerns the homeless community."

Harley wrinkled his brow, and Austin cleared his throat. "You see, uh, there's this kid named Pierce who says he's going to beat up a homeless person. I thought we should warn someone."

"Damn. Always some smart aleck who wants to make a statement. No use talking to the police. They won't do anything until afterwards. I'll put the word out to be careful."

Austin lowered his eyes. "I tried to talk

him out of it, but he's kind of crazy."

Harley chuckled. "He'd fit in with my crowd. Too bad he feels he has to take his aggression out on one of us."

"Yeah. I don't know what Pierce's problem is, but he's determined to cause trouble."

"Thanks for the alert." Harley turned back to the game. "Good overhead, Clyde. Way to show the young kids how it's done."

As Austin and I walked back home, he kicked a rock off the sidewalk. "What else can we do?" he asked. "I just wish I could find some way to prevent Pierce from hurting an innocent bystander."

"I think you've covered the bases for now. Keep an eye on Pierce, and if you get any indication of when he's going to try something, let me know."

"I won't have any warning. He's not speaking to me now."

"Probably just as well. Austin, you did the right thing to confront him on this. Let's see how it plays out."

He gave me a half smile. "I guess you're right. Too bad there have to be people around like Pierce."

I put my arm around his shoulder. "Makes me appreciate people like you, Austin."

His step seemed lighter and as I removed

my arm, I happened to look behind us. Damn. There was the same guy I had seen earlier.

"Austin, stop and pretend you're tying your shoelace again. Surreptitiously look back where we've been. There's a man following us."

"How do you know?"

"He was behind us on our way to find Harley, and he's there again."

Austin stopped and played out his role.

"The man in the gray baseball hat who stopped to look in the window of the store?" Austin asked.

"That's the one."

"I have an idea." He pulled out his cell phone. "I'll pretend I'm talking on my phone. Then I'll race back right past him and take his picture."

"Where's your camera?"

He gave me a disgusted look. "My cell phone can take pictures."

I scratched my head. "I thought it was for phone calls."

"Cell phones also take pictures."

"I'll be damned."

"I'll meet you at home." Austin acted like he was chatting on his cell phone. Then abruptly he turned and raced down the street past the guy in the gray baseball cap.

I finished my return journey. When I entered the gate at home, Austin was already in the yard.

"I have a great picture of him." He held out his phone, and I saw the ugly mug of the guy who had followed us — crooked nose, bushy eyebrows and a scowl. "Come on. Let's go inside and I'll print it out."

"How are you going to do that from your tiny phone?"

"I'll download it to my computer."

"Whatever the hell that means. I wouldn't know a download from a load of bricks."

Austin did his magic and within minutes he handed me a full-size color picture of our stalker.

"I wonder who this guy is," I said.

"I don't know, but you can show his picture around and see if anyone recognizes him."

"Good idea. Print me an extra copy."

After Austin gave me the additional picture, I carefully folded one and put it in my wallet. The other I took with me to show to Marion when she returned.

As I slunk across the backyard, I looked furtively over my shoulder, fearing a return of the mystery man who had been trailing me. In addition to Detective Quintana following me now I had to worry about this stranger. Damn. That's all I needed. Too many unknowns were descending upon my uncertain brain. I'd make some progress and then something new would be thrown at me. But I had to keep trying to put the pieces together. Eventually I'd solve this puzzle or die trying. Hell, that could be any moment for someone my age.

Marion wasn't back yet from running her errands so I settled into my easy chair for a moment of peace and quiet. The phone rang and I picked it up.

An oily voice announced too loudly into my ear, "Mr. Jacobson. You're the lucky recipient of a brand-new car. You've won the Bonneville Sweepstakes!"

"That's funny. I never entered any damned sweepstakes."

"Your name came up as the winner. Maybe a friend or relative entered your name. In any case, we have a brand new Pathfinder waiting for you."

"Well, send it over."

"We'll be happy to. We only require a low-cost service charge. Just five hundred dollars."

I thought back to what I had noted in my journal about senior scams. "I'll consider that after the car arrives."

"We'll have the car to you soon. The upfront fee covers the cost of delivery."

"Fine. Come pick up the fee. I'll be here."

He double-checked my address which I double-checked in my wallet, and then he indicated that a man would be over in an hour.

After I hung up, I retrieved Detective Quintana's card and called his number. He answered on the third ring.

"Detective, this is your favorite suspect, Paul Jacobson."

"What's on your mind, Mr. Jacobson?"

"Can you put me in touch with your bunko squad? I just received a call from a man trying to pull off a scam on old coots like yours truly."

I could hear him sigh on the phone. "What's the scam?"

"I received a phone call telling me I had won a car. All I have to do is pay five hundred dollars first and then it will be delivered."

"That one's been active lately. How did you respond to the contact?"

"I told him to send someone and then called you."

"When will a courier be there to pick up the money?"

"In an hour."

"I'll get an officer right over."

"And, Detective, I learned more regarding these art dealers in Venice. I'm convinced more than ever that either Brock or Theobault murdered both Vansworthy and Muddy Murphy."

"Interesting hypothesis, Mr. Jacobson. Trying to keep the focus away from yourself?"

I sighed. I wasn't going to get through to him.

"And someone has been following me, and I don't think it's one of your people."

In forty-five minutes I heard a knock on my door. A young fellow in a suit stood there. He had short-cropped blond hair and a serious expression on his thin face. He held out a police badge. "Mr. Jacobson, I'm Special Investigator Benson. I understand you've been contacted in regard to the car sweepstakes fraud."

"That's right."

He handed me a packet of bills. "Here's five hundred dollars of marked money. I'd like you to give this to whoever shows up."

I took the money. "I can do that. Then what?"

"I have three cars waiting. We'll tail the courier and take it from there."

"As long as you're here, someone has been following me."

I handed him the picture of the man with the bushy eyebrows. "Here, give this to Detective Quintana. This guy has been stalking me."

He left and I waited for the next visitor. Shortly, another knock and this time a sleazy guy in a ponytail handed me a document. "Congratulations! Here's your award certificate. Just need the five-hundred-dollar service charge."

I handed him the packet of money, which he counted. Then he turned to go.

"Aren't you going to give me a receipt?"

"Oh, yeah." He quickly scribbled out a note, handed it to me and scrambled out the door.

I shook my head. I hoped Detective Quintana's crew nailed these bastards.

Now having done my part to make the world a better place, I needed to help myself by finding out more of the workings of the art-dealer community. I found some notes I had made and decided to call the two art dealers who had been driven out of business in Venice Beach. I punched in the numbers for Pieter Rouen and once again heard a metallic click followed by an equally metallic voice informing me that I had reached the Rouen Gallery. I couldn't imagine it was doing that well if no one ever answered the phone. Next I tried James Farquart and finally reached a human being, one of the female persuasion.

"May I speak to Mr. Farquart, please?"

"And who may I say is calling?"

I stated my name in a tone as if everyone in the world knew that my piss smelled like lilacs. It seemed to work as she said she'd find her boss. I tapped my fingers on the table as I waited. Finally, a soft-spoken voice came on the line. "Mr. Jacobson, this is James Farquart."

I took a deep breath and launched into my spiel. "I understand you used to have dealings with Clint Brock, Vance Theobault and Frederick Vansworthy in Venice Beach, California."

There was a short pause. "That's correct. What is this call in regards to?"

"Vansworthy was murdered recently as well as a local artist named Muddy Murphy."

"Oh, dear. I remember Muddy Murphy. Very eccentric man."

"There are implications that both murders may be connected with either Brock or Theobault. Do you have any comment?"

I kept my fingers crossed that he wouldn't

go off on a tangent and ask who the hell I was and why I had called him.

"If you want my humble opinion, they're both capable of it. You couldn't find a better pair of vultures."

"I detect you don't hold them in the highest regard."

"No. And I'd be tempted to say Vansworthy deserved what befell him as well. The three of them systematically drove me out of business. They lied to my potential clients, and one of them — I've always suspected Theobault — planted a dead cat in the middle of a buffet table when I held an open house."

"Sweet guys, huh?"

"Each of them would be perfectly happy if all the other dealers in Venice dropped dead. One of them must be taking the steps to make that a reality."

"So between Theobault and Brock who would you suspect?"

"That's a hard call. Theobault is more blatant, and Brock comes across on the surface as friendly and smooth. Underneath they're both probably psychopaths. Take your pick."

"Muddy Murphy had stopped painting as a protest because he felt the Venice art dealers were taking advantage of him. Your perspective?"

"Muddy was a unique talent. He went through different styles as fast as he went through paintbrushes. But he had a fragile ego and would go into funks if he felt he wasn't appreciated. I could see him quit painting if he felt someone took advantage of him."

"But why would he be murdered?"

"It's the money. Find out who benefits the most from his death and that will lead you to the murderer."

"I've been trying to track down Pieter Rouen. Have you stayed in contact with him?"

Farquart laughed. "The only other honest man in the business, and he suffered the same fate I did. I understand he has a small gallery in Pittsburgh now. Haven't talked to him in two years. Now I have a client coming through the door so I must go."

After thanking him and hanging up, I thought over what I had heard. Everything continued to point to Theobault or Brock. I just needed to figure out which of the slime-balls had really gone over the edge.

Marion returned from shopping with Andrea and said, "Paul, I forgot. I was supposed to remind you to call Meyer Ohana."

"Uh-oh." I wagged my finger at her. "Is your memory starting to fall apart like mine?"

She kissed me on the cheek. "No, because I eventually pull things back out. With you, it's either your journal or me that does the remembering."

"And I'm damn grateful for both. I'll give Meyer a jingle right now."

"I've taped his number to the phone stand so you don't have to hunt for it."

"What a woman. How did I get by before I found you?"

"Not very well." She laughed.

I called Meyer, and a polite woman's voice informed me that he would be with me momentarily. I pictured a harem of women fanning him while he ate grapes and bon-bons.

When he answered, I said, "Is this the decrepit old fogy who keeps the care-home staff jumping?"

"The same, Paul."

"How did you know it was me?"

"Who else would call and insult me like you do?"

"Hell, I don't know. Maybe some of your other friends. So are you ready to hear a story or am I interrupting a tryst with a young nurse?"

Meyer chuckled. "I'm afraid the female adventuring is your domain. How's Marion?"

"She's keeping me young and alive."

"I can imagine the alive part, but you'll never be young again."

"It's all a state of mind. With my flawed memory I keep forgetting how old I am."

"All you have to do is look in a mirror to remedy that."

"Enough small talk. I have my O. Henry short-story collection here. Ready for action?"

"Yes. Pick one out."

"Okay." I leafed through and randomly selected a page. "Here's one called 'Memoirs of a Yellow Dog.' "

"An appealing title," Meyer said.

I proceeded to read a story from a dog's viewpoint about a woman owner and her henpecked husband. The yellow dog, learning of another dog that goes with his master to a bar, drags his own master into a bar, too. The guy is so grateful to be away from his wife that he decides to run off with the yellow dog to the Rocky Mountains.

When I finished, Meyer said, "I hope you don't do that to Marion."

"No way. I'm happily married to a wonderful woman and have no intention of leaving. I know when I have a good thing."

"You've traded away your single days. But before you met Marion, you and I had some interesting times with our tablemate Henry when we lived in the retirement home."

"I don't remember him."

"Henry enjoyed insulting you and, in turn, you always argued with Henry. He's recuperating from a heart attack."

"And how are you doing, Meyer?"

I heard a sigh. "I miss my dear departed wife."

"I'm sure I felt the same way until I found Marion. You just need a woman. Aren't there any old broads limping around that care home who you can hook up with?"

"Actually there's one who keeps wandering into my room thinking I'm her husband." He guffawed. "The first time she did that I woke up and she was six inches from my face, staring at me. I about had a heart attack."

"You don't have to let her scare the bejezzus out of you. There are other possibilities."

"So far I've set the record straight and sent her back to her own room. She calls me Harry, shakes her head and asks why I'm sending her away."

"Sounds like you've acquired a new girlfriend," I said.

"She's an attractive old gal, and when I first met her we spoke for a long time. She described her two grandchildren and how they both had successful careers on the mainland, one a doctor in Sacramento and the other a lawyer in Phoenix."

"Sounds like a good solid family, except for the lawyer, of course."

"You still down on attorneys, Paul?"

"Absolutely. Except for you, I don't trust any of them. So from what you've described of this young lady, I haven't heard anything that should hold you back."

"Initially she seemed really savvy. We had a delightful conversation and I thought that here was a lady who was with-it."

"So what's the problem?"

"The next day we began chatting at breakfast and she described her grandkids again almost word for word as the day before. Every day we have the same conversation over again."

"Hey, she's probably just like me. All she needs to do is keep a journal."

"But she doesn't attract any murderers like you, Paul."

"Each of us mental defectives has our own style. Does she know who you are each day?"

"Yes. When she's not confusing me with her dead husband, she launches into her spiel like the record player was stuck on the same groove."

"She obviously likes you. You'll have to accept the replay. Who knows? Some night she might just crawl into bed with you."

"They'd probably kick me out of here if that happens."

"You could always live on the beach. I've met some interesting homeless people here who do that, and the weather is better in Hawaii."

"With my eyesight, I'll stick with the care home."

"You could always marry the old biddy and make it legitimate."

"Let's not rush things. I haven't even met her kids or grandchildren yet."

"When you do, this may become serious."

"Right now I'll live my life as it presents itself," Meyer said.

"Well, if some broad prances into your room at night and presents herself, what then?"

"Paul, I think I'll limit my excitement to hearing O. Henry stories."

We signed off, and I once again thanked my lucky stars that I was here with Marion.

With nothing better to do, I updated my journal.

I woke up wondering where the hell I was. I lifted myself up on an elbow and looked around. Sand. I had been sleeping on a damn beach. I tried to think. Last thing I could remember was living in Hawaii. This didn't look like a Hawaiian beach — too wide and lined with vendor stalls. I saw some hazy mountains in the distance. Looked more like LA. Damn. What was I doing in Southern California?

Looking at my watch, I discovered it was two o'clock. Little good that did me. I didn't know the day or the century.

I stood up and ambled toward a boardwalk, still not knowing why I had come to the beach. My stomach growled. Crap. I decided to treat myself to a hamburger at a greasy spoon with a bright red sign that advertised the best burger in Venice Beach. Mystery solved. At least now I knew where I had awakened, although I had no clue why I would be here. I didn't think I had been abducted by space aliens, but who knew what had happened to me.

After ordering, I opened my wallet to pull out a ten-dollar bill to ransom the food. I found a slip of paper which I unfolded. It read, "If you don't know where you are, call Marion." A phone number and address appeared at the bottom of the note. Who was Marion? Was she head of the Paul Jacobson rescue squad?

I ate the hamburger while sitting at a dented metal table, and I watched strange people in various combinations of shorts, jeans and swim gear prance by. Then with my stomach filled and with change from the purchase of a good case of indigestion, I headed off in search of a pay phone. It took me five blocks before I found one and had to wait while some man holding a leash connected to a Dalmatian shouted, "Bitch!" and then slammed the receiver down. I suspected that he wasn't talking to the dog. He stomped off dragging the dog, which gave me a pathetic look. I hoped the guy hadn't broken the phone.

I dropped a quarter in the slot, punched in the digits and listened to the ringing. A woman answered.

"I found a note in my wallet to call this number and ask for Marion."

"Paul, where are you?"

"You know my name?"

"Of course. Did you fall asleep somewhere?"

"Yeah. I woke up on the friggin' beach."

Marion laughed. "Paul, I don't know what I'm going to do with you. Put you on a leash?"

"I don't know what I'm going to do with me either, but having just seen a dog being dragged along on a leash, I don't relish the thought. I can't remember how I ended up here. Can you give me any insights into what's going on?"

"Where exactly are you?"

"I'm on the path that runs along the beach near an outdoor café with checkered red and white tablecloths and a bookstore next door to it."

"Okay. I know where that is. Stay put and I'll be there in fifteen minutes."

"Thanks. Sending out the mounted police will be much appreciated."

After I hung up, I found an unoccupied bench and sat down to wait for the cavalry to arrive. In front of me passed a group of smiling twenty-somethings. They seemed to know what the hell they were doing here.

Then a young fellow in his forties with frizzy hair sat down on my bench. "Mind if I smoke?"

"Not as long as you don't exhale."

He chuckled. "I'm downwind from you. I'll keep the smoke away."

He lit up and put his arms back along the

top of the bench backrest.

In spite of his promise, I received a whiff of his smoke. Pungent. Not a tobacco cigarette. I remembered that aroma from the time I had stumbled into a group of pot-heads in a coffeehouse in Hawaii.

I glared at him.

"You want a drag?" He held out the glowing ember toward me.

"No. My brain's screwed up enough already."

"Speed? LSD? Meth? Coke?"

"No. Life."

Fortunately, he finished his smoke, spotted an acquaintance and charged off into the crowd. I resumed my people watching and was only accosted by a woman in a turban offering to read my fortune, a panhandler seeking change and a kid who wanted to sell me girlie pictures. I didn't realize I'd become such a popular guy.

Then an attractive biddy with shiny silver-gray hair and a pleasant smile approached me. "You here to retrieve me?" I asked.

"Yes, Paul. Time to go."

I lifted myself up from the bench. "You care to give me a rundown on who you are and why I'm here?"

"It's pretty simple. You must have wandered down to the beach and fallen asleep.

When you doze off, you forget things. We live half a mile from here and we're married."

"A sexy broad like you is hitched to me?"

"Yes. We're newlyweds and have a honeymoon cruise coming up in a week."

"Hot damn. Life is full of surprises. So what's happened to me since I lived in Hawaii? Did the Mafia abduct me and forget to drop me in the ocean?"

Marion proceeded to fill me in on the world of Paul Jacobson of the flawed brain. When she informed me that the police had interrogated me as a murder suspect, I flinched.

"I used to be such an upstanding citizen. What's happened to me?"

Marion squeezed my hand. "You haven't done anything wrong. You have a knack for getting in trouble, and you discovered a few dead bodies . . ."

"You mean as in more than one?"

She bit her lip. "As in three. But one was an accidental death."

"I'm glad of that. What am I, a dead-body magnet?"

Now a twinkle came into her eyes. "Well, you do attract my body."

This was getting interesting. "I must say the attraction is mutual. I'd invite you up to my place except I don't know where my place is."

She gave my arm a hug. "I'll show you where *our* place is."

CHAPTER 15

Marion led me up to a cozy apartment above a garage and instructed me to sit down to read a leather-bound journal. Then she informed me she would be gone for a while to gab with her daughter.

After catching up on the adventures of Paul Jacobson of the almost-in-jail squad, I sat there in stunned silence. I couldn't believe the things that had happened to me recently. After all the years that I could remember in my distant past when I had minded my own business, now I had become some kind of murder lure. And my family had been to visit me when Marion and I tied the knot. All of this pushed my aged brain to the limit. I felt like I had plopped down in someone else's life. On top of everything else I had been told by an attractive broad that we shared the same bed. Entirely too strange.

But I realized I had some work to do to

clear my good name. My notes indicated one task still left undone. I reached for the phone and punched in the number I had for Pieter Rouen. Miracle of miracles, a man's voice said in a clipped tone, "Rouen Gallery."

"Pieter Rouen, please."

"Speaking."

"Mr. Rouen, my name is Paul Jacobson. I'm calling from Venice Beach, California, and your name was given to me as an individual who knows the art community here."

"At one time that was correct."

I quickly thought how I wanted to steer this conversation. "It seems the remaining dealers here are involved in some sort of vendetta. One has been murdered, and two others may be implicated in his demise."

Rouen gave a bitter laugh. "If you mean the triad of Brock, Theobault and Vansworthy, any of them would eat their own mother for dinner given the right price."

"I take it you don't think very highly of them."

"They drove me out of business. They systematically stole business from me and smeared my reputation. Them and their Long Beach connection."

"Long Beach connection?"

"Yes. I never figured out the exact link, but some deep pockets helped them ride out the downturn in business we faced for two years. I couldn't weather it, closed my gallery and left."

I thought back to my journal. "I heard something about Beverly Hills financing but not Long Beach."

"I know nothing regarding Beverly Hills, but the evil triad seemed to have unlimited funding coming from some gallery in Long Beach."

"Do you know the name of the gallery?"

"No. I never pursued it. I had to declare bankruptcy and move."

"But they stayed on."

"Yes. And took over the clients I had. Very neat operation."

"Vansworthy is dead. I suspect either Brock or Theobault could be the murderer."

"Two good suspects."

"Anything you can think of, which would point to one or the other?"

"No. Maybe they did it together."

"But I was told Vanworthy and Theobault had some sort of partnership. Brock has never been mentioned as working closely with the other two."

There was a pause on the line. "That's strange. They all hated each other. Not as much as they hated the smaller dealers like me. I can't see Theobault and Vansworthy working together. Maybe someone else forced them into it. Is there anything else?"

"If you happen to think of any further specifics related to Theobault or Brock, please call me." I gave him my phone number.

"And what police department are you with?"

"I'm conducting a private investigation."

"Oh. I see. Well, good luck. I must return to a prospective client." With that he hung up.

I thought over what I had heard. Once again a confirmation of the unsavory character of Brock and Theobault. I needed to find out more about Vansworthy and Theobault's partnership. Also there now seemed to be some Long Beach link as well as the Beverly Hills connection. For every two steps forward, I was stumbling backward a step.

I decided to talk with Mallory Pitman, who I had noted in my diary was my "art consultant." I looked up the phone number of the Renaissance Restaurant and called. A man answered who sounded like I had interrupted his tea and crumpets. I asked to speak to Pitman and was informed, in no uncertain words, that the waitstaff could not be interrupted to come to the phone.

"Well, is he there?" I asked.

"Of course. He's preparing for a busy evening."

I slammed down the phone — my way of venting. I still needed to speak with Pitman, so I looked up the phone number of a cab company. They said a taxi would be by in fifteen minutes, and I indicated I would be out in front. Then on my dresser I noticed a picture of a man with bushy eyebrows. I snapped my fingers. My journal described a man like that who had been following me. I decided to take the picture along to show to Pitman.

Marion was still in the main house with Andrea, so I decided not to bother her and after fourteen minutes headed out the side gate to wait for my magic carpet ride.

The fifteen minutes only took thirty.

"Where to?" the cabbie asked after I had plopped down in a worn backseat that had seen a few too many fat fannies.

"Renaissance Restaurant as fast as you can."

He shot away from the curb with the tires squealing while I grabbed the seat in front of me to keep from being thrown against the side window.

"Whoa," I said. "I was only kidding."

He slowed to only twice the speed limit, and in minutes we screeched to a halt in front of the restaurant.

I paid the fare, thankful to still be in one piece.

Inside, I approached the maitre d'. "I have an important message for Mallory Pitman."

He pursed his lips. "I'm sorry. He's busy at the moment."

I felt the desire to shove miscellaneous utensils up part of that SOB's anatomy, but held my temper. No sense pissing him off. "Well, go get him or I'll cancel my fifty-person reservation here."

The guy shot off like he had a firecracker up his butt.

Moments later a man with red hair appeared and gave me a broad smile. He met the description I had jotted in my journal.

"Let's step outside for a moment." I motioned, and Pitman followed me out the door.

Once we were out of range of prying ears, I said, "I've tracked down some further information about the art-dealer community and wanted to ask your opinion."

"I only have five minutes," Pitman said, looking back over his shoulder. "They hate it when I'm not at my station."

"Tell them your grandfather is ill and if

he pulls through, there will be an expensive banquet at the restaurant."

Pitman chuckled. "Go ahead. What did you find?"

"I located two art dealers who were driven out of business in Venice and have moved east. They both gave scathing reports on the ethics of Brock and Theobault."

"Not surprising."

"Then one of them dropped some hints implying a connection to a dealer in Long Beach. This is on top of earlier indications of a link to Beverly Hills."

"Interesting. I need to look into that."

"Brock and Theobault have some sort of financial backing that allowed them to ride out the downturns, and the small guys were pushed out of business."

"But people don't casually throw money at financing art dealers." Pitman's brow furrowed. "There has to be more to it."

"With Vansworthy biting the dust, they must be trying to hide something deeper than just eliminating a competitor."

"I have a couple of people I can check with. I'll meet you at the graffiti wall tomorrow at two P.M. Then we can investigate further at the open house at Brock's gallery tomorrow night."

"Now one other matter. There was a guy

following me recently. Austin took a picture of him." I handed the photo to Pitman.

He shook his head. "No, I don't recognize this character. He'd be an interesting model with his distinctive eyebrows."

"I think I'd prefer a model of the female variety myself."

He handed back the photograph.

After Pitman returned inside the restaurant, I spotted a taxi and waved it down. I avoided mentioning the need to arrive at my destination quickly, so returned to the old homestead without the excitement of seeing pedestrians running for their lives.

I decided I'd show the bushy eyebrow guy's photograph to Marion. She might recognize him or have seen him following us.

When I dragged myself in, Marion was standing in the living room.

"Where have you been?" She had her arms crossed.

"I had some things to check out with Mallory Pitman."

"I was worried silly. I thought you'd gone off and fallen asleep somewhere again. You have to tell me when you're going out."

"You were busy with Andrea." I felt my neck getting hot. "Besides I don't have to check with you every time I go somewhere.

I'm not a goddamn little kid."

"What! In that case you can just leave again." She pushed me toward the door. "Get out!"

Uh-oh. Now I'd really blown it. I didn't realize how strong she was. Before I knew what happened, I was out on the porch. The door slammed and I heard it lock.

With a deep sigh, I sat down on the stairs, placed my elbows on my knees and cradled my chin in my hands.

Some old farts never learn. I still had my quick temper which got me in trouble, and then I suffered the consequences. What a pisser.

I had been wrong speaking to Marion the way I had. She was only concerned about me, and I had made a snide comment. I needed to think before I opened my big yap. I would have to find a way to apologize to Marion for my misdemeanor.

Not wanting to wander off, I just sat there feeling sorry for myself. I considered the options of living in jail, at the beach with the homeless people or camping right here on the stairs. I probably would have rusted into a statue if a gray tabby cat hadn't sauntered up to me. She mewed and rubbed against my leg.

I inspected the name tag hanging from a

blue collar and read the name, Cleo. Remembering from my journal, I realized this was the cat that lived with Marion's daughter.

"Giving some comfort to a dumb old poop?" I said.

The cat looked up at me with its green eyes.

"Stick with me, and you'll get in trouble too."

Cleo jerked her head. She must have heard something because she shot down the stairs and disappeared into a hedge.

Moments later a kid came in through the back gate. He saw me sitting there and approached the stairs.

"Whatcha doing?" he asked.

"Who are you?"

He rolled his eyes. "You've forgotten again. I'm your wife's grandson Austin. So why are you sitting outside?"

"I'm in the doghouse with your grandmother."

"You act like a jerk or something?"

Ah, the directness of youth. "You nailed it. I said something dumb, and she locked me out."

He smiled. "Yeah. That happens to me. I mouth off, and my mom sends me to my room."

"I'd be happy to be sent to my room, but I may have to spend the rest of my short life on these stairs."

"Tell you what. I'll speak to Grandma on your behalf."

"You willing to help me escape the penalty box?"

"Sure."

Austin climbed past me and knocked on the door.

"Go away," came the shout from within.

"Grandma. It's me, Austin."

Moments later the door opened a crack, and Austin scuttled inside.

I remained glued to the stairs, awaiting my fate as Austin negotiated to reduce my sentence. My stomach was in turmoil. I needed to return my life to a state of normalcy. First, make up with my bride, then redirect Detective Quintana so we would be free to cruise off to Alaska. Of course if Marion kept me locked out, the cruise might be a moot point anyway, although — worst case — it might provide room and board for a week for me.

Finally, when I was considering finding a tree to pee behind, the door opened. Austin came to me and pulled my arm to help me stand up. Then he pushed me into my living room. "What do you have to say to

Grandma?"

I hung my head. "I'm sorry. My temper got the best of me. You were right. I need to let you know where I'm going. I apologize for blowing up and acting like a jerk."

Marion eyed me. "Well stated. Are you going to follow through on that?"

"As best as I'm able with my sieve-like brain."

A smile crept across her face. "I guess I forgive you."

I opened my arms, and she leaned into them. We hugged.

"There," said Austin. "That's better."

I suddenly remembered reading in my journal how I had made Austin apologize to Jennifer when he had acted like a jerk at the wedding. This kid was learning.

I stepped back and looked into Marion's eyes. "The next time I do something dumb and let my mouth spout off, just slap me alongside the head."

"I don't think that's necessary," she said.

"Sometimes that's what it takes with someone past their prime like me."

That night I remembered I had a photograph to show to Marion. I decided I'd show it to her in the morning. Marion indicated I could share the bed with her, although I received vibes that it wasn't an opportune time to do more than just sleep there. Before retiring, I documented my day's adventures. I hoped for a calm Saturday to follow.

CHAPTER 16

The next morning I awoke with a start and found a warm and sexy woman lying beside me. Next thing I knew she snuggled against me and said all was forgiven. Hell, I didn't know what I had done, but suddenly my soldier went into a high salute.

"Um, I hate to say this but who are you?" I asked.

"Paul, I'm Marion, your wife."

"I'll be damned."

She rubbed my chest, and I put my arm around her. Before I knew what was happening, a nightgown and pair of pajamas were dispensed with, and we found ourselves exercising the springs of our mattress. I panted so hard I thought my lungs would collapse, but I pulled through like a trouper, achieving the right balance of exertion and mutual satisfaction. I lived to tell the tale without any side effects such as a heart attack or stroke.

Afterwards I lay in bed counting my blessings and enjoying her warmth against me. I didn't fall asleep again but just remained there in a state of marital bliss. Too bad I couldn't do this more often, but there was only so much I could expect of my old body.

Later, Marion stretched her arms and yawned. "I'm getting up," she said.

"I've already been up," I replied.

"I'll say. Now before you do anything else, read your journal." Marion pointed to a bound notebook lying on the nightstand.

"Yes, ma'am." I went through the journal, amazed at the life I lived. Then I hopped out of bed and prepared for the day.

After we feasted on scrambled eggs and toast, I retrieved the photograph referenced in my diary.

I gave Marion a peck on the cheek. "Take a look at this picture and tell me if you recognize this guy."

Marion squinted at it, and then a smile crossed her face. "I do, and obviously you don't recollect when we saw him."

"Apparently he has been following me."

Marion frowned. "I don't like the sound of that."

"So don't keep me in suspense. When did you see him before?"

"That day we went to Theobault's gallery.

He worked there."

I flinched. "I'll be damned. Theobault has been watching me. He's worse than that Detective Quintana. I wonder why he'd do that."

"He wasn't very pleased that day we spoke with him."

"That may break the tie between Theobault and Brock as my prime suspect in this chain of art-dealer crimes, although I'm going to keep both on my list for the time being."

Marion reminded me that we had office-assistance duty at the church that morning.

"Just as long as we're finished in time for me to meet Pitman at two."

She raised an eyebrow. "What's going on now, Paul?"

"He's checking out some background information on our favorite art dealers. We set up a rendezvous at the graffiti wall to debrief."

"We should be done by eleven so you'll be free then."

I picked up the *Los Angeles Times* and scanned through several articles about freeway congestion, housing prices and forest-fire danger. Then one caught my eye. I read a summary of a money-laundering scheme where drug money was being used to buy valuable antiques. Then it clicked. Yes, that could be it.

"Time to go, Paul."

I dropped the newspaper on the table, brushed my teeth and prepared to meet the world of paper cuts and dead bodies in storerooms.

As we strolled over to the church, I asked Marion, "You've known Clint Brock for a while. Does he seem to have more money than a normal art dealer would?"

"What kind of question is that?"

"I'm just wondering about his lifestyle and the money he would earn from an art gallery."

She came to a stop and looked at me. "You have some new suspicion."

"Yes. I'm still trying to piece this together."

We continued walking. "I can't say for sure, but he must be on the leading edge of art dealers around here," Marion said.

"Yeah. It's bugging me. I can see making a good income, particularly if you've driven other dealers out of business, but maybe he's just too successful."

When we arrived at the church, Marisa Young assigned Marion to file a bunch of invoices and asked me to clear out the storage room. I carefully opened the door and was relieved to have no body fall on my shoes. I moved things out and with Marisa's assistance determined what would be kept and what I would haul out to the Dumpster. An hour into it, I took a break and had a cup of coffee with Marisa.

"Is Clint Brock a member of your congregation?" I asked.

"Yes, he has been an active member for several years."

"I understand he's a very successful art dealer. Probably makes large contributions to the church."

"Why, yes. He's a leading patron of the church."

It all fit. I continued my cleaning exercise until eleven when Marisa excused Marion and me from our churchly duties. I took one last look at the white bell tower and red tile roof, and we headed home.

"I'm convinced that Clint Brock and Vance Theobault have something illegal going on," I said to Marion as we strolled along Venice Boulevard. "It could be one of them or both, but something shady is happening. I need to do a little more checking."

"I think you should leave it to Detective Quintana. This isn't something you should be handling on your own."

"I wish I could, but he seems more intent on accusing me than working these art dealers."

As we entered our apartment, I asked, "Any idea where I could find Jennifer's phone number?"

"We have an address book in the top dresser drawer."

"Perfect." I scurried as fast as my old legs could carry me into the bedroom and found the address book.

When I called, my daughter-in-law Allison answered the phone.

"I need to speak with my illustrious granddaughter."

"Just a minute, Paul. I'll have to pull her away from the computer."

Moments later I heard, "Hi, Grandpa."

"I need your nimble fingers to dance on the computer keys for me."

"Something to help solve the murders?"

"You got it, kid. I need to learn everything you can find that relates to money laundering in the art world."

There was a pause on the line. "So that's it. You think these art dealers are involved in illegal activity that led to murder."

"Right again."

"Okeydokey. I'll Google it."

I scratched my head. "Did you say you'd

noodle on it?"

"No Google. I'm going to search the Web."

"What the hell is Google? I used to be a fan of Barney Google in the funny paper. And what's this have to do with spider webs?"

Jennifer let out an exasperated sigh. "Grandpa, you have so much to learn. It means I'm going to search the Internet using the Google search engine."

"I don't know a search engine from a V-six, but you do whatever magic you need to do."

"I'll start immediately. You should also call your friend Meyer Ohana."

"Is he into money laundering?"

"No. But he was a lawyer and judge in Hawaii. He might know something on the subject."

"Good idea."

"I'll assemble background information, and e-mail it to Austin. He can print it out for you."

After we hung up, I found Meyer's phone number and called. A woman answered, said he was watching TV in the common room and would retrieve him.

Shortly, a man's voice said, "Hello."

"What's a geezer like you spending your day watching TV?"

"Paul, it's good to hear your voice. And with my eyesight I wasn't doing much watching. I was mostly listening to the news."

"There's nothing new anyway. You and I have heard it all. These young whippersnappers keep making the same mistakes we used to and cause the same problems in the world that our generation did. When are they going to learn how to avoid pissing into the wind?"

He chuckled. "I'm glad to hear the mainland hasn't softened the curmudgeon in you."

"Hell, they've turned me into a marshmallow. I'm an old softy living near the beach and trying to keep my butt out of jail."

"You need legal advice?"

"The police and I are doing a two-step. But why I called: do you know anything about money laundering?"

"You're not involved in illegal activities are you?"

"Other than fishing for grunion without a license, hell no. But I think I've stumbled upon a den of thieves disguised as art dealers who are doing some kind of money laundering. I thought I'd call upon your legal expertise on the subject."

"I heard a few cases before I retired."

"So tell me how an art dealer might launder illegally gained money."

"Let me tell you what I know of money laundering. First, the money has to be placed, that is, the illegal cash needs to be converted into some other form through a transaction."

"Such as buying a painting," I said.

"Correct. Moving money into a foreign bank or buying an object of value are two possible forms of placement. Then comes layering. A sequence of transactions is performed, sending the money on a complex journey, to mask the money's source and destination."

"So several art dealers could buy and sell a painting, creating a chain from the buyer of the work to the ultimate disposition of the money."

"Exactly. Then the final step is integration. The funds become available through a legitimate business."

"If an art dealer purchased paintings from an artist, there would be no suspicion. He could write a check to the artist from his gallery account, and it would appear completely legitimate."

"And if the paintings passed through several layers of art dealers, the whole three-step process would work."

I thought for a moment. "That fits right in. You've been a great deal of help. Now, from what I've reviewed in my journal, I sometimes read short stories to you over the phone. Are you up for that rather than listening to news on TV?"

"Absolutely."

"Let me retrieve my O. Henry collection."

I found my book and returned to the phone.

"What kind of story would you like to hear today?" I asked.

Meyer sighed. "I've been reminiscing — remembering the good times with my dear departed wife Martha. Why don't you select something romantic?"

"A tough old retired judge and lawyer like you?"

"We all have our soft undersides, just like you, Paul."

"Are you accusing me of being all bluster?"

"No, but you're much more than the crusty exterior you project. How many codgers would bother to read to their friend over the phone?"

"I like the way you said friend. I only wish I remembered you more without the assistance of my journal and Marion."

"You and Marion will have to come back

272

to Hawaii and visit me one of these days."

"After our Alaskan cruise, I'll add that to our social agenda."

"You do that. Now, as you always say to me, are we going to yak or hear a story?"

"Okay. Okay. You want something romantic . . . hmm." I scanned the table of contents. "Here's one titled 'The Romance of a Busy Broker.' That sounds almost as good as The Romance of a Bored Care-Home Detainee."

"Or The Romance of a Forgetful Scofflaw."

"Touché." I thumbed through and found the beginning of the story. "Make yourself comfortable. I don't want this to put too much pressure on your aging heart."

"I think I can manage."

I proceeded to read the story of Harvey Maxwell, the frenetic broker who charges around transacting stock deals. He's informed he plans to replace Miss Leslie the stenographer but things are so frantic that he orders her to continue. After being consumed with his work, Harvey has a free moment and discovers he's in love with Miss Leslie and proposes marriage to her. She gently informs him that they were married the night before.

"I can identify with that guy," I said after

putting the book down.

"You're right, Paul. He has as bad a memory as you."

"Damn straight. If it weren't for my journal, I'd wake up every morning unaware of being married to Marion."

"Well, not every morning, Paul. I assume there is still enough romance in your life that occasionally your wires receive that extra spark to keep them connected."

"True. Once in a while I'm fortunate enough to experience that benefit of marital bliss."

"I'll let you return to your wife. I appreciate you taking the time to read to me."

We signed off, and I once again thanked my lucky stars for Marion's open-mindedness in accepting me. Could I have put up with me if I were in her place? It would be pretty tough being around an old coot whose memory reset every day. That would require inordinate patience to reeducate someone morning after morning.

And how did I thank her? By getting bollixed up in a series of murders. Marion deserved better than that. I had to clear up the whole art-dealer mess so our lives could return to some semblance of order. I'd keep doing what I could to resolve this strange sequence of events.

I checked my watch and saw I had some time to catch a bite to eat before meeting Pitman. I ate a banana and some blueberry yogurt and had just wiped my mouth when I heard a knock on the door.

"Come on in," I shouted.

The door opened and Austin stood there with a handful of paper. "Jennifer sent this to me for you."

"Excellent."

He raised his eyebrows. "Are you studying money laundering?"

"Yeah. I think one or more art dealers here in Venice may have a money-laundering scheme going on."

His eyes widened. "Cool. Can I help?"

"Sure. Come on in and let's review these together."

We sat down at the table and both read through the stack of sheets.

"Seems like a lot of examples of money laundering through art dealers," I said.

Austin pointed to one article. "The main thing is to keep the cash transactions under ten thousand dollars. This says the Patriot Act now requires art dealers to report cash transactions larger than that."

"But as long as they stay below that limit everything could work fine. So the Venice crooks would have to move lots of paintings at just under ten thousand dollars." I thought back to what I had read in my journal. "And that seems to be the approximate asking price of Muddy Murphy works. How convenient."

Austin left, and I sauntered down to the beach. I had some time to kill before meeting Pitman, so I found a nice smooth spot on the sand and plunked my old body down. The heat from the day's sun felt good so I took off my shoes and socks and wriggled my toes into the warm sand.

I craned my neck up to view the blue sky and listened to the surf crashing into the breakwater. The aroma of hot dogs, hamburgers and popcorn wafted past my twitching nose. A retired geriatric like me should be enjoying the sun and beach and not worrying about art dealers and murderers. What cesspool had I fallen into?

I couldn't even escape to a Pacific island. Detective Quintana would be on me like one of those dogs that sticks its nose in your crotch. I felt trapped.

It was ironic me living near the ocean. I hated expanses of water. If I waded in over my ankles, it gave me the heebie-jeebies. So I guess a Pacific island was out as well. I'd have to adjust to my newlywed pad in Venice and leave it at that.

My ruminations were interrupted by a tap on my back.

I turned around to see a guy in a dirty beard and ratty clothes.

"I've been looking for you," he said, pointing a grimy finger at me.

"Me?" I put my hand to my chest.

"Yeah. You were interested in Muddy Murphy."

"I am. I hate to be impolite, but with my short-term memory loss I don't recognize you."

"I'm Harley Marcraft. We've spoken several times.'

The name clicked. "Now it's coming back to me. You have an update for me on Muddy?"

He dropped down on the sand beside me.

"Sure do. Good old Muddy." He shook his head. "We all miss him."

"So what's the news?"

"I learned something last night. One of the other guys mentioned what Muddy had said to him before he died."

Now he had my attention. "What's that?"

"Muddy had some plans."

"Plans? Don't keep me in suspense."

"Yeah. Muddy had something else up his sleeve, even though he usually wore sleeveless shirts." Harley chuckled. "Muddy apparently had his own agenda."

He paused and looked out toward the ocean. It was obvious he wanted me to encourage him.

"I'll bite. What do you think he was up to?"

"Muddy was a painter, so he had experience with chemicals such as turpentine, thinner and linseed oil. He hinted to my buddy that a painter could concoct a device that would make an arsonist proud."

"Yeah. Some of those painting materials are highly flammable. So what?"

"I can't say for sure, but Muddy might have been planning to do some damage."

"You mean set a fire?"

"Precisely. He still had money squirreled away and could walk into an art-supply store to buy the materials he needed. Then when he wanted . . . varoom, a big blaze."

"That seems pretty bizarre. Did your buddy find out why he would do this?"

"No, but I can speculate."

Again he paused and smoothed the sand with one hand while looking up at the sky. I wondered if he was searching for a seagull, but then figured out he just wanted me to egg him on. "Okay, take a shot at it."

"He hated art dealers. Enough said."

"So you think he may have decided to

break into one of the dealer's galleries or warehouses and start a fire?"

"He may have intended to burn up some of his own paintings that the dealers had in storage. He hated that they were taking advantage of him."

I thought for a moment. "That would be a hell of a way to get back at them. Obviously he never carried out such a scheme."

"No, but he may have been getting ready to. Muddy could be very determined. I once saw him sit on a bench for six hours to prove a point. When he set his mind to something, it was hard to sway him otherwise."

"And if one of the art dealers got wind of it, maybe he decided to take preventative measures against Muddy."

"It could have contributed to Muddy's demise." Harley flicked away a sand flea.

"It all makes sense in an absurd kind of way. One of the art dealers could have killed Muddy to prevent the loss of paintings as well as to move along the appreciation in value. Two benefits from one murder."

"That could have been what happened to Muddy. The poor bastard never had a chance." Harley wiped his brow with the back of his left hand.

"I wouldn't like someone burning down

my place, but I wouldn't resort to murder to prevent it," I said. "I wonder if the police know of this."

"Probably not. They're so closely tied to the moneyed interests that they never check out what's really going on."

I'd have to bring this up with Detective Quintana the next time he showed up to accuse me of something. Maybe he'd then spend more time pursuing the real killer than bugging me.

Harley jumped up. "Now if you'll excuse me, I'm going to watch some more paddle tennis."

I slowly raised myself up. It was time to mosey over to the graffiti wall and find my art consultant. Once there, I spotted two teenagers working together to make large purple and black letters and a man with wild red hair who was spraying paint in crisp geometric shapes.

"Pitman," I shouted.

He turned and waved. "Give me a minute to finish." He constructed a purple octagon, orange triangle and red pentagon, then stepped back to admire his work. "There." He dropped the spray cans in the sand and turned toward me.

"I don't get this," I said. "How can you spend time painting on this wall when someone else will cover it up again and you'll have to start all over?"

Pitman waved his hands in the air and turned a color to match his hair. "You brush your teeth again every day, take your clothes on and off every day, eat meals over and over, go to sleep again. This is life! This is existence!"

"Yeah. Yeah. To me this is crapola but don't work yourself up. I don't want you having a conniption before we go to the gallery open house tonight."

"Speaking of which, I have some information for you." He looked like the cat that had eaten a canary convention. "Let's sit down."

He strutted over to a cement wall and plunked himself down. I followed.

Pitman moved his right hand in a big circle. "These art dealers are connected like spokes in a wheel, like stars in the milky way, like grains of sand in the beach . . ."

"All right, Pitman. Contain yourself to the subject at hand."

"You'll never guess what I found out!"

"Brock and/or Theobault are involved in a money-laundering scheme," I replied.

CHAPTER 17

Pitman's mouth dropped open. "How'd you know the art dealers were involved in money laundering?"

"I put the pieces together. They stayed financially solvent when others folded. They have some sort of arrangement with dealers in other cities in Southern California. I read in my journal that you told me that dealers didn't work together as a rule. I had been given the advice to follow the money. Just a lucky guess."

He pouted.

"Hey, don't let me spoil your surprise. Tell me what you found out."

He perked up. "Well, I can't prove anything, but I did discover that both Brock and Theobault regularly sell paintings to an art dealer in Long Beach. Not little piddling transactions but big-ticket deals of, say, five to ten thousand dollars."

"So large amounts of cash flow from Long

Beach to Venice."

"Correct."

"And the Beverly Hills connection?"

Pitman tweaked his chin. "Nothing specific there yet. But I suspect there may be transactions taking place between Beverly Hills and Long Beach."

"Masking the receiver from the source."

"Exactly."

"I suppose they could keep a set of books but actually transfer a lot more cash under the table." I thought for a moment. "Or they could move paintings as a means to mask the movement of cash." I waved my hands like Pitman had done. "Your spokes of the wheel."

He scratched his head. "I don't get it."

"Long Beach buys a painting from Venice for say, six thousand dollars, transferring cash to Venice. Venice ships the painting to Long Beach. Long Beach sells the same painting to Beverly Hills for eight thousand dollars. Beverly Hills sells the painting to a scam artist for just under ten thousand dollars. The scam artist moves the dirty money to the source. Long Beach and Beverly Hills receive compensation along the way and Venice ends up with the majority of the proceeds."

Now Pitman's eyes lit up. "Now I get it.

Everybody in the chain makes out."

"Yeah. This scheme works if ever they're audited."

"It certainly supports why I never trusted art dealers. So who do you suspect? Theobault or Brock?"

"It could be one or both of those guys," I said. "I did have one piece of evidence fall in place which points to Theobault. You remember me showing you a picture of a guy with bushy eyebrows who had been following me?"

"Yes."

"Turns out he works for Theobault."

"Wow." Pitman's eyes grew as large as coasters.

"We need to keep after these slimeballs."

"Let me see what else I can uncover this afternoon," Pitman said.

"Good. You snoop around and then we'll get together tonight at the open house and compare notes." I patted him on the back. "We're getting close to catching these crooks."

Pitman charged off like he had a chili pepper up his butt, and I meandered over to the boardwalk to see what the street vendors had to offer. I rejected a henna tattoo, five colors of sandals and fighter-pilot dark glasses but stopped at a table where a skinny man in a white sun hat was selling books on the history of Venice Beach. I picked up a copy and thumbed through it, looking at pictures of early construction, amusement parks on piers and canals of various dimensions.

"Venice originally was planned to be an art colony," the man said, tweaking his Van Dyke beard. "Abbott Kinny's vision was to attract artists from all over the world."

"And now we have a graffiti wall and a building with a picture of some old rock star."

"A far cry from Kinney's original thinking. But the street named after him has a thriving art community with galleries and antique stores."

"But the canals didn't quite make it."

"No." He sighed. "There were attempts to keep more but many of the original canals were bulldozed over to make way for real estate. A real shame."

I thought about saying that more canals would only lead to more floating bodies but held my tongue. "So tell me. I lived in the Los Angeles area after World War II but never came to Venice. What was it like then?"

"During the war Venice was a center for entertainment. Many GIs came through for

R and R. After that, the place decayed. Then it became a hippie haven in the sixties and is on the upswing now."

"But there are a lot of homeless people here."

He shrugged. "With the good weather, the beach and lots of tourists, it's the perfect place to hang out, panhandle and survive inexpensively."

"I suppose," I replied.

With my history lesson under my belt, I headed back to my place to gather my thoughts before an evening full of art-gallery talk. I felt a growing excitement that I was getting close to solving the art-dealer puzzle. I had established a motive for either Brock or Theobault to knock off Vansworthy and Muddy Murphy. They both were around town when the murders took place so they had access. Now I just needed to figure out which of the slime bags had actually committed the murders.

Then my euphoria changed as I sensed a tightening in my gut. If the murderer had killed twice, he'd have no qualms doing it again. I was an old fogy and had no training in dealing with criminals. I should turn it over to Detective Quintana and his twitching mustache. No, that wouldn't work. He never believed me anyway. He'd think I was trying to divert attention away from myself. I'd have to suck it up and see what I could learn tonight, but I would need to be on my toes with the likes of Brock and Theobault to deal with.

I carefully checked in with Marion regarding my plans. "I read something in my journal that you're not accompanying me to the reception sponsored by the criminally disposed art dealers."

"That's right, Paul. You'll be on your own. I promised to join Andrea and George at Austin's band concert this evening."

"Damn. I guess I'll have to hold my own with the help of Mallory Pitman."

"Is he still acting as your art consultant?"

"Something like that. I'm sorry I'm missing Austin's concert, but I need to collect all the information I can regarding the slimy art dealers."

"The concert is close by and should be over by eight, so you can call Andrea and George if you want a ride home."

I explained the money-laundering hypothesis to her and she said, "That sounds possible. But why the murders of Vansworthy and Muddy Murphy?"

"They must have somehow bollixed up the gears of the well-tuned money machine. Muddy stopped producing and maybe

287

Vansworthy got cold feet and was going to blow the whistle on the whole damn scheme."

"And how does that employee of Theobault following you fit in?" Marion asked.

"I don't know for sure yet. It does make Theobault seem mighty suspicious."

"I suppose so. In any case, you be careful tonight, Paul." She tilted her head and looked into my eyes.

"Yes, ma'am, I will. Mallory Pitman can act as my bodyguard."

"I'm concerned he'll do more damage than good in that role."

"Well, I can't be picky. He's willing to help me. I just need to see if I can turn over a little more evidence to hand to Detective Quintana. Then he can get off my case."

"Speaking of Detective Quintana, I'm still worried that he'll try to stop you from going on our Alaskan honeymoon cruise. It's only a week away."

"You have a point. Damn. I need to solve this art-dealer mess so I can be a free man. All the more reason to get to the bottom of it tonight."

"See what you learn. Maybe you can sit down with Detective Quintana tomorrow and explain things to him."

"I'll be happy to try, but he doesn't seem to value my opinion that much."

There was a knock on the door, and Marion ambled over to open it.

Austin stood there, chatted with Marion for a few moments and then pointed toward me.

"Paul, Austin has something to show you on his computer."

I joined him and asked, "What's up, sport?"

"I received another e-mail message from Jennifer. She asked me to have you come over to read it."

I followed him down the stairs, across the backyard and into the big house. We entered his room. On his computer TV screen, I read, "Have my grandpa look at this URL." Then I saw a funny run-together name with dots and slashes.

"What the hell is a URL?" I asked.

Austin rolled his eyes. "It's a link to a Web site. Here, let me bring it up for you."

He punched some keys, the computer TV flashed and a new set of writing appeared.

I bent over to read it. An extract from the *Los Angeles Times* from several months back described a fraud investigation. Senior citizens received notification of winning an automobile and to activate the award had to pay a service charge. Once the service charge was paid, the scam outfit disappeared.

"Hey, I know this one. I read in my journal that someone tried this on me, and I helped the police trace the culprits."

"Cool," Austin said.

I continued reading the article. It described how a task force had been tracking this crime. Then the punch line caught my eye. "The only arrest so far is James Bardell, an employee of the Vansworthy Gallery in Venice Beach."

CHAPTER 18

Damnation. Jennifer had uncovered an article linking the deceased Vansworthy's operation to the automobile scam. Was that the cause of his murder? Was he connected with possible money laundering? Had someone tried to eliminate Vansworthy as a partner or competitor? Was I dealing with every imaginable form of crime wrapped into the local art-dealer community? Would I be able to figure this out in time to go on my cruise?

All these thoughts raced through my dysfunctional brain. I would definitely have a lot to discuss with Detective Quintana during our next friendly chat.

My musings were interrupted by Austin. "There's something else I need to tell you." He paused.

I refocused my eyes on Austin instead of the computer TV screen. "Go ahead."

"Well . . . uh . . . tonight is when Pierce is

planning to beat up a homeless person."

"Do you know where this is going to happen?"

He hung his head. "No. I overheard Pierce bragging about tonight, but that's all I found out."

I reached over and raised his chin. "Look at me. You've done the right thing on this." I thought back to what I'd read in my journal. "We warned people. Maybe Pierce will come to his senses."

"I doubt it. He's pretty stubborn."

"Tell you what. If you want to make one last effort, take a walk down to the beach and see if that guy Harley Marcraft — who we talked to before — is hanging out by the paddle-tennis courts. If he's there, you can pass on the latest information."

Austin's eyes lit up. "Okay. I'll do it. I have some time before I need to get ready for my concert."

"I'm sorry I'm going to miss it. I have an art-gallery event to attend tonight to see if I can learn more to clear myself of accusations. I hope to make your next performance."

"There'll be one more at the end of the summer. You can come to that when you get back from your cruise."

"Yeah, our cruise." I definitely had to wrap

this investigation up by then.

Austin looked at his watch. "I better leave now."

"All right. You get your butt over to find Harley."

"I hope he's there."

We both left the house. Austin dashed off toward the beach, and I returned to my apartment above the garage.

As I mounted the stairs, my brain engaged and I saw how the pieces were starting to connect in some strange way. I could understand how the art-dealer laundering could be tied to collecting money from the automobile-award scam. I just wasn't sure how all the art galleries played together. Time for a little snooping.

I found the trusty yellow pages and under Art Galleries located a listing for the Vansworthy Gallery in Venice Beach. I flexed my fingers and punched in the numbers. A pleasant female voice answered, "Theobault Galleries."

I recoiled. "Isn't this Vansworthy?"

"Yes. This used to be the Vansworthy Gallery, but we've merged with Theobault and took on that name. We now have two locations in Venice."

So Theobault hadn't wasted any time after Vansworthy's death in consolidating the "partnership."

"I'm trying to reach an employee of yours named James Bardell."

"I'm sorry, he's no longer with us."

"What happened? He go to a competitor?"

"No. Apparently he had some sort of legal problems and quit."

Yeah. From what Jennifer found for me, Bardell certainly did have a legal problem if he had been arrested for his participation in the automobile scam.

"You sure he wasn't fired?"

"Not that I know of."

So he probably was operating under the auspices of the gallery and not going solo.

"Could you inform me of who took his place?"

"No one has specifically been named yet. After the consolidation of the two galleries, Mr. Theobault asked that any queries for Mr. Bardell be directed to him."

"Is the big cheese, Mr. Theobault, there by any chance?"

She giggled, then caught herself and coughed. "Not at the moment. He will probably be at our other gallery this evening. Do you want the number?"

"That's okay. Thanks for your assistance."

After I hung up, a feeling of suspicion ran through me. I ruminated on the latest bit of information. A Vansworthy employee was involved in the automobile scam. Vansworthy gets bumped off, and Theobault picks up the operation and becomes the contact for any queries for Bardell. Why would Theobault be personally involved unless he knew something about Bardell's misconduct?

It should have been obvious to the police that Theobault knocked off Vansworthy to take over the operation, but if it were that simple, they would have had the whole case wrapped up by now.

Then another thought struck me. The Bardell thing could have a simple explanation. Theobault as the new boss might simply be taking any calls directed to an ex-employee. I had done that once when an employee suddenly quit a clerical job at my auto-parts store.

On the other hand, one of Theobault's employees had been following me. That would lend further support to Theobault being the culprit.

I could go on for the rest of the day arguing both sides of this equation.

But there was still something missing. I'd have to pry into it some more that evening with my weirdo art buddy, Mallory Pitman. Between the two of us we'd have to see if we could assemble the final pieces of the puzzle. Then I'd be free to sail off into the sunset.

Now it was time for me to prepare for the evening's festivities.

I looked through my closet, trying to decide what to wear to an art-dealer confrontation. Rejecting the extremes of Bermuda shorts or a suit, I settled on black slacks and a white shirt. No beret or tie-dyed wrap. I'd leave that to Pitman.

Andrea gave me a ride over to the shindig. "When the event is over just call and I can come pick you up," she said.

"Only in an emergency. It's not that far and I can walk back."

"We'll be returning from Austin's concert by eight-fifteen if you change your mind."

I waved good-bye and entered Brock's gallery. The place was packed with a diverse assortment of ages, wardrobes and lifestyles. The soft background melody from a string quartet melded with the hum of dozens of conversations. I sniffed the aroma of women's perfume mingled with bubbling meat dishes that lined a long table covered by a white cloth.

First, I cruised the buffet to build up my energy for the evening. I feasted on Swedish meatballs speared by toothpicks, four different kinds of cheeses on a variety of crackers, baby tomatoes, broccoli and cauliflower. And I topped it all off with a chocolate-covered strawberry. I passed up on the champagne for bottled water. I needed to keep my wits about me — whatever was left of them anyway.

Once sated, I scanned the mob and spotted Mallory Pitman, his red spiky hair visible through the throng. I meandered over and listened to him expound on color, form and canvas finish as he waved his arms in the air. One woman had to step back so as not to be smacked in the kisser. Finally he ran out of steam, and I pulled him aside for a little chat.

I leaned toward Pitman's ear and whispered, "Is Theobault here tonight?"

"Yes, indeed. See the guy over there talking to the blonde in the slinky green sheath? That's him."

I stared at the man Pitman pointed out to me. He wore dark slacks and a blue sports shirt and held a drink in his hand. So that was one of the suspected slimeballs.

I waited until the woman sashayed away. Then I approached Theobault.

"I have a question to ask you," I said, staring directly at him.

He did a double take. "I remember you.

You and your wife invaded my office."

"No, we merely came to conduct a civil inquisition. I'm surprised that you're here at a party put on by your competitor, Brock."

"This is a small community. We all keep in touch."

"So tell me, are you and Brock in the scam and money-laundering business together, or are you each doing it solo?"

His eyes flared. "I don't know what the hell you're talking about." His voice went up fifty decibels.

People turned toward us.

"Don't shout at me, you crook. People like you should be eliminated." I wanted to reach over to the buffet table and find a pie to smash into his face.

"How dare you insinuate that I'm involved with Brock. I think you're the one who was spying for Brock, when you and your wife pretended to be interested in Muddy Murphy art and showed up at my gallery."

"Is that why you had me followed?"

He flinched, and I saw that I'd hit a nerve.

"You and Brock stay out of my way," he shouted and pushed past me.

"What an asshole," I muttered. I looked up and saw Brock watching the encounter, a smile on his lips.

Then I felt a tap on my shoulder. I spun around to find a short man in an ill-fitting suit. His dark eyes appeared above a small nose and a twitching mustache. That could only have been — "Detective Quintana?"

"Very good, Mr. Jacobson. You're not making many friends tonight. Getting kind of heated, aren't you?"

"Damn straight. You better be investigating these art dealers, Detective."

He scowled. "Are you threatening me now?"

I took a deep breath. "No. It's only a strong suggestion. Between Brock and Theobault, one or both of them are up to no good."

"What are you doing here, Mr. Jacobson?"

"Reconnoitering. I should ask the same question of you."

He frowned. "Seemed to be an interesting gathering with all that has happened in the last week, especially with you here, Mr. Jacobson."

I wagged a finger at him. "You didn't follow me, did you, Detective?"

He shrugged his shoulders.

"Say, Detective, there's something you should look into. I suspect some of these art dealers are involved in money laundering."

"What makes you think that?"

"I've looked into the history of the art-dealer community. Brock, Vansworthy and Theobault survived while other dealers went bankrupt during a downturn in the economy. That is, Vansworthy survived until someone did him in. But these guys had financial staying power that indicates a unique source of funding. Maybe from scams like the automobile-contest one I helped your guys with."

Quintana regarded me thoughtfully. "An interesting theory. Sure you're not trying to distract me from your involvement in the murders?"

I sighed. "We've been over this ground before. I just happened on the dead bodies. These art dealers could be the cause of the murders. A good detective like you should be able to ferret out the plot."

"I'll see what I can find out."

"And another thing," I said. "I read an article indicating a guy arrested in the automobile-sweepstakes scam worked for Vansworthy."

"I'm aware of that."

"Good. I'm sure you're figuring out how to lock all these art dealers up. Also, I heard a report that Muddy Murphy may have been planning a little arson event to destroy paintings at the gallery of one of the art dealers. That might have contributed to Brock or Theobault doing him in."

Quintana raised an eyebrow. "You're a wealth of information tonight, Mr. Jacobson. Where'd you hear that?"

I tapped my ear. "You just have to listen to the homeless community."

"I'll follow up on that. In the meantime I've got my eyes on you, Mr. Jacobson."

I leaned over, cupped my hands and whispered, "I'm pretty vicious. I destroyed a whole plate of finger food."

Quintana gave me a half smile and disappeared into the crowd.

After my brief encounter of the Quintana kind, I took several more deep breaths. I needed to watch my damn temper. If I wasn't careful, it would get me in deeper doo-doo than I was already in.

I spotted Pitman's red coiffure again and meandered over to separate him from a man who looked like an escaped midget from a sideshow. They were debating preferred types of pallet knives.

"You find out anything new?" I asked.

"Yes. I met an art dealer from Beverly Hills named Louis Autry. He's a piece of work — arrogant, obnoxious and full of himself."

I thought this was quite a statement coming from Pitman. "So? A lot of people are that way."

"He also acted very buddy-buddy with Clint Brock."

"That's worth checking out. Where is he?"

"He's the tall fellow with black hair standing by the Pollard."

"What's a Pollard?"

Pitman rolled his eyes. "That sculpture over there." He pointed.

I stared at what appeared to be a stack of bricks. Nearby stood a tall man with black hair, wearing a white turtleneck and navy-blue blazer.

"Thanks. Keep working the crowd, and I'll see if I can make the acquaintance of Louis Autry, another of the scumbag art dealers."

I moseyed over and joined a group of four other people listening to Autry expound.

". . . the essence of the program is to provide funding for a core of artists who have been approved by the Foundation Board. This select group will be mentored much like the patron system in Renaissance Italy."

I stepped in. "Would someone like Muddy Murphy have qualified?"

Autry brushed his sleeve like trying to get rid of an unwanted speck. "Muddy Murphy was not the type of artist who would have either applied for a grant or followed the guidelines established by the Foundation. We seek young artists eager to develop their skills in a controlled environment."

"In other words, ones who toe the line."

Now he made eye contact. "And who are you?"

I reached out a hand. "Paul Jacobson."

He regarded my hand as if someone had offered him a turd on a plank. "I don't believe I've heard of you."

"You may not run in the right circles. Paul Jacobson of the Jacobson Foundation."

He frowned and looked upward like he wanted to pull my name out of a Rolodex embedded in the ceiling light fixture.

Before he could say anything else, I jumped back in. "I understand you're pretty cozy with Clint Brock."

"What's that supposed to mean?"

"That the two of you have some pretty tight business dealings."

His eyes flared. "I don't deal with him directly."

"How about paintings that transfer from Brock to someone in Long Beach to you?"

He gave me a dismissive wave of the hand. "I don't know what you're talking about, Mr. Jacobson."

"You mean you've conveniently forgotten the money-laundering scheme?"

He flinched like I had slapped him. He turned and stalked off. Moments later I saw him speaking with Clint Brock and pointing toward me.

I plastered on my most innocent smile and waved.

Deciding not to press my luck, I returned to the goodies and grazed a little more. After a few fruits and veggies, I fed my sweet tooth by stuffing two baby chocolate éclairs into my mouth, wiped my lips on a purple napkin and then scanned the crowd. I spotted Pitman's spiked red head flouncing up and down in one corner. Hopefully he was uncovering some good poop.

This time he was expounding on form, function and the use of perspective to a bevy of beauties — a group of four rapt young women.

"Pitman. Give your harem a break. We need to talk."

"Excuse me, ladies."

He bowed to them and then hopped over to me like an excited teenager. "Yes?"

"Something I forgot to mention to you. My detective buddy is working the crowd. I explained our money-laundering theory. He didn't react much, but hopefully I've planted a seed with him. Anything new on your front?"

"Yes. I've located the Long Beach connection. It's the bald guy over there." He pointed out a squat bowling ball in slacks and a white shirt, dressed just like me except for the difference in stature and shape.

"Did he divulge anything worthwhile?"

"I didn't have a chance to spend time with him alone," Pitman said.

"Okay. Let me take a shot at him." I sauntered over to where my target stood with a group of two women and two men.

One of the men was describing how he had discovered new art talent in the beach communities.

I jumped in. "Yeah. All you have to do is hang out around the graffiti wall here in Venice. There're all kinds of talent. Artists like Mallory Pitman."

The bald man crossed his arms. "Pitman did some interesting work in Colorado but hasn't produced anything since he moved to California."

"That's because he's been pursuing culinary art," I said.

"Culinary art?"

"Yes. It's the latest fad. Turning the presentation of food into an art form."

He turned away from me and resumed the conversation with one of the men. After a few minutes the others departed, and I was left with Baldy.

"I understand you work closely with Clint Brock," I said.

"Where'd you hear that?"

I leaned close to his ear and whispered, "Word gets around. You seem to have connections with a dealer in Beverly Hills as well."

He shot straight up like I had thrust a corncob up his fanny. "Who are you?"

"I'm Paul Jacobson." I reached out a hand.

He avoided it like I had forgotten to wash after visiting the little boys' room.

I eyed him. "I'd think you'd be more friendly toward a patron of the arts."

"You're no patron. You're just a snoop."

"So my reputation precedes me. How'd you decide to enter the money-laundering business, anyway?"

"This conversation is over." With that he stomped away. I watched him hook up with Brock. They both looked over toward me and then put their heads together. I was making all kinds of friends on this lovely evening.

CHAPTER 19

I decided to find Quintana and after circling the room saw him standing off to the side, watching Clint Brock. Approaching him, I said, "I'm glad to see you have your eyes on one of the suspected villains. I still think Brock, Theobault or both are the prime movers of crime in this community."

Quintana turned toward me. "There are many interesting people here tonight, including you, Mr. Jacobson."

"Nah. I'm not nearly as fascinating as this artsy-fartsy crowd. And you should check out Louis Autry." I scanned the room. "I don't see him right now, but he has some special deal going. I think Brock also sells paintings to that dealer in Long Beach." I pointed toward the short squat guy. "He, in turn, resells them to Autry in Beverly Hills. A nice chain to cleanse some illegal money."

Quintana looked thoughtful. "Yes. There could be something to that."

"Good for you, Detective. You're starting to see the light."

"Now if you'll excuse me." He shot off and disappeared into the crowd.

So much for a significant exchange with the good detective.

With nothing better to do, I looked for the carrot top and spotted Pitman by the munchies.

"Okay," I said to him while he masticated. "I've stirred up the hornet's nest. Let's see what happens. By the way, have you seen Theobault? I haven't spotted him recently."

"No. He seems to have disappeared."

I shrugged. "I'll look for him later. Now I need your expert opinion on an artistic matter."

"Sure." He licked his fingers.

I led him toward the door to Brock's office, which was open a crack. "Quick. Duck inside."

We moved quickly, and I closed the door behind us. I marched past Brock's large desk and opened the door to the storage room. "I read about this in my journal. There should be some artwork here for you to check out." I entered and turned on the light.

"Take a look at these paintings. Could be Muddy Murphy's work."

Pitman began moving canvases. "Very interesting."

"What'd you find?"

"See the signatures at the bottom." He pointed to three paintings he had lined up against the wall.

I stared at what appeared to be two intersecting letter M's all in the same shade of orange.

Pitman put a finger to his chin. "That looks like Muddy's signature, but there's a problem."

"Problem?"

"Yes. All three signatures are the exact same color. A little-known fact that I learned once when I bought Muddy dinner: he always used different shades of colors to sign his name. He never would have repeated the identical color formulation like on these three paintings."

Then I understood. "So the signatures are forged."

"Yes. And the paintings are knockoffs."

"How do you know that?"

"I've studied Muddy's work."

"I've studied it too," I said, staring at a picture with colored blobs thrown on the canvas. "Most of these paintings look like someone upchucked."

Pitman clicked his tongue. "Muddy's

pictures have texture and consistent brush-strokes. For once your observation is correct. This picture doesn't exhibit Muddy's flair for composition."

"So we now have Brock pawning off fake Muddy Murphy paintings after he or Theobault knocked off Muddy to drive the value up. But if you can spot the fakes, aren't there others who would reach the same conclusion?"

He shook his head. "I'm not sure anyone else knows of Muddy's signature idiosyncrasy."

"So Brock could easily go on having someone produce Muddy Murphy pictures with forged signatures and doling them out from his infinite inventory."

It was all starting to fall in place. "It's not Theobault at all." I punched my right fist into my left hand. "This is all Brock. Theobault believed I was working for Brock and that's why he had someone follow me."

"What are you talking about?"

I shook my head. "Man, sometimes your memory is as bad as mine. I told you this afternoon how the guy with bushy eyebrows who works for Theobault had been tailing me."

His eyes lit up. "Oh, yeah. Now I remember."

"Theobault had him spy on me. When I confronted Theobault earlier tonight, I found out that he suspected me of being in cahoots with Brock. Theobault's not the murderer. Brock is."

"If that's the case, we better get out of here," Pitman said, twisting his head to look over his shoulder.

"You go ahead," I said. "I want to look through the inventory a little more."

Pitman shot out of the storage room like his stomach was calling him to return to the feeding frenzy.

I scanned the storage area. There had to be three hundred paintings here. At ten thou a pop, this represented three million dollars of potential income.

Brock had put quite an operation into place. I turned to go back to the reception, but my path was blocked.

"What are you doing in here?" a voice demanded. Brock stood there with the bowling ball from Long Beach.

"Just admiring your Muddy Murphy collection. When are you going to be offering these for sale?"

Brock narrowed his eyes and turned to the short squat guy. "You're right, Harvey. He's definitely interfering in matters where he doesn't belong."

Brock grabbed my arm and dragged me out into the office. He pushed me down into an easy chair that matched the blue couch facing the mahogany desk. Then he extracted some heavy twine from a cupboard and proceeded to tie me up and bind me to the chair.

"Hey, this is no way to treat an old guy," I shouted.

"Enough noise." Brock stuffed a handkerchief in my mouth and secured it with a strip of duct tape.

"This should work out well," Brock said to Harvey. "I was wondering how we'd get him aside, and he's conveniently obliged."

"The old goat won't know what hit him." Harvey chuckled.

I wanted to tell him to watch who he called an old grazing animal but couldn't utter more than a muffled gurgle.

Brock patted me on the head. "We'll carry out the rest of the plan after the reception is over."

The lights went out and the two of them left the office. I heard a key in the door and knew no one else would be wandering in like Pitman and I had done. Damn. My snooping had landed me in deep yogurt.

I tried to move my arms behind my back, but I was securely constrained. Crapola. I had been too wrapped up in looking at the fake paintings to consider that Brock might show up, and now I was really too wrapped up. As my eyes adjusted to semidarkness, I swiveled my head. Nothing within reach, not that I could move anyway. I tried to lift up. The chair was too heavy to move even a fraction of an inch. I could twist my head, but that was all. I faced a window that overlooked an alley, dimly lit by the remaining light of dusk. No one there, just a bunch of trash bins. It would be a perfect time for a break and enter. No such luck. I continued to assess my options.

None.

My arms and shoulders began to ache. I shrugged my shoulders and wriggled my arms as much as possible, which wasn't much.

Hell. What kind of manure dump had I landed in? I had a bad feeling in the pit of my stomach on where this would all end up. I needed to find some way to get out of here. But in my current condition, I could do nothing but wait for my captors to return. Having memorized everything in the room including a dimly visible plaque on the wall, probably from the Society of Abusive Art Dealers, I peered through the window at the alley again. I could barely see the brick wall of the neighboring building. Then a figure appeared pushing a shopping cart. I could make out a person in an oversized overcoat and baseball cap who bent over one of the garbage bins. His hands and arms disappeared into the container and then, periodically, a hand emerged to drop something into the shopping cart.

I tried to shout, but only a faint sound emerged from my gagged mouth. Even if I could catch his attention, what good would it do me?

The street person finished one can and proceeded to the next. This must have been a prime spot for good pickings as he took his sweet time.

Then off to the side, I spotted another figure. This appeared to be a big kid with a baseball bat. He approached the homeless man, who must have heard something as he jerked his head around just as the kid swung the bat.

I tried to scream again. Nothing.

The homeless man ducked and the bat struck the wall across the alley.

With amazing agility the street guy grabbed the kid's arm, and the bat disappeared from my line of sight. Then with hands and feet, the homeless man proceeded to beat the snot out of the kid. I wanted to cheer.

Finally the kid had enough and half ran, half limped out of the alley, holding his arm.

The street guy watched the retreating figure for a moment, then straightened his baseball cap and returned to the garbage can to continue collecting junk. Finally, he put a lid on the last can, added the baseball bat to his collection and pushed the well-laden shopping cart out of sight.

So much for my evening entertainment. I could have used that guy to help me with the art-dealer mafia.

Now my thoughts returned to my predicament. I had to shortly deal with an irate, criminal, mayhem-embracing art dealer and his equally ugly cohort. And I didn't have any damn bargaining chips.

Pitman was my only ally, but the red-topped twerp couldn't get into the locked room and might not have even known that I was still in here, trapped and immobile.

With all this time on my hands and since I couldn't even as much as twiddle my thumbs, I set my clunky old mind to work at trying to connect the pieces of this crime jigsaw puzzle. Brock was the kingpin of this operation. It was obvious from the way he had taken charge when he found me snooping in his storeroom.

Both Vansworthy and Muddy Murphy had gotten in Brock's way and been eliminated. With Vansworthy gone, Theobault definitely benefited from taking over the partnership, but that had been a convenient ruse for Brock in deflecting attention from himself. I now suspected that Theobault was innocent. He had someone follow me because he truly believed I was hooked up with Brock. What a joke. As if I would be part of his scumball operation. Theobault just didn't appreciate what a sweet guy I was.

Brock had set up the perfect moneymaking scheme. With income from the auto-sweepstake scam, plus handling real and fake Muddy Murphy paintings now that the value had increased, it was almost like printing money. Then he had his connections with the Long Beach and Beverly Hills flunkies to provide a neat chain of laundering. I had inserted myself in the gears of this well-oiled machine. No wonder Brock wanted me out of the way.

And the automobile-contest scam. An employee of Vansworthy had been involved. I had my suspicions that Brock had set that up as another diversion away from himself. I would have to see if Brock would divulge anything to support this idea. I just had to find a way to get out of my current predicament. And I didn't know if I wanted time to myself or for Brock and company to return to see what would happen next.

My reverie was interrupted by the sound of a key scraping in the lock of the door. I heard a creaking sound and the light flashed on. Then my nemesis and his short hench-man strolled over to stand in front of me. "Look, Harvey, our intruder is still here."

The short guy came over and stuck his face two inches from mine. "Enjoy your rest in the dark?"

I mumbled through the cloth in my mouth.

"He can't answer." Brock leaned toward me. "I'll even let Harvey remove the gag if you promise to be quiet."

I nodded my head.

With a satisfied smile, Harvey ripped the duct tape off my mouth along with a little skin.

I spit out the handkerchief.

"Have a good time by yourself?" Brock asked.

"Just peachy," I replied.

"You didn't doze off by any chance?"

"No. I stayed awake thinking about you, Brock."

He chuckled. "Too bad. When I had that nice chat with you and your wife after your

wedding, I learned how you forget everything when you fall asleep. If you had nodded off, you wouldn't remember why you
were here or what had happened."

"No such luck. I remember it all very
clearly."

"Maybe that can be remedied."

I didn't like the sound of that.

"I have something to tell you, Brock."

He paused and stared at me.

"I have you all figured out."

He sneered at me. "Do tell."

"You used one of Vansworthy's employees
for the automobile-sweepstakes fraud. That
way if anything went wrong it would reflect
on Vansworthy. When the minion was arrested, I suspect that Vansworthy put two
and two together and realized you had your
grubby hands in the affair. I bet dollars to
doughnuts that you bumped off Vansworthy
to keep him from squealing about your
money-laundering operation and the source
of income being that automobile-contest
scam."

Brock chuckled. "Very good, Mr. Jacobson. Go on."

"And the Vansworthy death cast suspicion
on Theobault because of the partnership
between Theobault and Vansworthy. The
police must have been tracking that motive."

"Right again. At first I was surprised that they didn't immediately arrest Theobault."

"That's because the cops are waiting for you, Brock."

"I don't think so. After tonight they'll know that one Paul Jacobson is the mastermind of the crime wave here in Venice Beach."

"Even Detective Quintana will never believe that my tangled brain could have conjured up all these murders."

He wagged a finger at me. "I think the police will be convinced of what you've done. It was very convenient that you stumbled onto the scene. The police didn't go after Theobault because they're suspicious of you, Mr. Jacobson. You obligingly argued with Vansworthy the night before he died. Then when Muddy Murphy made noises about planning to destroy my inventory, I had to eliminate him. You once again stumbled right in to help me. Besides, it was time for Muddy's paintings to ratchet up in value."

"You seem awfully complacent telling me all this."

"It won't do you any good."

I felt a shiver run down my spine.

Brock opened his hands toward me. "You gave me the perfect cover when I had to kill

Muddy. Having heard of your episode with the candleholder at the church, it gave me the ideal way to hide my involvement in Muddy's murder and point suspicion at you."

Bingo. I thought back to what I read in my journal. "So you obviously wore a glove to bash Muddy over the head with the candleholder that had my fingerprints on it."

"Very convenient, I must say. And on top of that I overheard you arguing with Muddy before he met his demise."

"Damn."

"Your temper gets you in lots of trouble, Mr. Jacobson. Like tonight. You made quite a scene with Theobault."

Uh-oh.

"I even understand a police detective saw that whole encounter." Brock guffawed. "He'll remember that when Theobault turns up murdered."

Pucky. I had stepped in it again.

Brock leered at me. "In fact, you're going to have a chance to spend some time with Theobault very soon."

"What the hell are you saying?" I asked.

Brock smirked. "We have quite a surprise waiting for you."

"Maybe we should take this old putz for a

little car ride," Harvey said.

Brock gave me an evil grin. "Yes. I think it's time for a trip over to Theobault's office."

Theobault's office? Now what?

"The police will be all over your butt," I said.

"I don't think so, Mr. Jacobson. If you're expecting that crazy Pitman to notify anyone, he thinks you went home sick."

"Now I'm really feeling sick," I said.

"Good. Let's go." Brock took a Swiss Army knife from his drawer, opened the blade and sliced through the cord holding me in the chair. Then he unceremoniously grabbed my shoulders and yanked me upright, sending pain shooting through my stiff arms. He pushed me toward the door, and I stumbled forward.

The place was deserted. Not even a maid or janitor cleaning up the mess from the reception. I could have bellowed to my heart's content, and no one would have heard me.

I suddenly craved a glass of punch to wet my cotton mouth. With a not-too-gentle shove, I found myself outside and then thrust into the backseat of a black Lexus. Brock drove and Baldy sat in the backseat with me.

"I appreciate you chauffeuring us," I said to the back of Brock's head. "But why a visit to Theobault's office?"

"It will be a little special treat for him and you."

"I thought at first that you and Theobault might be in this together, but now I know this is all your doing."

"I have no use for Theobault. He's as much trouble as you are."

"You going to get rid of him like you did with Vansworthy?"

Brock laughed. "The police will conclude that you killed Vansworthy as well as Muddy Murphy. And after your argument with Theobault earlier, I think the authorities will have a perfect pattern established."

Damn. I had sure given Brock lots of cover because of shooting off my big mouth.

"Detective Quintana would like to prevent me from roaming the streets, but I think he'll be more inclined to haul you in, Brock."

"After tonight it will be conclusive that an old man was on a murder spree. You'll be identified as the murderer of Vansworthy, Theobault and Muddy Murphy."

Damn, I thought. Something's going to happen to Theobault tonight. I may not have liked the guy, but we didn't need another body littering the landscape.

We pulled to the curb, and I saw the sign for the Theobault Gallery. It didn't look like a cozy place for a nighttime gathering.

"I never saw Theobault again after my earlier encounter with him at your shindig," I said.

"That's because he was tied up." Brock chuckled again.

We entered the building, and I received another push which propelled me into an office. Autry, the Beverly Hills art-dealer mafioso stood behind a bound man who I recognized as Theobault.

"Okay, Louis, untie Theobault," Brock commanded.

Autry removed the cords from Theobault's hands, which fell limply at his sides.

"You already kill him?" I asked.

"He's just taking a little snooze," Autry said, rubbing his hands together.

"Now comes the fun part," Brock said as he reached in his pocket.

He extracted a handgun and a bottle of pills.

I'm sure my eyes widened, and my heart started beating at a rate that wasn't safe for a geezer my age. I could feel drops of perspiration forming on my forehead.

"Suddenly not so confident, old man?" Brock said, as he emptied a bunch of pills into his hand. "Swallow these."

"I hate taking pills," I said.

"You'll hate it more if you don't take them."

His cohorts pried my mouth open, and he stuffed them in. I began gagging. Somehow I swallowed the mouthful.

"You have the note ready?" Brock said turning to the tall guy.

"Yes. Right here."

Autry put it in front of me and held a pen out to me.

I didn't raise my arm.

"Sign it," Brock ordered me.

My eyelids were growing heavy, and my aging body felt limp. I only had enough energy to try one thing. Instead of using my writing hand, I grasped the pen in my left hand. I scrawled my left-handed signature on the sheet.

I was barely awake now. I heard a voice say, "Clint, what if he survives the sleeping-pill overdose?"

"That's the best part. He has short-term memory loss so he won't remember any of this if he happens to be revived and wakes up."

Then I felt a gun being placed in my right hand.

"Wait a minute," a voice said. "I saw it clearly. He's left-handed. He signed the note with his left hand."

Someone grabbed the gun out of my right hand and put it in my left hand.

So sleepy . . .

I heard a gunshot as everything went blank.

CHAPTER 20

I woke up with my face in a toilet bowl. White porcelain and flushing water weren't my idea of good neghbors. Where the hell was I? My head throbbed and my stomach felt like someone had kicked it. A man in a white uniform was holding my head.

"I think it's all pumped out now," he said.

I tried to clear my foggy brain. Then it started coming back to me. Brock and the other two art dealers. Theobault sitting limp in a chair. Damn. Good thing Marion had helped me with a memory boost. Too bad my old body couldn't participate in that more often.

I put my left hand to my face, but my hand was covered with a paper bag, secured by a rubber band. "What's this?"

The man who I now noticed had a paramedic's badge on his uniform helped me to my feet. "A policeman put that on your hand. They want to test it for gunshot residue."

"Gunshot residue? Why do the police want to test my hand for gunshot residue?"

"Just be calm, sir. Detective Quintana will be here momentarily."

My stomach felt like someone had used it for a punching bag. My nose itched, so I had to use my right hand. Memories of what had happened continued to return. I had been in Theobault's office. He was in a chair. So sleepy . . .

"Mr. Jacobson, what have you done this time?"

I looked up to see the black, twitching mustache of Detective Quintana.

"I don't feel so hot, Detective, but I have some news for you. Clint Brock is the murderer. He killed Vansworthy and Muddy Murphy."

"What about Vance Theobault?"

"Last I saw, Brock and his two goons had him in a chair in his office."

"You mean this building?"

"I guess. I'm not sure exactly where I am."

"You're outside Theobault's office."

"Okay. I last remember being in his office."

"I thought you had trouble remembering things."

"I recall this. Brock kidnapped me from

his gallery after the reception. He brought me to Theobault's office. With Brock were two art dealers — one from Beverly Hills named Louis Autry, and Harvey something from Long Beach. Didn't catch his last name."

"An awful lot of detail for someone with a memory as bad as yours, Mr. Jacobson."

"And Brock stuffed me with sleeping pills and put a gun in my hand. I heard a gunshot and passed out."

"Very interesting. When did you write the note?"

"What note?"

"The one with your signature on it."

"Oh, yeah. Brock had me sign something. But I fooled him. I'm right-handed. I signed the note with my left hand."

Quintana regarded me with intense black eyes. "And the content of the note?"

"I have no clue. He never let me read it. Only forced me to sign it."

"It's a suicide note."

"Suicide note?"

"Don't touch it but read this." His latex-gloved hand spread a typed sheet of paper out on the receptionist's desk. I read a confession of having killed Vansworthy, Muddy Murphy and Theobault. Ended with, "And now I'm going to take my own life." The signature was my left-handed scrawl.

"The only thing that's mine is the signature. I'm not about to take my own life. Don't have that much time left, so no sense squandering it. Besides I hate taking pills. I'd never try to bump myself off that way."

"I need to test your left hand."

"Help yourself."

He carefully removed the brown paper bag and proceeded to swab my hand and fingers. I smelled the lingering aroma of smoke and noticed the soot.

"You need to haul Clint Brock in before he does any more damage," I said.

"We'll discuss that in due course, Mr. Jacobson."

I was still dazed. "How did you track me down?"

Detective Quintana flipped open his notepad, checked something and said, "A call came to the nine-one-one operator from your wife. She reported that you were in danger."

"How'd she know that?"

Quintana flipped a page. "She received a call from a man named Mallory Pitman. He had been told by Clint Brock that you weren't feeling well and had taken a cab home. Since you never returned, your wife reported that you had disappeared."

"I'm glad she called out the cavalry, but since I started at Brock's gallery and then he abducted me to this place, how did you find me here?"

"Someone reported a gunshot, and a police officer on patrol a block away investigated. He saw three men in a black Lexus drive away."

"That's the car Brock drove when he brought me here."

"The police officer did see the license number and we've verified that the owner is Brock."

"Did the policeman nail them?"

"No, Mr. Jacobson. The officer was on foot and his first priority was to see if there had been a shooting victim. He found the door to the building open and upon further investigation discovered Mr. Theobault shot and you unconscious. He called the paramedics who revived you."

"Damn. I'm appreciative of the personal attention. I'm lucky to still be alive and kicking."

Quintana nodded his head. "Another half hour, and the sleeping pills would probably have killed you. Unfortunately, it was too late for Mr. Theobault. He was already dead from the gunshot wound."

"Those bastards shot him and made it look like I had done it. Brock staged this whole thing to knock off Theobault and blame it on me."

"That appears to be the case. I thought at first that you had shot Mr. Theobault, but it quickly became apparent that the scene was staged and you were set up."

"Thank you for noticing."

Quintana chuckled. "You may have thought I was ignoring the art dealers, but I've been tracking the details of their activities. You brought Brock out in the open as the kingpin, and there is now enough evidence to connect him to a whole litany of crimes."

"I'm glad he will be rotting in prison. He's not a nice fellow." I let out a sigh. "You seem to believe me this time, Detective, or you'd have my butt in jail."

He eyed me. "There are some matters to clear up, but your story holds up, so far."

"Have you nabbed Brock?"

"We haven't been able to find him or his car yet. It's a matter of time."

I smiled at Quintana. "I appreciate that you believe me."

"Fortunate for you there is a supporting witness."

"Who's that?"

"There's a homeless man who bunks across the street. He happens to be very observant and keeps track of what goes on in this neighborhood. He described three men arriving in a black Lexus and going into Theobault's building. Two of them were strong-arming an old man."

"That was me."

"He also heard the gunshot and saw three men leave and climb into the Lexus. The third man was now a tall, younger man."

"And obviously I haven't gotten taller and younger. It's nice to know that the homeless community is looking out after my best interests. My stomach is starting to feel better now, but since it's approaching my bedtime, any chance of a lift home?"

"Not yet. But I'll provide a ride down to police headquarters for a few other details we need to attend to."

So once again I received an all-expense-paid ride to the police station in the back-seat of Quintana's standard-issue unmarked police car.

As I was led inside, I said, "I don't know what good it will do plunking my tired behind down here. I've told you everything I know already."

"Humor me, Mr. Jacobson."

I shrugged. "It's your nickel. I have nothing better to do other than sleep. I am thirsty though."

Quintana disappeared for a moment and returned, handing me a bottle of water. I drank some, careful not to overdo after my stomach being pumped.

"First, I'd like to collect handwriting samples from you." He put two sheets of paper down on the table in front of me and handed me a pen. "Please sign your name three times with your right hand."

I proceeded to do so.

He wrote a notation on the bottom. "Now do the same with your left hand on the other sheet."

When completed, he scribbled at the bottom and then looked at the two sheets. "Distinctly different signatures. May I see your ID card?"

I extracted it from my wallet and handed it to him.

"This is your right-handed signature."

"Very good, Detective. That's the way I sign. This other one is a little trick I learned, and this is the first time I've used it in years. Now, in addition to finding Brock, you should get a search warrant for his office to check out the stock of phony Muddy Murphy paintings. You can also verify that part of my story with Mallory Pitman."

"Please be patient. Now I need to leave you for a few minutes."

"Fine. I'll twiddle my toes and await your return."

I felt impatient and wanted to get this all wrapped up so I could return to my bride. After fidgeting for a few minutes, I realized that Quintana was going to take his own sweet time. I took a deep breath and exhaled.

Calm yourself.

Alone with just my old body, heart, mind and soul, I settled in to assess my situation. I felt uncomfortable about my predicament. I'd given Quintana enough to provide a reasonable doubt regarding me as the perpetrator of this crime wave. He could verify all the fishy stuff Brock was involved in, but the murders were still a problem. The thing I had going for me was lack of motive. Brock had reason to knock off these people. I didn't. I hoped I could clear my name.

And I had my bride waiting to go on a honeymoon cruise with me. I had to wrap this thing up.

I resisted the urge to count ceiling tiles or lick the one-way mirror to gross out the people behind it but instead sat there being a model interrogatee.

Finally, Quintana reappeared.

"Have you let my wife know that you've incarcerated me?"

"Yes. She's been informed that you're here. I also had a chance to speak with Mr. Pitman."

"And what did my red-haired buddy have to say?"

"He corroborated your account of the paintings in Mr. Brock's storeroom. He also confirmed that Brock told him you had felt ill and left the reception."

"There you go, Detective. My wife and I are reliable witnesses."

"So far."

"What's that supposed to mean?"

"There's still quite a bit to clear up regarding your presence in Theobault's office."

"Yeah, I'd like to understand that little stunt that Brock pulled. He seemed actively dedicated to eliminating his competitors. You going to search Brock's place?"

"You seem very impatient, Mr. Jacobson."

"Hey. I don't know how much time I have left on this mortal coil. I need to clear my good name and live out whatever is left for me."

"I'll release you for the time being."

"Good news. My bride and I thank you."

CHAPTER 21

A nice police officer the size of Godzilla escorted me out to a waiting car. As we drove along the streets of Venice Beach, I was glad to still be alive. I admired the reflection of lights off store windows. I took a few more sips from the police-provided water bottle. My queasy stomach was doing better now. The big guy dropped me off in the front of my place and I climbed the stairs.

Marion opened the door and gave me a hug. "I was worried when you didn't come home."

"You and me both."

"When Pitman called, I knew something was wrong and alerted the police."

"What a wise woman I married."

"Then someone called to say you were at the police station."

"It's good to be back in the comfort of my home."

"Well, you just stick around and don't wander off."

I helped myself to some iced tea and swallowed several mouthfuls. I guessed the sleeping pills had worn off since I was now wide awake. And with a pumped stomach, I needed a snack. I offered to fix sandwiches for both Marion and me, but she wasn't hungry so I slapped together just one "Jacobson" — a strip of turkey, a slab of ham, American cheese, lettuce, tomatoes, mayonnaise, mustard and a row of gherkins between pieces of wheat and white bread.

Marion shook her head when she saw my work of art and adjourned to get some shuteye. I demolished part of my creation, deciding not to overdo. After wrapping up the rest in cellophane and depositing it in the refrigerator, I put on my blue waterproof windbreaker and went outside to sit on the back steps. After the excitement of the evening, I found it relaxing to lean back and stare up at the sky. Even with all the city lights, I could make out a few stars. A gentle onshore breeze rippled through the trees and I felt a tingle on my neck. From the hedge came the cyclic "crick" from crickets.

Out of the corner of my eye I caught the flicker of motion and flinched. Then I let out a breath as I saw a gray tabby cat climb the stairs toward me.

It nuzzled against me, and I inspected its tag to see that it matched the name I remembered from my journal.

"Hello, Cleo. Out chasing mice?"

She purred and turned her head toward me so that her wide eyes flashed green reflected from the ambient light. Then moments later she shot down the stairs and disappeared.

I returned to my thoughts, relaxing in the pleasant evening.

Then a shape moved out of the shadows below me.

My heart started thumping like a percussion band, but then I saw it was Austin.

"What are you doing up in the middle of the night?" I asked.

"I couldn't sleep so I came outside."

I noticed a cell phone in his hand. "You calling your stock broker at this hour?"

He smiled. "No. When I can't sleep I check in with some of my friends. Benny and I were talking before I saw you sitting on the stairs."

"Yeah. I wasn't ready for sleep either so I needed a little time to myself."

Austin paused. "I can leave you alone if you like."

I waved my hand toward my chest. "I'd

welcome the company. Come join me."

"This was an exciting night," Austin said as he sat down next to me. "You'll never guess what Benny told me about Pierce."

"What?"

"Pierce tried to beat up a homeless man, but something went wrong, and he ended up at the hospital with a broken arm. Pierce's mom called Benny, asking if he knew what happened — she said Pierce wouldn't talk about it."

I thought back to the scene I'd witnessed through the window in Brock's office. "I'd say that Pierce picked on the wrong person and received his comeuppance. Hopefully, he'll learn from the experience."

"Yeah. I don't think Pierce will try that again."

"I just finished a snack, and if you're hungry, there are some cookies in the kitchen."

"Okay." Austin went inside and closed the door.

A feeling of contentment rippled through my chest. I had escaped the bad guy, the police were on his tail, and all was good in the universe. Austin had even resolved his problem and seemed in vastly improved spirits. I could now resume the life of a retired gentleman without a care in the world. I'd sleep in tomorrow and spend the day with Marion doing whatever she wanted to.

I looked up at the sky again and then down at the shadows in the yard.

Suddenly another shape emerged.

CHAPTER 22

I squinted at a shape in the yard below. Was Austin's mom or dad looking for him? Then I could see it was a man. He came right up to me. I let out a gasp. It was Clint Brock.

Uh-oh. I was in deep poop.

"You enjoying the night air?" I said in my most casual voice.

He pointed a pistol at me. "It's fortunate that I have a source in the police department. I found out that you're still alive and here."

"The police are going to get you, Brock." I hoped for Austin and Marion's sakes that neither would hear and come outside.

Brock grabbed my arm. "We're going for a little ride."

"Don't you think we've been through enough of that tonight?"

He pulled me down the stairs and gave me a push toward the gate that led to the alley. Suddenly a gray object shot by me.

There was a snarl, and then Brock gasped. "Something scratched my leg."

I smiled in spite of my predicament. Cleo had taken her best shot at rescuing me.

The cat disappeared after the fly-by assault so Brock collared me again and directed me out the gate.

"You're a very persistent cuss," I said. "Why are you bothering me again?"

"Louis was arrested. I received a call from his lawyer that some old man had set the police on him. You weren't supposed to remember anything even if you survived."

I gave him my most sincere smile. "Hey, stuff happens."

He shoved me again as a response.

"The police are going to nail you with or without my assistance," I said.

"Not if you're not around to testify."

I didn't like the sound of that. *Think.* I had to do something. "I filled out a full report on you, Louis and Harvey. It doesn't matter what you do to me. You're going down, Brock."

"In that case, I'll make sure you disappear on my way to Mexico. Get in the car." He pushed me inside his black Lexus.

"This is all such a waste of your time and effort. You should be trying to escape on your own without me slowing you down."

He laughed. "You won't slow me down much. Not for very long anyway. I'll be on my own after you take a little midnight swim."

"But I hate swimming."

"Good. It'll be a most appropriate way for you to go."

"I'm not ready to cash in my chips yet."

"You may not have any choice."

With that he stepped on the gas, and we shot down the alley. Then he slammed on the brakes as a black cat meandered across our path.

"I'd say that was a sign of bad luck for you, Brock."

"No, I think it was meant for you."

He turned the corner, driving at a normal speed. I guessed he decided he didn't want to attract attention. There wasn't any traffic, but Brock waited patiently at each light and made full stops at every stop sign.

"Nice of you to drive safely."

He only scowled at me.

I thought briefly of opening the door and making a run for it, but I couldn't move very fast. I kept looking for a friendly policeman to wave to, but the streets were nearly deserted.

What the hell did this psycho have in mind now?

My question was answered five minutes later when we pulled into a slip at Marina Del Rey. Damn. We were around boats.

He exited the car, came around to the passenger's side, opened the door, grabbed my arm and lifted me out.

"Easy does it," I said. I looked out and saw three sports fishing boats moored to the pier. Uh-oh. We *were* going for a little moonlight cruise.

He shoved me toward the largest boat and made me step aboard. I thought about screaming, but there was no one around, and I didn't want to give Brock an excuse to shoot me right there.

I didn't like this one little bit.

Then he pushed me down a ladder, and I slammed onto the floor of the cabin.

"You wait there."

I heard noises above. I looked around the sparsely furnished cabin — two bunks, a table, cabinets and, between two portholes, a picture of a sailboat. It took him ten minutes or so, and then the engine started.

"Come up on deck," Brock shouted.

I figured I'd go see what was going on.

I scaled the ladder and came out. We were slowly motoring out of the slip.

"You'll never get away with this, Brock."

"Sure I will. I'll dump your body at sea

and then cruise down to Ensenada where no one can arrest me."

I looked all around. At this time of night, we were the only boat moving in the harbor. Brock kept the throttle at a slow speed to avoid attracting attention, not that anyone was watching us.

We were now moving along a jetty that separated the beach from the channel. I had to do something. My lips were dry, and my heart beat double time at the prospect of dying at sea. I noticed the gun crammed in Brock's belt. I could imagine the final scenario here.

Then I heard a siren.

"Hell," Brock said. "The harbor patrol." He slammed the throttle forward and the engine roared. Then he reached toward the gun in his belt.

In an instant I knew what I had to do.

I removed my jacket, and, as the boat accelerated, I vaulted off the side. Flying through the air, I held the jacket over my head like a parachute.

I hit hard and went under water. I held onto the jacket for dear life, and when my head bobbed to the surface, I collapsed the edges of the jacket to form a bubble. I gathered in the jacket and held the bubble in my right hand. It wasn't much, but it supported me enough that I didn't turn into an anchor.

With my inability to swim, I knew I'd sink without that air pocket to hold me up.

I heard the sound of gunshots, but the boat had moved well past me.

I ducked under water, still clutching the jacket bubble as fear surged though my whole body. I was going to either get shot or drown.

Think.

I had to escape from Brock. I spotted the jetty. I sloughed off my shoes and started kicking and paddling with my left arm.

Brock's boat seemed to be changing direction. The patrol boat continued to approach me.

I desperately waved with my free hand toward the flashing lights, but the police boat aimed toward Brock's.

The bubble gave me a little support so that I could keep my head above water. I resumed a lame kick to propel myself toward the rock jetty.

It was so far away.

Could I stay afloat?

I kicked and one-arm paddled.

The bubble began deflating.

It was losing air.

I had to reach shore.

I kicked. I flailed.

What was in the water with me?

Don't even think about that. Just move your tired body.

I could hear waves lapping on the rocks.

How much farther?

My head bobbed up and I saw Brock's boat had circled around.

Uh-oh. He had spotted me in the water.

I continued my pathetic one-arm crawl and kick, trying to keep a little air in the jacket bubble.

A small swell smacked me in the face.

I spit out water and saw Brock's boat aiming right at me. He was within fifty yards when I heard a horn off to the side that caused me to flinch so that I almost lost my grip on the jacket.

Brock's boat veered off, and I was swamped by a wake as the police boat with flashing lights sped past.

Brock's boat tried to get away, but I could see the police boat pulling up alongside.

Good. They had nabbed the bastard.

But I was sinking. With all the wakes from the two boats, my bubble had burst, so to speak.

Apparently no one on the police boat had seen me in the rush to catch Brock. I struggled to the surface and lifted my jacket above the water to capture some air.

I swallowed water again, but was able to reform a bubble. I resumed kicking like mad and aimed for the rock jetty.

I gained purchase, and my legs propelled me forward.

Damn. I was actually moving in the right direction.

So close, yet so far.

If only I could stay afloat on my own.

My bubble gave out again.

I sank, but hit something solid. I propelled myself to the surface. The jetty was almost within reach.

I kicked frantically, released the jacket and stroked with both arms.

A swell caught me and thrust me against a rock.

I stuck out my arm and grasped a sharp piece of rock, cutting my hand.

Then slowly I lifted my old body up on the jetty.

I clambered above the waterline and paused to catch my breath.

I felt like I had swum across the English Channel. I shook my head in amazement — imagine me paddling to shore. Damn. Maybe someday I'd even learn to take pills and love lawyers.

Having determined that I only had a small

cut on my hand and would live, I climbed to the top of the jetty.

I plopped down on a flat rock and watched the two boats now tied together and bobbing farther out in the channel.

I didn't know how the police boat had arrived in such a timely fashion but, boy, was I glad they had given me a chance to escape from Brock's clutches.

With Brock in custody, I shivered in the cool night air. The adrenaline rush of the last few minutes subsided, and I suddenly wanted to take a nap. No, I needed to return home. Marion and Austin would wonder what the hell had happened to me since I last left sitting on the steps.

I climbed down the other side of the jetty onto the sand and limped toward the bike path. I spotted a group of people, wrapped in blankets, sitting on the sand. It looked like a Boy Scout campout, except they were all adults.

As I approached, a bearded man stood up. "Look what the ocean spit up."

"Yeah. Just out for a little night swim."

"In case you don't recognize me, I'm Harley Marcraft." He threw a blanket to me. "Here, dry off."

"Thanks." I grabbed it and wrapped it around my soggy body.

"No. The thanks goes to you. The warning from you and your grandson paid off."

"How so?"

"You said that a big kid was going to attack one of us tonight. We were all keeping a watch out." He chuckled. "Turns out the kid picked the wrong guy to attack."

"Yeah," I said. "I understand the kid had the piss beat out of him."

"Exactly. Alex looks like a weak, defenseless old man, but he once was a karate black belt."

I sighed. "For once, justice was served."

"You want something to eat?" Harley asked, holding out a half-eaten sandwich.

"No, I had a snack a little while ago."

After the blanket had soaked up some of the water from my clothes, I excused myself and headed home, hobbling gingerly in my sock feet. When I arrived back, there were lights on in our apartment, the main house and in the yard between.

"Looks like a party's going on," I said.

Marion raced out and gave me a big hug. "We were all so worried about you."

George, Andrea and Austin all appeared.

Austin had a big smile on his face. "You're safe."

"Damn straight. I lucked out. A patrol boat saved my butt."

Marion put an arm around me. "You have Austin to thank for that."

I peered at him. "Obviously, there's a story here."

He beamed at me. "I heard what happened on the stairs. I called nine-one-one on my cell phone and reported that you had been kidnapped."

"Good work. How did the police think to send out a patrol boat?"

"I jumped on my bike and followed the car," Austin said. "When you went to the boat, I was still on the cell phone with the police and told them what was happening."

"Smart lad."

"I stayed at the marina until I saw the police boat chasing you, then rode my bike home. Man, am I glad you're okay."

Just then there was a knock on the door.

Marion opened it to a short man with a black twitching mustache. "Come in, Detective Quintana."

"Welcome to our party," I said.

"I need to take a statement from you, Mr. Jacobson, and from Austin Kanter."

"Be my guest, Detective. You can speak with Austin first while I go change into some dry clothes."

I walked across the carpet with a few drops of water falling from my pant cuffs.

After a brief shower, I put on Bermuda shorts and a T-shirt and returned to the living room as Austin completed recounting his part of the story.

"Now, you, Mr. Jacobson."

"It was pretty simple. Clint Brock kidnapped me for the second time tonight. These young twerps never seem to learn when dealing with old farts like me. He was going to shoot me and chuck my body into the Pacific on his way to Ensenada. You gotta admit that he didn't give up. Fortunately, Austin got word to the constabulary, and a police boat picked up Brock's tail. I managed to swim to shore."

"But you hate swimming and the ocean," Marion said.

"I still do and can't swim worth a tinker's damn. But somehow I made it to the rock jetty. And, Detective, Brock has a spy in the police department. You better check it out."

"What do you mean?"

"Some informer told him where to find me."

"I'll look into that right away." He jotted down a few notes in his pad and then looked up at me. "That's enough for now, Mr. Jacobson. I'll stop by tomorrow for any further questions."

"You do that, Detective. Then you can

clear my good name of all these spurious charges."

Quintana actually smiled. "We'll see, Mr. Jacobson. We'll see."

CHAPTER 23

"I don't know about the rest of you, but my old body is ready for some sleep now," I said to Marion and her family as I stretched my arms.

I excused myself and went into my room. But before hitting the hay, I sat down and documented the adventures of Paul Jacobson, kidnap victim extraordinaire.

Needless to say, I slept late the next day. I woke without even a hazy recollection of the wild events of the night before. Reading my journal refreshed my memory of the Brock episodes. I couldn't believe that someone with as much mileage on his ticker as me had been through all that turmoil the night before.

I ambled into the kitchen to search for some vittles.

"Well, Sleeping Beauty is finally up," Marion said.

I gave her my dentist-perfect smile. "I had a tough night."

She hugged me. "You certainly did. I've already eaten, but I'll fix something for you."

"Thanks, but I'll rustle up a big bowl of cereal and make some toast."

After I finished my brunch, I was contemplating what to do for the rest of my life when I heard a knock on the door. I opened it to find a short guy in a suit with a black mustache. "Detective Quintana, come in. Your mustache isn't twitching today."

He winced, like I had slapped him, then a brief curl at the corners of his mouth appeared. He almost looked sheepish. "I guess I feel calmer today. A large amount of my caseload has been resolved."

"Well, I'm anxious to hear all the details. My bride is hoping that you'll give me the green light for our upcoming Alaskan honeymoon cruise."

He stared at me, his mustache still not twitching. "We'll discuss that."

I pointed to the easy chair. "Please sit down and give me the latest police-beat poop."

He sank into the chair, and I plunked down on the couch.

Marion appeared. "May I join you gentlemen?"

Quintana nodded. "By all means, Mrs. Jacobson."

Marion sat on the couch next to me.

"To begin with, Mr. Jacobson, you were implicated in several crimes."

"Yes. I've been a busy guy this summer."

He looked at me askance and then continued. "Let me review the list. First, you reported finding the floating body of Frederick Vansworthy. We've now determined that Clint Brock committed that murder."

"Good job, Detective."

"Next, you were in the room when Harold Koenig died at Saint Andrew's Church."

"Poor Harold," Marion said. "Have you learned more about his death, Detective?"

"Yes. Mr. Jacobson is in the clear. Mr. Koenig died of a heart attack."

"I'm sorry he died," I said. "But I'm glad I'm no longer a suspect."

"Third, Mr. Jacobson, you found the bludgeoned body of Mr. Maurice Murphy."

"I don't know any Maurice Murphy."

Quintana cleared his throat and stared at me. "He was known as Muddy Murphy."

"Oh."

"As I was saying, you found his body also at Saint Andrew's Church and were implicated because your fingerprints were discovered on the murder weapon."

"But Clint Brock set me up. He had overheard me talking about Harold Koenig's death and the candleholders."

Quintana held his hand up. "I know, Mr. Jacobson. I'm just recounting the facts. That murder was also the work of Clint Brock."

"Whew," I said. "I'm glad we're in agreement on that."

"And I used to think Clint was such a nice man," Marion said, shaking her head.

"You wouldn't if you had been tied up, had pills stuffed down your gullet and been shot at by him," I said. "Brock knocked off Muddy because he wanted the value of both the fake and real paintings to increase in value."

"Yes," Quintana said. "And also because Mr. Murphy was threatening to destroy Brock's collection."

"So Brock did him in before he could ruin any paintings."

"Exactly."

"What happened to Brock's two confederates, the art dealers from Beverly Hills and Long Beach?"

Quintana chuckled. "Oh, yes. Louis Autry and Harvey Milligan."

"So that was Harvey's last name."

"We arrested Mr. Autry last night and Mr. Milligan early this morning. They both confessed to their part in the money-laundering scheme and agreed to testify against Mr. Brock in order to lessen their sentences for accessory to murder."

"Excellent. I'm glad to hear they sang like tweetie birds."

"So, Mr. Jacobson, your tip to me concerning money laundering was right on the money."

"And here I thought you didn't believe anything I said."

"I'm just a natural skeptic."

"But I'm glad you checked it out."

"There's another thing I think you'll appreciate, Mr. Jacobson."

"I'm in an appreciating kind of way today, Detective, so fire away."

He smiled and his mustache still didn't twitch. "Thanks to your foresight in calling the police when you were approached to put money into the automobile-sweepstakes scam, we were able to trace the marked money you handed to the courier."

"Good work, Detective."

"The money was consolidated with other payments and used to purchase a painting at the gallery of Louis Autry in Beverly Hills."

"The same guy you arrested last night."

"The very one. And since we had a search

warrant for the sweepstakes sting, we seized Autry's records early this morning as well. The painting that was sold was painted by Muddy Murphy."

"Imagine that."

Quintana gave me a sideways glance and chuckled. "You can't fool me, you sly old fox."

"Definitely old, Detective. Definitely old."

"Autry's records show that the painting had been purchased from the gallery owned by Harvey Milligan in Long Beach."

"The short, round guy who assisted Brock in kidnapping me last night."

"The same. And one final piece of evidence you will appreciate. When we searched Brock's records this morning as a result of a friendly judge's quick warrant, we discovered a transaction selling that same painting from Brock's gallery to Milligan's gallery."

"And the chain is complete. Well done, Detective."

"I just wish we could have shut down the operation before all the killing started."

"At least they are all locked up now. And, Detective, if it will be any help to you in building your case, I spoke with two art dealers who used to have galleries in Venice Beach and were driven out of business by

359

Brock's shady dealings."

"Give me the names and I'll follow up immediately."

I searched through my room and found the note with the phone numbers for both Farquart and Rouen. I handed it to Quintana. "Here, Detective. They will enjoy hearing from you."

He looked at the names and tucked the paper in his pocket. "Another matter, Mr. Jacobson. From the comment you made last night, we tracked down a dispatcher who had been feeding information to Brock. She's now under arrest."

"Well done."

Quintana raised an eyebrow. "And concerning the briefcase you found on the jetty by the beach."

I thought back to my journal. "And I pointed out a suspect to one of your police officers."

"That's right. And he turned out to be the guilty party."

"So what the hell was that guy up to anyway?"

"We determined that he was part of an ecoterrorist plot. We found his prints as well as yours on the briefcase handle. He wanted to disrupt the concert in order to keep the beach less crowded. He thought people would stop holding and attending such events with a little explosion."

"But he could have killed quite a few people along the way."

"Yeah. Apparently he had second thoughts. That's why he was searching among the rocks when you spotted him. Anyway, he's safely locked up, and the suitcase was detonated by the bomb squad."

"That's a relief," Marion said.

"Yes, Mrs. Jacobson, your husband helped us a great deal. With the automobile-sweepstakes fraud resolved, fewer elderly people will be swindled."

"Watch who you call elderly," I said.

"My views on aging have significantly changed since I've met you, Mr. Jacobson. In spite of your memory, you're an active, robust, contributing citizen."

Marion gave me a hug. "You're absolutely correct, Detective."

"So it sounds like I'm clear of all charges and ready to head off to Alaska with my beautiful bride."

"Not quite, Mr. Jacobson. There's still the matter of fishing for grunion without a license." He tapped his fingers on the armrest of the chair.

"You're not going to hold that against me with all these major crimes solved?"

Quintana shook his head. "In fact I tried to have the charges dropped because of everything you had done, but the fish and game division was adamant. They would make no exception. So I paid your fine." He pulled a rolled document out of his coat pocket. "Here's a present for you, Mr. Jacobson." He stood up, stepped over to the couch and handed me the paper.

I opened it to find a receipt indicating that my fine had been paid in full.

"Well, thank you, Detective."

"Paul, we'll have to frame it and add it to your other memorabilia on the dresser."

I looked toward Quintana. "I guess I'm going to miss you and your twitching mustache, Detective, not that I'd remember you tomorrow if I didn't read my journal."

Marion whispered in my ear. "You never know. You might get lucky and be able to remember tomorrow."

I felt all warm and tingly inside. Maybe my old body would be put to the test tonight.

"One last thing, Detective. I understand a homeless man outside Theobault's office helped identify Clint Brock and his gang entering and leaving the building last night."

He raised an eyebrow. "I thought you couldn't remember overnight?"

"I can't. But this morning when I woke up, I read it in my journal. I must have been so hyped up last night after all the festivities that I wrote down everything that had happened."

He shook his head like trying to rid himself of a fly that had landed on his forehead. "Yes, a homeless man who sleeps on Windward Circle witnessed the comings and goings."

"What's his name?"

"He had no ID. But the officer on that beat told me everyone refers to him as Old Ollie."

"Thanks, Detective. I'll have to show him my appreciation."

Quintana stood up, and we shook hands.

After he left, I dropped into an easy chair, feeling like a heavy weight had been removed from my shoulders. I was a free man. After all the crap Detective Quintana had given me, he turned out to be a nice fellow. And there were no accusations left for anyone to harass me over. I could resume the life of Riley.

"What are you going to do with yourself now?" Marion asked.

"Nothing. I'm looking forward to being a lazy slob for a few days."

She bent over and kissed my forehead. "I

can't see you doing that."

I sighed. "I suppose you're right. But it sure is a relief not having the police breathing down my neck."

Marion put her hand to her cheek. "Oh, I meant to tell you, Paul. Something came for you in the mail yesterday." She reached on top of an end table and handed me a package.

"What could this be?" I asked.

"It has Meyer Ohana's return address. Why don't you open it?"

I tore away the wrapping and found a box of chocolate-covered macadamia nuts with a note that read: "Here's the box of chocolates I owe you for the bet we placed on the O. Henry story."

"I'll be damned," I said to Marion. "I wrote about this in my journal, but I didn't think any more about it. Meyer and I made a bet, and I won a box of candy. Have a piece."

We pigged out on the treats, and then I snapped my fingers. "I better give Meyer a call. I need to thank him for upholding his end of the wager and to read him a story."

"And I forgot to remind you to phone him," Marion said.

"There you go. I'll have to watch you to make sure you don't end up with soggy brain cells like mine."

Marion laughed. "I'm not worried about that. You're in charge of the interesting mental traits for this family."

I found a phone number and Meyer's name taped to the phone stand, and I punched in the digits.

When Meyer came on the line, I said, "Is this the Hawaiian representative for Geriatrics Anonymous?"

"Paul, you haven't forgotten me after all."

"Actually I did for a while. But I received a box of chocolate-covered macadamia nuts from some reformed gambler in Hawaii, and it jogged the old brain. Thanks for the goodies."

"You're welcome. I guess I should know better than to bet against someone who successfully wooed Marion and escaped from numerous murder allegations."

"Speaking of which, I'm a free man again."

"You mean Marion got tired of you and kicked you out?"

"No, you old poop. I'm free of criminal accusations. The bad guy's arrested, and I'm no longer on the Most Wanted List. My bride and I are free to sail off into the sunset in Alaska."

"No grass grows under your feet."

"Hell, no. I'm a vigorous old codger even

if I can't remember squat. How are things with your new girlfriend?"

"She and I are still having the same chat about her grandkids every morning."

"To move things along I've selected an O. Henry story for you called 'The Exact Science of Matrimony.' "

"That sounds foreboding."

"Hell, I don't know what it's about. I just like the title."

I proceeded to read the story of Jeff and Andy who work up a scam to collect money from men who woo a widow named Mrs. Trotter. They planned to abscond with the money, but in the meantime provided some of it for Mrs. Trotter to hold in good faith. Mrs. Trotter fell in love with one of the suitors and gave him two thousand dollars of the duo's collected money. Jeff thought the two thousand dollars was lost, but Andy handed Jeff the money at the end of the story. He had disguised himself as a suitor and "protected" the money.

"O. Henry had a devious mind," Meyer said.

"Either that or he didn't trust women."

"Having had his own encounter with the law, his stories often involve a crime."

"Given my own involvement with the more hardened criminal element lately, I'd prefer gentle conniving to what I've been through. Although I did see the backside of a scam that was cheating old relics like us. I helped put a stop to it."

"Paul, you never cease to amaze me, solving crimes, getting married. What can't you do?"

"I can't remember yesterday."

There was a pause on the line. "I guess we all have our deficiencies."

"Damn right. Now, did the story provide any inspiration of the matrimonial sort?"

"No. I'm going to continue my repeated conversations and just leave it at that."

"Too bad. Maybe you two could find ways to help each other like Marion helps me with my memory."

"I doubt that. You just happen to have a very perverse set of wiring in your brain."

"That's for sure. Well, I'll sign off now and let you return to your grandkid discussions."

After I hung up the phone, my mind churned on all the recent events. I couldn't complain of boredom. My life was certainly filled with interesting and challenging events. Retirement provided more activity than I had ever expected. At least I knew what was in store for me next: a trip to the forty-ninth state. That would be calm and relaxing. I could watch whales, see beautiful forests and glaciers, eat good food and not have to worry myself over murders. I pictured myself on a deck chair wrapped up in blankets, viewing icebergs floating by. Damn. I hoped the name of the ship wasn't the *Titanic.* With my luck, my tranquil cruise would turn into some weird adventure. But enough of that kind of thinking. I had some final planning to do with my bride, and then we'd be ready for the Alaskan wilderness. Bring on the eagles, bears and salmon.

Marion told me to read the cruise brochure and start thinking about which shore excursions we should select. Then she went over to George and Andrea's house, to see if she could rustle up a frame for my fishing fine receipt.

I sat back down feeling both sad and relieved. I would not be seeing Detective Quintana again, but the cloud of all these accusations was removed from above my gray head.

I picked up the brochure which described panning for gold, salmon bakes, city tours, railway rides, a lumberjack show, helicopter rides, a zipline through a rain forest, fishing, whale watching, kayaking — you name it. That was too much for my befuddled brain, so I put the brochure down and almost dozed off, catching myself in time so as not to do the Jacobson reset.

Marion sauntered in with my document under glass in a wooden frame and held it up for me to see.

"Come with me," she said.

"With an invitation like that, how can I resist?"

I extracted myself from the couch and followed her into the bedroom.

Marion placed the frame on the dresser, and I admired my trophies: a monarch butterfly collection, a picture of the Boulder County jail and this receipt for a paid fishing violation.

"All your souvenirs from helping solve crimes in Hawaii, Boulder and now Venice Beach."

"I've been quite the world traveler."

"And you've helped a number of detectives along the way."

"Just think if I'd started this crime spree as a young man."

"It's a good thing you waited until your eighties. We'd have no room in our bedroom."

"As long as there's room for you, Marion."

We hugged, and I felt an arousal send a surge through my body. Damn, it was nice having such a good woman married to me.

We disengaged.

"Now," she said. "The shore excursions."

I saluted. "Yes, General."

Marion grabbed the cruise brochure, and we reviewed all the options, settling on visiting the Mendenhall Glacier in Juneau, the White Pass Railway in Skagway, a rain forest and whale-watching excursion in Ketchikan and the Butchart Gardens in Victoria.

She sighed. "That will be a lovely trip. I can't wait to see Alaska."

"Yes. I have my life planned for me with no dead bodies and no Detective Quintana. That will be quite a change. By the way, where are we staying in Seattle before we sail?"

"It's a nice older hotel called the Lincoln."

"That's good, because I'm a nice older guy."

"You are." Marion kissed me on the cheek.

Just then the telephone rang so I picked it up.

"Hello, Grandpa."

"Is this my long-lost granddaughter?"

"I'm not lost. I'm right here in Boulder."

"And I'm right here in Venice Beach. What's up?"

"I'm calling to see how things are going with the art dealers."

"Swimmingly. They're all locked up, and

your grandpa is a free man again."

"Cool. Now you and Marion can go on the cruise."

"Exactly. We have the itinerary all planned. Alaska will never be the same again." I thought back to what I had read in my journal. "And thanks for the work you did on your computer. Between you and Austin, we tracked down the leads I needed to clear my good name. And by the way, Austin isn't a jerk anymore."

"I know that, Grandpa. We've been text messaging each other."

"What the hell is text messaging?"

"Oh, Grandpa. You're so behind the times. It's the best way to communicate. We send each other messages on cell phones. I don't have my own yet, but Mom lets me borrow hers."

"What's wrong with telephone calls or writing letters or even coming to visit?"

"I'm hoping my folks will bring me out to see Austin . . . and you."

"Wait a minute. I sense a little change in priorities here."

There was a pause on the line. "As you said, Austin isn't a jerk anymore."

"I'd love to see you, so you drag your mom and dad out here as soon as you can."

With Alexander Graham Bell overused, I

hung up feeling proud at how well my granddaughter had turned out and that she and Austin were now friends. I watched the phone to see if it would ring again. What a world. Computers, cell phones and art dealers. Oh, well. Somehow I would survive . . . for the time being anyway.

CHAPTER 24

That afternoon the phone rang and I answered to hear a male voice say, "This is Pieter Rouen. May I speak to Paul Jacobson?"

"This is Paul."

"Mr. Jacobson. I got a call earlier today from a detective in Los Angeles. He asked questions about Clint Brock, just as you did recently. He told me that Brock has been arrested and that the Vansworthy, Theobault and Brock galleries will all have new ownership."

"That's right. Two dead and one in jail."

"With that trio no longer in business, I'm considering returning to Venice Beach."

"There's definitely a need for an upstanding, legitimate art dealer here," I said.

He chuckled. "I mentioned to the detective that I had received a call from you. He told me that you were instrumental in bringing Brock to justice and that you were the one who gave him my phone number."

"Only doing what a law-abiding citizen should do."

"I heard it was more than that. When I reopen my gallery, you can stop by and select a painting free of charge as a thank-you for clearing the way for my return."

"Glad to have been of service."

That evening I said to Marion, "You up for a promenade followed by a bite to eat?"

"If it means I don't have to fix dinner, I'm all for it."

"I think you deserve a nice meal. I want to wander over to Windward Circle and then we can go to the restaurant where Pitman works."

"I enjoyed our meal there before."

"Then all we have to do is find Windward."

"I can guide us there."

"Good. I must have married you so you can show me where to go and prevent me from being a lost soul."

"I hope that's not the only reason."

I gave her a hug. "I also get lonely at night."

After a pleasant stroll at dusk we arrived at Windward Circle. The Theobault Gallery still had yellow crime-scene tape around it.

Across the street I spied a man in an old overcoat, hunkered down next to a brick building.

When we approached him, I asked, "Are you Old Ollie?"

"The same."

He didn't look that old. Couldn't have been a day over sixty, although he had weathered hands, a scraggly beard and wild gray hair poking out from under a dirty blue baseball cap.

"What's your favorite meal, Ollie?"

He looked up at me, and a sparkle came into his eyes. "Lamb chops with mashed potatoes and peas."

"And dessert?"

He licked his lips. "Chocolate cake."

"Okay. I'll see what we can do."

As we sauntered on toward the restaurant, Marion asked, "What do you have in mind?"

"I thought we'd bring Old Ollie a little surprise."

When we arrived at the Renaissance Restaurant, I requested Mallory Pitman for a waiter so we were seated at one of his tables. Shortly, I spotted a red-haired guy in black pants and a white shirt bouncing our way, and although I didn't recognize him, I knew it had to be the crazy artist.

When he saw who his customers were, his eyes grew wide. "Paul, the police talked to me last night. Are you all right?"

"Yeah. They nabbed Brock and his cohorts. Thanks for your assistance in identifying the fake paintings."

"It's good to see you safe and alive, Paul."

"It's good to still be around, and thanks for calling Marion last night to check on me. How's the wonderful world of art?"

A smile crept up the sides of his face. "That reception inspired me. I'm ready to start officially painting again."

"It's time for you to give up the graffiti wall, anyway. See if you can make a contribution to the art world. Besides, someone needs to take Muddy Murphy's place."

"That's right. Venice needs another home-grown artist."

"Just don't do that weird stuff. Paint something sensible that ancients like me can appreciate."

He chuckled. "I'm not going to do Grandma Moses."

"As long as it isn't blobs of paint." I picked up the menu. "Now for the matter at hand, what do your suggest we feast on tonight?"

"I would recommend the lobster and steak."

I turned to Marion. "How does that sound?"

"Just perfect."

"Okay, make that two orders with house salads. And I need you to fix a special meal to go."

After dinner he brought the bill and a large bag. I left Mallory a huge tip to help finance some painting supplies, and we waited out front for the cab the maître d' had called for us.

When the taxi arrived, I told the driver to stop at Windward Circle. At the requested location, I lumbered out of the vehicle and handed the bag to Old Ollie.

"Here's a little snack for you."

"You were here earlier."

"That's right. I'm your catering service for the evening. Enjoy."

I hopped back in the cab.

"That was a nice thing to do, Paul," Marion said.

I shrugged. "That's the least I could do to thank him for supporting my story that Brock abducted me."

The next Saturday I sat in my easy chair contemplating the upcoming cruise.

"We have to leave in ten minutes," Marion called from the bedroom.

377

"Where are we going?"

"You're hosting a party for the homeless people at the church today."

"I am?"

She squinted at me. "Didn't you write anything in your journal?"

"Apparently not. So what is this?"

She sighed. "You set up a catered lunch for the homeless community. You also invited Mallory Pitman, Marisa Young and Al Bertrand to join us."

"I'll be damned."

"Now get ready."

"Aye, aye, Admiral." I went into the bedroom to change into a pair of long pants and a long sleeve shirt. I might be hosting homeless people, but I didn't have to dress like them.

After a quick swipe of a brush to my locks, I headed into the living room just as there was a knock on the door. I opened it to find Austin all spruced up, in other words, he had shoes and long pants on.

"You here to kidnap me?"

Austin smiled. "We're all ready to drive to the church."

"I understand you've been sending messages to my granddaughter."

His cheeks reddened. "We've been keeping in touch."

I wagged an index finger at him. "No funny business." Then I put my arm around his shoulders. "Just kidding. You're a solid young man, Austin." I felt him straighten his shoulders. He'd turn out all right after all.

We all clambered into George's car with Austin wedged between Marion and me in the backseat for the short ride to the church. Marion had made all the arrangements, I learned, and a caterer had been hired for the event.

"My lottery winnings financing this?" I asked.

Marion peered at me across Austin. "You insisted on paying for it. You told me the homeless people deserved a first-rate meal."

"I'll be darned," I said. "Can't argue with that. I'm surprised I didn't write it down in my journal."

She winked at me. "You're full of all kinds of surprises."

I decided to take that in a positive way.

When we arrived at the church, we all pitched in to move folding tables and chairs out into the courtyard. As we entered the building for another load, Marion said, "Now stick with me so you don't get in any new trouble here."

"I don't know about that," I replied. "But

in any case you're stuck with me."

She smiled. "I consider that an honor."

The caterer arrived with white tablecloths and enough food to feed an army, and then the army arrived. I spotted a mob strolling along Venice Boulevard in every imaginable, God-awful costume you could imagine: a patched flower dress, pants with one leg torn off, a hat that looked like it had been stolen from a dairy horse, a faded aloha shirt with no buttons, a gray sweater with a large grease stain in front. But everyone seemed happy and dove into the victuals.

A man strolled over and pumped my hand. "Thanks for sponsoring this, Paul. You're the man of the hour."

I looked sheepishly at him. "I hate to admit it, but with my poor memory, I've forgotten who you are."

"No offense. I'm Harley Marcraft."

"Okay. I read your name in a journal I keep."

Harley ruffled Austin's hair. "And thank you, young man, for giving us the warning about the psycho kid on the loose. You both need to meet Alex." He waved over a short, stooped man who must have been in his sixties.

"Alex, these are the two who passed on

the word regarding the kid who attacked you."

Alex looked up from his scuffed mismatched wingtips and eyed the sandwich in his hand momentarily. "Kid came after me with a baseball bat. Didn't know crap."

Austin's eyes widened. "You took care of Pierce. He's six inches taller than you and must weigh fifty pounds more."

Alex took another bite. "Kid had no fighting skills. Thought he was hot stuff. A few karate moves and he was history."

"Do you think you could teach me karate?" Austin asked.

Alex smiled. "No one's asked me that in ten years. Sure."

"I've saved up some money so I can pay for lessons."

Alex gave a dismissive wave. "I don't care about money. I'll do it for lunch."

They made plans to start the next day.

I turned to Harley. "There's one other thing. Does there happen to be a guy named Old Ollie here today?"

"He's not with us."

My smile faded. "Oh, no. Did he have an accident or die?"

Harley chuckled. "Nothing bad like that. He had an interesting experience. After all the years of scrounging food, someone gave

381

him a complete gourmet meal a week ago. He enjoyed it so much he decided to apply for a job, so he could afford good food on a regular basis. He used to be a waiter and heard there was an opening at the Renaissance Restaurant, so Old Ollie cleaned himself up to go interview today."

"Imagine that," I said, shaking my head.

Then I spotted Mallory Pitman. He was matching a bag lady bite for bite along the goody table. As I approached, I heard snippets of phrases: ". . . conditioned colors . . . mauve motif . . . prism swatch . . ."

"You find a kindred spirit, Pitman?" I asked.

"Yes, indeed. Carol here is a retired artist. She used to give Muddy Murphy a run for his money." Pitman bounced up and down like a pogo stick in overdrive.

"But I had to give up painting," she said. "Arthritis in my fingers."

"You should try finger painting," I said.

Her mouth fell open. "What a wonderful idea." Then she filled her puss with a chocolate éclair.

Pitman slapped me on the back. "You're quite the idea man, Paul."

I shrugged. "These things just pop into my screwed-up brain from time to time."

Pitman sighed. "We made Venice Beach a

safer place for artists."

"We did. Thanks again for your assistance. I'll look forward to seeing some of your paintings on display in galleries along Abbott Kinney Boulevard."

"It won't be long. I started painting again this week. And thanks to your recommendation, I have a lawyer to help me."

I wasn't sure what he was referring to, but let it pass.

Pitman gave me a huge grin. "I feel the old inspiration surging through my body. I've even made contacts with an art dealer."

"I hope you found someone reputable."

"I have. There is a new owner for what used to be the Theobault Gallery."

"Anyone I know?" I asked to humor him.

"Actually you do. It's Pieter Rouen. He's back in town."

"I'll be damned. Small world."

"He's asked me to assemble a collection of my new work. I'll send you an invite when I hold my first show." He thumped his chest and dashed off to raid a bowl of chips.

Moments later a man came up and shook my hand. "You may not remember me, but my name is Al Bertrand."

The name clicked from my journal. "Yeah, you helped me one morning when I was wandering around lost."

He chuckled. "Glad to have been of service. And I want to thank you for inviting me to this lunch and recommending me to a new client."

"Oh? Who's that?"

"Mallory Pitman. I'm helping him negotiate a studio lease and a contract with an art dealer."

"Excellent. He could use some sound representation."

Marisa Young stopped by to say hello to Marion and me, and I promised not to cause any more problems in her church office in the future.

Within an hour nearly every crumb of food had disappeared. I turned to Marion. "Nothing goes to waste with this crowd. Like a horde of locusts came through."

"I think they enjoyed the meal. This was a great idea, Paul."

"Yup, everybody seemed to have a good time. And Austin is on his way to becoming a Black Belt."

Afterwards, I carefully wrapped up the one remaining meatball in a paper napkin and stuck it in my pocket.

Marion saw me. "Paul, what are you doing? Didn't you get enough to eat?"

"This isn't for me. It's for Cleo."

"You've become quite fond of that cat, haven't you?"

"Damn right. I read in my journal that she tried to save me from Brock, so this is the least I can do for her. I need to reward our watch cat."

Then we bagged all the trash, and the caterer whisked away all the silver containers and tablecloths.

I took a moment to look up at the blue sky and palm trees swaying in the gentle breeze. The lingering aromas of cinnamon cookies and roast beef drifted by. I felt contented. My life was in order, the bad guys were locked up and the police were off my tail.

Marion came over and hugged me. "We catch our flight late this afternoon and tomorrow is our cruise. A whole week to ourselves, surrounded by lovely scenery."

"Then we'll be feasting like these folks did today." I patted my stomach. "I'll have to be careful if I want to keep my youthful figure."

"You deserve to be fattened up and spoiled for a week at sea."

"Just as long as I don't have to go in the ocean or the sloshing swimming pool. I'll be perfectly content to watch the sights from the comfort of our balcony. Since you'll be with me, Marion, that's all that counts."

We kissed.

"Please, not in front of kids," Austin said. He gave me a wink and dashed off with two folding chairs in each hand.

"Quite a change in that young man," I said.

"And we both know who helped him." Marion gave my arm a squeeze. "There's a wedding this afternoon, so we need to finish up here. Austin will carry the rest of the furniture inside, but would you take the coffeepot back to the office?"

"Sure." I picked it up and sauntered into the church and set it down on a table. I looked around the room and noticed that the door to the vestibule was ajar. I heard a rustling sound. Being the nosey old coot that I was, I stuck my head inside.

A man stood there inspecting a table piled high with presents. Everything I had read in my journal that morning flashed through my weird brain, and I hightailed it out of there before you could say, "Detective Quintana."

ABOUT THE AUTHOR

Mike Befeler turned his attention to fiction writing after a career in high-technology marketing. His debut novel, *Retirement Homes Are Murder,* was published in 2007. The second novel in his Paul Jacobson Geezer-lit Mystery Series, *Living with Your Kids Is Murder,* appeared in 2009, and was nominated for the Lefty Award for the best humorous mystery of 2009. Mike is active in organizations promoting a positive image of aging and is vice president of the Rocky Mountain Chapter of Mystery Writers of America. He grew up in Honolulu, Hawaii, and now lives in Boulder, Colorado, with his wife, Wendy.

If you are interested in having the author speak to your book club, contact Mike Befeler at mikebef@aol.com. His Web site is www.mikebefeler.com.